A Collection distributed by Heron Books

THREE INQUISITIVE PEOPLE

DENNIS WHEATLEY

DENNIS WHEATLEY

THREE INQUISITIVE PEOPLE

Frontispiece Portrait by
MARK GERSON

Original Illustrations by
SHIRLEY BELLWOOD

Distributed by
HERON BOOKS

Published by arrangement with
Hutchinson and Co. (Publishers) Ltd.

First published 1940

© *1973, Illustrations, Edito-Service S.A., Geneva*

4184

CONTENTS

CHAPTER I

REX VAN RYN MISSES
MR. COWARD'S NEW REVUE

MR. REX VAN RYN placed one gigantic hand upon the glass doors of the Mausoleum Club, pressed lightly, and passed within.

Green marble columns and a marble floor, a broad stairway carpeted with thick red pile, two enormous portraits so darkened by time as to be almost featureless in the dim light that struggled to combat the all-pervading fog of the November night.

Two strides brought Mr. Van Ryn opposite the absurd little roofed-in mahogany box, an oasis of brightness in the big, empty hall, which housed an elderly man in dull livery.

The elderly man was casting up figures in a small book; he had a bald head, and his wrinkled face was slightly reminiscent of an antiquated turtle.

"The Duke de Richleau," said the tall visitor. "Would he be in?" And the manner of his words rather than his intonation disclosed the fact that he was an American.

The turtle-faced man did not look up, he sucked the stub of his pencil, jotted down a total and inquired: "Have you an appointment with His Grace?"

"I have," declared the American briefly.

"Thank you, sir." Without glancing to right or left, the porter struck a small hand-bell, which gave one clear single note; out of the darkness of the hall appeared a diminutive page. "And your name, sir?" The man looked up at last.

"Rex Mackintosh Van Ryn."

"Thank you, sir. Boy, Mr. Rex Mackintosh Van Ryn to see His Grace the Duke de Richleau."

With his eyes alone the turtle-faced man indicated a long and apparently uncomfortable horsehair settee opposite the box. "If you will kindly be seated, sir, we will hascertain if His Grace is in."

"Mr. Rex Mackintosh Van Ryn to see the Duke de Richleau," piped the page in a shrill treble.

"*'Is Grace* the Duke de Richleau,"corrected the bald man sharply, flashing into momentary animation; after which he drew the racing page of the evening paper towards him and returned to his seemingly endless computations.

Van Ryn did not accept the proffered invitation of the horsehair bench. It needed more than the solemnity of this aged institution to awe the fifteen stone of well-shaped matter and lively mind that made this young American such a popular figure among his contemporaries from Long Island to Juan-les-Pins.

Instead, he thrust his large hands into the voluminous pockets of his well-cut dress trousers, and began to pace the hall.

At the moment he was busy wondering what this foreign duke would be like. He recalled his last interview with Van Ryn the elder.

"Now, Rex," the President of the Chesapeake Banking and Trust Corporation had said, "you've got a whole stack of introductions to the right people on the other side, and you wouldn't use the half, even if I let you stay twice as long as I've a mind to in that London office of ours, but I do want you to make contact with the Duke. We people spend a lot of time seeing the Pyramids, and Notre Dame, and Stratford, and places—well, the Duke, to my mind, is all these in one, he'll give you the idea what Europe really stands for—and, incidentally, why on this side we're not quite so marvellous as we sometimes like to think. That's not our fault, mind—we started late, and you can't get seven-year-old whisky out of a home still. But it is up to your generation to make the difference—get that?"

Yes, Rex had "got that," and the old man was a great sport, but when he said a thing he meant it—otherwise Rex would never have been moving slowly up and down like a large fish in the dim green waters of this vast tank-like hall.

All the same, it was a bore, Rex reflected; more than a month had elapsed since his arrival in London before he had even sent in the letter of introduction to the Duke, and during that time his friends in the American Club had seen to it that he never had a dull moment—but even now he wished that he had wriggled out of the polite invitation that he had received a few days before.

2

He had had to leave the Mowbray's cocktail party early, and tonight was the first night of Coward's new revue—he had wanted to take Felicity to that, and now she had probably gone with some other fellow—he'd see her at Irma's dance later, of course, still it would have been more fun to dine Felicity first, do the show with her, and then go on. Perhaps she was at home this evening—he'd slip away after dinner just as soon as he could ring up—suggest calling for her, and then, with any luck, have half an hour alone with her if her mother was not in.

His square, ugly, attractive face lit up at the idea, then a frown creased his brows: "Damn the old man and his antiquated Duke, they'd be bored to death with each other for sure!"

An end was put to his reflections by the reappearance of the small page.

"If you please, sir, will you step this way," he piped.

Up the broad stairs of that tank-like hall, down a long corridor, and then through silent doors into a gust of warm light—a lofty, well-proportioned room, with great fires blazing beneath handsome chimney-pieces, soft carpets, and tables strewn with literature of every kind, only a scattered handful of black-clad men, the nearest of whom rose to greet Van Ryn.

So this was the Duke de Richleau. The young American studied him closely. A slim, delicate-looking man, somewhat above middle height, an aquiline nose and greying hair, a thin, delicate face that seemed as if it should have ended in a pointed beard; beneath grey "devil's" eyebrows were grey eyes flecked with yellow, of an almost piercing brilliance. It needed only the cordon of some distinguished order across the white shirt-front of his almost too perfect evening dress to imagine him the accredited representative of some great foreign power in the days before the war.

Quite suddenly the rather grim face broke into a charming smile, the Duke extended both his slender, fragile hands.

"My dear boy," he said slowly taking Van Ryn's hands in his for a moment, "it is a great pleasure that you give an old man by sacrificing one of your evenings."

For a moment Van Ryn was at a loss, the words so aptly expressed exactly what his feelings had been only a few moments before, yet as he looked into the almost supernaturally brilliant eyes which regarded him with shrewd, humorous kindliness he

3

had a feeling that it was the Duke who had sacrificed an evening to him; but only for a moment, a broad smile dawned slowly on the younger man's ugly, attractive face. "It's good of you, sir," he murmured, "to have me come."

"On the contrary." De Richleau led him to a deep arm-chair.

"People like myself are no longer of any moment in this world of ours—even the fact that we have inherited an ancient name nullifies any little aptitude for affairs which we may have, whereas your father's voice is a power in your great country; and what he is today you may be tomorrow."

Van Ryn smiled again; he had been far too busy indulging in his passion for sport, surf-riding and dabbling in the lighter kinds of love, these last half-dozen happy years since he had left Harvard, to take a serious interest in world affairs; but occasional talks with his father, and his father's friends, had given him enough understanding to appreciate the truth that underlay the half-humorous statement of his host. He gave another glance at the broad forehead and clever, sensitive face, and it drifted through his mind that this man might be a great force in the world if only he cared to enter the turmoil of modern business. He voiced something of his thoughts.

"But you, sir, why d'you say you're old? I believe you could give my old man points—if you sat down to it."

"You think so?" The Duke gave his charming but ever so slightly cynical smile.

"How nice of you. Well, sometimes I have dreamed for a little of sinking my identity, to start life again in your great country. The big business man, eh? But no—truly—I am not so old, only perhaps a little more than twice your age, yet I am old in spirit. I have seen and done too much in my fifty-six years for anything really to be worth a great effort any more. Besides," he added on a lighter note, as he reached for the decanter that waited upon the little table before them, "I should be forced to give up the very passable sherry we have in this club. I hope that you will forgive that I cannot offer you a cocktail."

Van Ryn took the proffered glass. Like all his educated compatriots, he was just a little supersensitive about his race; the lighter literature of the last decade has not made life easier for the cultured American in Europe; too many people have been apt to accept the portrait of the rich, but vulgar, Middle

4

Westerner as typical of the whole. The young man's face was clouded by a frown.

"I like cocktails," he declared firmly, "and lots of 'em; but in this place they just wouldn't do—and this sherry," he sipped appreciatively, "I'll say it's a marvellous wine."

The elder man leaned forward and placed a hand upon his knee.

"My dear fellow," he began, "forgive me. I, too, at times drink cocktails—but that leads to the reason why I have asked you here to dine. It would have been easy to take you to Claridge's or the Ritz, and, since they have no sherry that I care to drink, we should assuredly have drunk cocktails together, but I felt that you must know these places as well as I, and that if you were in any way your father's son, it would interest you to step back into the days of Queen Victoria for an hour or so. Therefore I asked you to dine in this quaint old place, behind closed doors through which the word socialism has never penetrated, and women do not come."

"That was a marvellous idea, and a very kind one, too," Van Ryn grinned. All his natural good-humour had returned to him.

"You know," he added ingenuously, "I didn't want to come, not a bit, but the old man made a real show about my meeting you, and now I have—honestly, I'd have kicked myself if I'd missed the opportunity."

The Duke pulled for a moment at his long Turkish cigarette.

"That is the charm," he said suddenly, "of you Americans, your utter frankness—a most delightful trait; and I, even with the interest I have in youth—so often disappointed yet always tempted to try again—I feared to waste another of my precious evenings, in which there is always so much to do, upon another commonplace young man. Come, my dear fellow, another glass of this excellent sherry; then let us make the best of each other and dine."

5

CHAPTER II

THE DUKE DE RICHLEAU IS INQUISITIVE

SOME two hours later M. de Richleau and his guest sat entrenched behind long cigars; they had just savoured the last drops of a sixty-year old bottle of Madeira, and both were filled with the sense of well-being that succeeds a carefully chosen dinner and fine wines.

"What are your plans for the evening?" the Duke inquired. "If you are free, I am entirely at your disposal; as it happens, my old friend Wilberforce is laid up with a sprained ankle, he is bound to be at home, and since you are interested in aeroplane design, it might amuse you to meet him; few people know more about the history and, perhaps, the future of the aeroplane. But there, at your age I imagine your evenings are devoted to more pressing matters?" He lifted his slanting eyebrows with a smile.

"Well," Van Ryn hesitated, "that's really kind of you, and I'd just love to meet Wilberforce some time, he's a great man, but tonight I'm supposed to drop in on Lady Ingram's party."

"Ah, well, in that case, since you are to stay in your father's London office for some time, it is easily arranged. We will go then to my flat in Curzon Street and we will look up those addresses in Paris which I promised you, then my car can take you on. Would you care for a liqueur brandy before we go?"

"No, thanks all the same, that Madeira was just too marvellous —I'd hate to ruin the flavour of that yet awhile."

Van Ryn rose as he spoke, the two men passed out of the club, and the waiting footman tucked them into the Duke's great Hispano Suiza that stood ready at the entrance. Slowly the big car made its way through the gloom of the fog-laden streets, but the distance was short, and a few moments later they drew up before Errol House in Curzon Street.

M. de Richleau's flat was on the first floor of the blocks and they did not therefore use the lift, but walked up the wide stone stairway.

Just as they reached the landing and the Duke was about to insert his key in the lock, the front door of the flat on the other side of the staircase shut with a click, and they both stood aside to allow the young man who had come out to pass.

He wore a shiny topper and evening dress, with a silk muffler loosely wound round his neck; there was nothing to distinguish him from the average young man of the upper classes except his markedly Semitic appearance. His strongly developed Jewish nose in his thin face stood out like the hooked bill of some great bird. That and his pendulous lower lip caught the attention of both the Duke and Van Ryn, as his quick, intelligent, rather narrow eyes flickered over them from behind his rimless pince-nez as he passed them on his way downstairs.

Once inside the Duke's flat Van Ryn's attention was taken up by the curious assortment of beautiful and interesting things which decorated the big lounge.

Rapiers of Toledo steel, etchings by Rembrandt and Dürer, figures in Chinese jade and in ivory; a beautifully chased Italian "ceinture de chastité" of the cinquecento; a book of hours, once the property of the Duke's great ancestor, and framed maps and documents of the greatest historic interest; Greek Tanagra figures and Egyptian gods. Van Ryn felt that it would have taken him days to do justice to this rare collection, and the Duke delighted to tell the history of his treasures, but the small neat head of Lady Felicity Standish kept intruding itself upon the young American's mental vision, and, after ten minutes or so, he begged that he might be allowed to come again some other time. De Richleau, having carefully written down the promised addresses, escorted his guest to the door.

For a moment, on the landing, Van Ryn stood, rendering thanks, then quite suddenly, as he was about to start downstairs, the front door of the flat opposite was flung open, disclosing a white, frightened maid. Immediately Rex paused to look at her, and the Duke, too, remained with his door half open, staring at the hysterical woman, who stood there capless, her hair awry, dead white, and with staring eyes.

It was De Richleau who spoke; "Is there anything the matter? Can we—er—be of any assistance?"

"My mistress—" gasped the woman, "she's dead—" With

7

that she swayed forward and Van Ryn was only just in time to catch her as she fell.

The Duke stepped out on to the landing. "Dear me," he said quietly, "I fear that you and I are about to be drawn into some unpleasant business; can you manage her, or shall I help?"

Rex Van Ryn grinned. "No, you go ahead. I'll bring her right along." And with a simple, easy motion, impossible to anyone with less than his unusual strength, the powerful young man lifted the dishevelled maid in his arms.

De Richleau led the way into the opposite flat, the front door opened on to a long corridor, and he walked down it, opening the first door on the left. As he supposed, it corresponded with his own flat, and was a large sitting-room. A cheerful fire blazed in the grate, but although the windows were closed it seemed that the fog had penetrated a little—it dulled the light and caught one in the throat.

Van Ryn laid the still unconscious maid upon a big sofa and looked about him. He noted that the room was the exact counterpart of the Duke's, except that the door and fireplace were at opposite ends, but, unlike De Richleau's, it was a very ordinary room, not distinguished by grace or beauty in any way. The furnishings were modern and expensive, but expressed no individuality; everything there might have been bought at one time from any first-class store.

"What'll we do now?" he said, glancing at the older man.

"If you would stay here," said the Duke, "and endeavour to bring that woman round, I will explore."

Van Ryn nodded. "Go right ahead," he agreed briefly. "I'll handle her."

He crossed to a large silver tantalus, evidently a presentation piece, since it bore an inscription which the American did not stop to read, and mixed a stiff brandy and soda. Returning to the woman, he put his arm under her and forced her to swallow a little, then he set it down, and taking up a white cardboard folder that lay upon the nearby desk, he began to fan her.

After a moment the woman opened her eyes and gave one look at Van Ryn, then closing them again tightly she began to beat a sharp tattoo with her heels on the sofa.

8

"Now, that'll be enough of that," said the American quickly. "Just take a sip of this and tell us all about it."

As he spoke he tilted the glass towards her mouth again. She spluttered and sat up.

"Oh, sir," she moaned, "I don't rightly know. Miss Winifred—the mistress' sister that is—called me out of the kitchen just as cook and me was having a cup of tea before going off to bed, and there was the poor mistress lying in her bath—and I had been with her these twenty years!"

At this she burst into a loud fit of sobbing.

Van Ryn coaxed her to her feet, and out into the passage. "Now, don't you worry," he advised kindly. "Just put me on to where this bathroom is." She pointed dumbly to a door a little farther down the passage on the opposite side, and then broke down again. "I can't go in," she wailed, "I can't go in!"

"All right, now, all right." He patted her on the shoulder. "You step back to the kitchen with cook, and just don't move from there. We'll look after things, don't worry."

He opened the door which she had pointed out. It proved to be a large and comfortable, almost luxurious, bathroom, with its tiled walls, neat white-painted cupboards, and glass shelves lined with rows of bottles. But his eyes went immediately to the porcelain bath.

In it lay a woman, quite still and half-submerged beneath the water, from which faint wisps of steam still rose.

At once glance he saw that there was nothing to be done.

She gave the impression of being some fifty years of age, and had, when younger, most certainly been good-looking.

On a chair beside the bath sat a small, grey-haired woman, dry-eyed, but clasping and unclasping her hands in a state of the highest agitation.

When Van Ryn entered she was staring at De Richleau, who had evidently just come into the room by another door, with wide, frightened eyes.

Suddenly she made a movement to fling a bath towel over the nude body, but with a gentle gesture Rex stopped her.

"Excuse me," he said, "don't worry about that, you will be Miss Winifred, I expect, the dead lady's sister? You must be just terribly upset."

The Duke came forward. "I am your neighbour," he said

kindly. "I hope that you will forgive our intrusion, but my friend and I found your maid on the landing. Is there anything we can do?"

Miss Winifred continued to wring her frail little hands. "Oh, yes," she said vaguely, "very kind I'm sure—I can't realize it—it's too awful—poor Elinor—what an awful thing—"

Van Ryn sat down on the edge of the bath, with his back to the body, shielding it with his broad shoulders from the gaze of the elderly little lady, and reaching out one of his large hands, took one of hers in his.

"There, there," he murmured soothingly, "don't take on so, just you try and tell us what happened, and how we can help. Is there anyone you'd like us to call on the 'phone?"

She looked at him pitifully. "Oh, it's all so confused—I don't quite know—Elinor was going out to supper tonight with her husband, Gideon—Sir Gideon Shoesmith, you know—he should be here at any minute, and I always help Elinor dress when she is going out late, because she doesn't like the maids kept up—I came along only a few minutes ago and was putting her dress out in the bedroom—she seemed rather a long time in here, and I couldn't hear her moving about, so I knocked—and there was no reply—no reply at all, but Elinor never locks the door and so I came in—and this—this is what I found—I can't realize it."

"Wouldn't it be better," the Duke suggested, "if we went into another room? Van Ryn, perhaps you would take Miss —er—Winifred, and might I prescribe a small brandy and soda?"

"But I couldn't drink brandy—I never touch anything at all," protested the faded little woman nervously.

"Maybe," said Van Ryn, taking her gently by the arm, "but just this one time it wouldn't do you any harm at all, you come right along with me." And he led her from the room.

De Richleau remained behind. He regarded the dead woman critically. "A heart attack—I wonder?" he mused. "I don't think so, more probably the poor lady slipped, struck her head upon the edge of the bath, and became unconscious—let us see."

Carefully avoiding wetting his cuffs he dipped his hand into the water, but drew it back sharply. "Dear me, how very hot, I should hardly have thought it possible for anyone to take so

10

hot a bath in comfort." He stooped again, and this time inserted his hand below the dead woman's neck. Lifting her head and steadying it with his free hand, he carefully felt in the thick, greying hair at the base of the skull. As he lifted the head the water showed a very slight discoloration, and he nodded to himself.

"Yes, she slipped and fell, a definite abrasion." But as his sensitive fingers moved softly under the dead woman's hair an expression of deep thought overspread his features.

"Now, I wonder," he mused, "yes I wonder." Then he gently let the head slip back into its original position.

He continued to stare with his bright searching eyes as he slowly dried his wet hand upon his cambric handkerchief, then he took the thermometer from its hook on the wall and held it for a moment under the water.

"One hundred and twelve degrees," he said softly to himself. "Enervating—terribly enervating, quite unusually hot."

He then returned the thermometer to its place on the wall and slipped out into the passage, closing the bathroom door quietly behind him. He next went along to the telephone in the hall, dialled a number, held a short conversation, and replacing the receiver, rejoined Van Ryn and Miss Winifred in the drawing-room.

Rex rose to meet him. "I understand Sir Gideon Shoesmith is out at some big dinner—some show at the Park Lane Hotel, that's only round the corner in Piccadilly, and he's due back any time now. It is hardly worth trying to call him up.

De Richleau nodded thoughtfully. "I fear it will be a great shock for him to learn that Lady Shoesmith has died so suddenly, but we shall have no choice other than to inform him, besides"— he returned to the little grey-haired woman—"there is the official side of it."

"You mean the police," exclaimed Miss Winifred, in sudden horror. "But this has nothing to do with them."

The Duke shrugged his slim shoulders very slightly. "Un-fortunately, failure to inform the police of any death in such tragic circumstances would be a serious breach of the law, but I assure you there's no cause for alarm. In order that you should not be troubled by the importunities of subordinates I have myself telephoned Scotland Yard."

11

CHAPTER III

HOW THE LETTER "S" MAY MEAN MURDER INSTEAD OF ACCIDENTAL DEATH

IT was the Duke who received the police when they arrived some twelve minutes later.

"I'm Superintendent Marrofat," the big, bluff-looking individual introduced himself; "I understand that you telephoned to the Assistant Commissioner at the Yard, and he asked me to step round"—he jerked his big round head with its shock of curly ginger hair towards the tall man in plain clothes beside him—"but Inspector Gartside here will take charge officially. What's the trouble, sir?"

The Duke spoke slowly: "I'm not certain that there is any trouble, at least, trouble which would call for the attention of an officer of your seniority, Superintendent. Lady Shoesmith, who lives in this flat, died suddenly this evening, about half an hour ago, perhaps—and I thought it right in such a case that the police should be informed—you had better see the unfortunate lady—then you will be able to judge better than I, if your presence is required."

As he spoke he led the way to the bathroom. Superintendent Marrofat and Inspector Gartside followed him, the latter having posted a uniformed constable on the door, with instructions to let anyone in, but nobody out, and to report all arrivals; the fourth member of the police party, a seedy-looking little man, who carried a large tin box, was left in the hall.

De Richleau threw open the bathroom door, and the Superintendent paused on the threshold, his great bulk almost filling the doorway. For a moment he stood, his heavy overcoat thrust back and his hands buried deep in his trousers pockets, as his sharp blue eyes travelled carefully over every inch of the walls, ceiling and floor.

He seemed to be registering the room in his mind, the doorways, the window, the shelves and cupboards, and it was not

12

until he had completed this careful survey that he allowed his eyes to rest on the woman in the bath.

"Who found her?" he asked at length.

"Her sister who, I think, lives here," replied the Duke. "Miss Winifred—I don't know her full name."

"How did you come into this, sir?"

"I live in the flat opposite, and I was saying good night to a young friend of mine on the landing, when one of the maid-servants here came running out—quite hysterical, poor girl—and fainted; naturally we came in to render any assistance which we could—my friend is with Miss—er Winifred now."

"I see, nothing has been touched, I hope?"

"Nothing as far as I know, with one exception. I took the liberty of examining the dead woman's head."

"What?" Marrofat swung round. "That was very wrong, sir, as a gentleman like you should know—a body should never be touched until the police doctor's seen it."

"Very wrong, Superintendent," agreed the Duke blandly, "I perfectly agree, unfortunately, like the Elephant's Child, I suffer from an Insatiable Curiosity—but I assure you I was most careful not to disturb the position of the body."

"Very wrong all the same, sir—still what's done is done, perhaps you'll tell us why you did it?"

"As I have said, Insatiable Curiosity—I know enough of death to feel quite certain that this was not heart or apoplexy; it occurred to me therefore that she had slipped and struck her head. I'm afraid I was far too impatient to find out if my idea was correct to wait for the police surgeon."

The big detective regarded De Richleau with not too kind a look. "And did you?"

"I found there were contusions at the back of the head."

"That'll be about the size of it," the Superintendent nodded, "she slipped and struck her head, then slipped under water—death by misadventure—eh? There's nothing to indicate otherwise—the doctor will be here shortly—he'll verify what you say, of course. I thought from what the Assistant Commissioner said that there might be some special trouble—as it is the Inspector will take any notes that are necessary, and I'll get back to the Yard. I may be wanted this evening on a job down Houndsditch way." He turned on his heel with an air of finality.

13

"I see," said M. de Richleau quietly—so quietly that the Superintendent swung round on him quickly and gave him a long stare.

After a moment, he said, cocking his head on one side: "Look here, sir, what do you mean by saying that—in just that way?"

"Perhaps you did not hear exactly what I said before?"

"Perhaps not—so, if you don't mind I'll trouble to say it again."

"I said 'contusions'," murmured the Duke, very quietly and distinctly.

Superintendent Marrofat regarded the slim, delicate-looking man thoughtfully for a minute, then his blue eyes suddenly brightened, and he nodded his big round head.

"So that's what's at the back of your mind, eh?" He smiled broadly. "Very good of your Grace to give us that pointer— mind you," he added quickly, "I should have seen the doctor's report later, and even if I had let that pass, Gartside would have spotted it. But since we've got so far let's go a bit further— what's the deduction? as the detective novels say."

"My friend," said De Richleau amiably, "if you have not already made the deduction my words would have been meaningless to you—One slip—one contusion—a fatal accident perhaps; but *two* contusions—*three* contusions. No—one does not keep on having fatal accidents, and getting up each time to fall once more in the same way—striking very nearly the same place. With two or more contusions at the base of the skull we are inclined to say—Is this a fatal accident? No—I believe it is murder."

"The gentleman's not far wrong, sir," nodded Inspector Gartside, who had been listening to the conversation of the other two with the greatest interest.

"Right," said the Superintendent briskly. "Now we know what we're up against, and all thanks to you, sir. A bit irregular —moving the body before the doctor's seen it, but it will save us a lot of time—good thing we brought Sammy. Gartside—get him in."

As he spoke, the big man began to examine the two doors and the window, carefully refraining from touching them with his hands; there was no trace of any force having been

14

used upon these. The window was a little open at the top, but there were strong bars outside, and after a short survey, Marrofat turned to the seedy little man who had been called in from the hall.

"Case of murder, Sammy," he said briefly. "See if you can get us a few prints—doors and windows—usual thing—take the handle of the back-brush, too, looks innocent enough, but it's just possible that this job might have been done with that—We'll have a little talk with the people of the house." And he led the way from the bathroom.

Inspector Gartside followed, and the Duke brought up the rear. As he left the room he spoke casually to the fingerprint expert. "I should be grateful if you would do the taps. It would be interesting to know who prepared the bath—don't you think?" And he followed the others down the passage.

CHAPTER IV

THE POLITE YOUNG MAN WHO WORE WHITE KID GLOVES

In the sitting-room Miss Winifred was seated by the fire, still clasping and unclasping her hands. Rex van Ryn stood near her.

"Now, Madam," Superintendent Marrofat addressed the frail little, grey-haired woman in as soft a key as his big, booming voice could command. "Sorry I have got to trouble you, this is a sad business, but I'm from the Yard, and I've got to make a report. Of course, you needn't answer me if you don't wish, but I'd like to ask you a few questions, and I shan't keep you long."

"Yes, I understand, Inspector," she answered quietly.

"Thank you, Miss—now, what's your full name?"

"Winifred Lucy Eaton."

"Good—now you're the dead lady's sister, I understand."

"Oh no, *sister-in-law*."

"I see—and who are the other occupants of this flat?"

"There's Sir Gideon and Lady Shoesmith, myself and a cook, a house-parlourmaid and a between-maid—but she's not here, she had an accident last week and went to hospital, so there are only the two servants at present."

15

"Right. Sir Gideon Shoesmith, now. I know his name, of course, but what exactly *is* Sir Gideon?"

"Oh, he's an accountant, you know—his real business is in Sheffield, but he's lived in London since he married, though he goes up there now and then."

The Superintendent nodded. "Exactly. Has Sir Gideon been married long?"

She shook her head, and took out a minute pocket-handkerchief with which she dabbed at the corner of one eye. "Only last April—it's too terrible," she sighed.

"And there are no menservants living in the flat?" Marrofat inquired.

"No, there is the chauffeur, but he lives out."

"Now when did you see Lady Shoesmith last? Now— now—" he encouraged as Miss Eaton showed signs of breaking down.

"Well, I must think," she replied slowly. "It must have been about a quarter past nine; I left her with Richard."

"Who's he?"

"Oh! Richard is Lady Shoesmith's son by her first marriage—Mr. Richard Eaton."

"I see; and when did he go?"

"Well, I don't quite know, but I think I heard the front door shut about a quarter to ten."

"Where was Lady Shoesmith, then?"

"She was in her bedroom, just starting to dress to go out to supper."

"Right. Now Sir Gideon—what about him?"

"He's out at a dinner tonight—he left here just after seven o'clock."

"And not been in since, eh?"

"No, he should be in very soon now; he was to take Elinor—Lady Shoesmith—out to supper."

"And you've been in all the evening?"

"Yes."

"Whereabouts have you been sitting?"

"I don't sit here, I sit in the sewing-room which is next door to my bedroom, down in the servants' end of the flat."

"Now, would you hear anyone who came in, from your room, do you think?"

"Well," she looked at him vaguely, "I might, but on the

16

other hand I might not; I don't think I should because I was doing some sewing on the machine."

"And you were there from the time Mr. Eaton came till when?"

"Until about twenty minutes ago when I went along to Lady Shoesmith's room to help her dress."

"And you heard nothing in all that time?"

"No, not after Richard went."

"Well, I don't think I need trouble you any more for the moment, Miss. I expect you'd like to go to bed."

Miss Eaton rose awkwardly. "Yes, I think perhaps I would. I shan't sleep—it's too awful—but why do you ask all these questions? There's nothing—about Elinor's death—is there? I mean—" she broke off lamely.

He evaded her question skilfully. "I'm afraid you find us an inquisitive lot, Miss, but the poor old Yard has to make up for not being spectacular by being thorough, and perhaps we waste a lot of time asking questions that don't mean anything at all."

She looked round vaguely and pitifully, as though in search of some help or assistance, and then with a little nod to the four men walked out through the door which Van Ryn held open for her.

Inspector Gartside drew a line with his pencil under the shorthand notes which he had been taking and looked questioningly at his superior.

"Better see the maid next," said the big man; "perhaps one of you gentlemen would be good enough to bring her along. I don't want to scare the girl, and she's seen you before."

"I'll get her along right away," volunteered Van Ryn, and after a minute, during which the Duke, the Superintendent and the Inspector stood in thoughtful silence, he returned with the flustered woman, who seemed to have recovered from her hysteria but was still a little incoherent.

"Now, my girl," said Marrofat, after having given her the usual warning, "what do you know about this, eh?"

"Oh, sir, I don't know anything—I was just having a cup of tea in the kitchen, before I went to bed, and I heard Miss Winifred calling from down the passage, and when I went into the bathroom there was her poor Ladyship. Oh, it was awful, sir."

17

"Quite so; now, what's your name?"

"Susan Brent, sir."

"And when did you last see her Ladyship?"

"It must have been about half past eight, sir. Her Ladyship had dinner in the morning-room, and after she'd had coffee she rang for me to clear."

"And Miss Eaton—when did you last see her?"

"Miss Winifred was with her Ladyship at the time."

"Has anybody called here this evening?"

"No, sir, not that I know of."

"Now be careful, my girl; just think."

"Oh! Mr. Richard, sir, he came just in time to have coffee with his mother."

"There, now, I told you to be careful. Anybody else?"

"No, I'm sure there was nobody else, sir."

"What time did he go?"

"I don't rightly know, sir—I think he let himself out—I didn't see him go."

"You have no idea when he went?"

"No, sir, I was at the other end of the flat with cook."

"What time did Sir Gideon go out?"

"Just after seven I should say, sir. I put his clothes out, and he dressed and went out to a dinner."

"And you're quite certain that you didn't hear anything at all while you were in the kitchen?"

"No, nothing at all, sir, until I heard Miss Winifred call."

"All right, that'll do. Just ask cook to step along here for a moment, will you? By the way, Brent, how long have you been with the household?"

"I've been with her Ladyship for nearly twenty years, sir, but of course we've only been here these last eight months—since she married again."

"No other servants are there except you and the cook and the girl who's away?"

"Only Mr. Jevons, sir."

"Mr. Jevons? Who's he?"

"That's her Ladyship's chauffeur, sir, but he lives out."

"Good—you can go now. Send cook, will you?"

"Yes, sir; very good, sir."

18

As she left the room a tousled head was thrust round the door. "Doc's come, Boss; 'e's in the 'all."

"Right-o, Sammy. How're you getting on?"

The finger-print expert made a grimace. "Same old gime," he grumbled. "I never 'as no luck; don't seem as if no one can't keep their 'ands off nothing—door-plates is a mass of smears, and I should think they opens and shuts them windows a 'undred times a day. I'll have plenty for you, but I doubt it'll do you much good. Shall I tell Doc to get busy?"

"Yes. I want to hear what he's got to say as soon as possible, and you'd better go straight back to the Yard when you've finished so that I can have your stuff first thing in the morning. Report to me again before you go in case there is anything else for you to take."

"Ho! anover all-night sitting, eh!" the little man sniffed wearily. "Orlright, I'll show the Doc the corpse."

The Superintendent smiled at De Richleau as he lit a cigarette. "You wouldn't think that little chap was the cleverest print expert we've got, would you? It was a bit of luck that he was in my room when you telephoned; it makes all the difference if you can get markings when they're fresh, that's why I brought him along—on the chance."

Gartside, who was standing near the door, beckoned in the waiting cook.

She was a portly woman of some fifty years, with a sour expression of face, but perfectly self-possessed.

"You're the cook here?" questioned Marrofat.

"I was, but I shall be leaving tomorrow," she answered with some asperity. "I'm not used to such goings on—police and all."

The big Superintendent suppressed a smile. "I'd just like to ask you a few questions; you need not answer unless you wish."

"I've got nothing to hide, I'm sure," she flashed.

"Good. May we have your name?"

"Hiskins—Mary Elizabeth Hiskins, and fifteen years with the Dowager Lady Glenack."

Superintendent Marrofat gave a little nod. "Most excellent qualifications, I'm sure—and how long have you been here?"

"Seven months and two weeks come Monday, and I wouldn't have taken the place but what it was good money and the lady seemed a respectable woman, as you might say."

19

"And when did you see her Ladyship last?"

"Eleven o'clock maybe, when she give the orders. I know my place, and I will say the poor lady knew hers, she never come in my kitchen."

"Quite. You cooked dinner for two, I understand."

"Yes. 'Dinner for two at eight,' she says, 'and see the coffee's strong, because Mr. Richard will be in after, and he complained last time,' though why he should *I* don't know—he's that pernickety."

"And after you'd cooked dinner?"

"Me and Susan listened to the wireless for a bit, then we had a game of ludo, and after, I was just insisting on her having a plate of meat with her tea, because she's too thin by a long sight to my mind and wants feeding up, when Miss Eaton starts calling down the passage."

"I see, and did you see or hear anyone walking about the flat during that time?"

She bridled. "It's not my place to take notice of what goes on outside my own quarters."

"Nevertheless, my good woman, did you hear anything that you can remember?"

"I'm not your good woman, and I'd be very sorry ever to be so," she snapped, "and if you must know—I did not."

Van Ryn was grinning broadly behind her stiff back, and the Duke turned aside to hide a smile as Marrofat said amicably: "Thanks, Mrs. Hiskins, that's all I wanted to know. If you really are leaving tomorrow will you please give the officer who will be on duty here your address before you go. Good night."

Gartside smiled at his superior. "She doesn't seem to care for us, does she, sir?"

"Pompous old fool," said Marrofat genially, "but I'd rather have her than some, at least she's telling the truth all right." He turned to the Duke. "You'd be surprised the twisters we come across in our game, sir, trying to hide up their silly little personal secrets, and costing us hours of trouble sometimes to get down to the bottom of things."

The four men were standing together on the hearth and they did not hear Miss Eaton come back into the room until she spoke in her low, frightened voice. "Inspector, I've just remembered, I didn't tell you about the strange young man."

20

"What's that you say?" The Superintendent turned quickly.

"The strange young man I found in the passage; all this trouble had driven it out of my head."

"Come now, Miss, I'd like to hear all about this; take your time and don't miss out anything."

"Well, it was when I came from the sewing-room to put out Lady Shoesmith's dress. I found a strange young man standing just inside the front door. I asked him what he wanted and he said, was Sir Gideon in, and when I told him that Sir Gideon was out he seemed very surprised and said that he had rung up on the telephone only ten minutes before and somebody had said that Sir Gideon could see him if he came round at once. I told him Sir Gideon was out at a dinner and he said he thought that there must be some mistake, and after hesitating a little he went away."

"Do you know how he got in?"

"No. I asked him how he got in and he said that he found the front door half-open."

"Did he give any name?"

"Yes, it was a Jewish name, but I can't remember what it was now."

The Duke and Van Ryn exchanged a quick glance. "That'll be the bird we met on the step," said the latter.

Marrofat turned to them for a moment. "You saw him too, eh? Could you recognize him again?"

Both men nodded, and Van Ryn smiled. "I'd know that face in a thousand."

"What was he like, Miss Eaton?"

"Oh, quite a nice young man, very polite, not a bit casual, like so many young men are nowadays."

"But what did he look like?"

"Well, he was very slim—rather stooping shoulders—and in evening dress."

"Top-hat, and a scarf wound loosely round his neck," added Van Ryn.

"Yes," she agreed. "He had a stick, too, and white kid gloves —so few young men carry gloves now, I think it's such a pity."

"You may add a very pronounced Semitic nose, a pendulous lower lip and very quick, black eyes to your description, Super-

21

intendent," supplemented M. de Richleau. "Also he wore pince-nez."

The door opened suddenly and Sammy's ugly and rather grimy little face appeared.

"I done, Boss," he chirruped. "If you 'aven't nothing more I'll cut along."

"Nothing else, Sammy," the big detective gave a curt nod. "Get down to it as soon as you can."

"Right you are, Boss, see you liter." The small head disappeared and the door slammed.

"That's a piece of real good luck that you all saw him," Marrofat went on, continuing the conversation. "I should like ten minutes' quiet talk with that young man; a pity you can't remember his name, Miss."

"Oh—no—it's quite, quite gone. You see, directly he left I went straight into Elinor's room, and I'd hardly time to wonder who he could have been, or think how strange it was about the door being open, when I found—I found—"

"Now, Miss Eaton, you've been just marvellous; wouldn't it be better if you went straight back to your room?" Van Ryn coaxed her, "that is if the Superintendent has finished saying his piece?" He took her by the arm.

"Yes, I'm done," Marrofat agreed. "Everything will be all right, Miss, you go along to your room and try and get a little rest. If you'd like to see the doctor I'll send him along presently."

But at this moment the uniformed officer who had been stationed in the hall put his head inside the door and said: "Sir Gideon Shoesmith, sir."

CHAPTER V

THE MISSING PEARLS

A PORTLY, middle-aged man pushed past the constable. His glance fell on the group of strangers who occupied his sitting-room.

"What's all this about, Winifred?" he asked sharply, turning on her almost as if he thought her responsible.

The poor little spinster seemed almost more frightened of him than she had been of the Superintendent.

"Oh! Gideon," she exclaimed, "an awful thing has happened —I don't know how to tell you."

"Look here, Miss," the Superintendent intervened, "I think perhaps you'd better leave it to me to break the news to Sir Gideon. Inspector, take the lady and these other gentlemen into another room. I'm Superintendent Marrofat of New Scotland Yard, sir," he explained to the frowning owner of the flat, "and there has been serious trouble in your absence tonight."

Gartside held the door open for Miss Eaton, De Richleau and Van Ryn; meanwhile the Sheffield magnate threw the butt of his cigar into the fireplace and, walking over to the tantalus, mixed himself a drink.

"All right, Superintendent," he said, looking straight at Marrofat with his bright, round, hazel eyes which seemed to stand out in his heavy, rather white face, "what's been happening here?"

"I'm afraid it will be rather a shock to you, sir—it's Lady Shoesmith."

"Well—what's she done? Nothing about which there will be any undesirable publicity, I trust?"

"It's not what she's done, poor lady—she's met with an accident—a fatal accident."

"Good God!" Sir Gideon set his glass down quickly on the mantelpiece. "You can't mean—*she's dead*?"

The Superintendent nodded. "That's it, Sir Gideon, and I'm afraid it's my duty to inform you that there are circumstances connected with Lady Shoesmith's death which give us grounds for believing that it may have been murder."

"Good God," Sir Gideon exclaimed again, and he lowered himself, heavily, into the nearest arm-chair.

The burly detective walked over to the other side of the room— by turning his back he was, to all appearances, respecting the grief and shock which Sir Gideon would naturally feel—but actually it was his business to observe people under the stress of emotion, and therefore he remained for a few moments—not studying the rather indifferent collection of novels in the big bookcase, but Sir Gideon's reflection in the glass.

The elderly magnate sat slightly forward in the chair, his hands quite still on the arms—his eyes on the floor.

Suddenly, without altering his position, he spoke:

"How did it happen?"

Marrofat turned towards him again and gave him the brief facts as far as he had ascertained them.

"How, then," Sir Gideon looked up with his hard hazel eyes, "do you know that it was murder?"

For a moment the Superintendent felt slightly uncomfortable. "I don't," he said shortly, "I haven't had the report of the police surgeon—but if that confirms certain ideas of mine, then there will be very little doubt. In the meantime, would you mind if I asked you a few questions, sir—as I don't doubt you know, you need not answer if you do not wish."

"No, that's all right," said Sir Gideon dully. "If you're right, anything I can do to help the police goes without saying, but, poor woman, she'd not got an enemy in the world—it's incredible."

"Thank you, sir," Marrofat stepped to the door and sent the constable for Gartside. "You won't mind my having my right-hand man present, will you, Sir Gideon?" he asked. "I might get taken off this case for something else, then Inspector Gartside would carry on, and we won't want to bother you more than necessary."

Sir Gideon Shoesmith gave a short nod of consent, and sat staring at the fire while Gartside, who had joined them, settled himself unobtrusively, with his note-book, in a corner.

"Now, sir," the Superintendent began, "I understand Lady Shoesmith and yourself have not been married very long?"

"No—just over eight months."

"She was married before, I believe?"

"Yes."

"And yourself, Sir Gideon?"

"No, I've led a very strenuous life with little time for marriage, but now I had hoped to take things easier and settle down."

"Quite so, sir; a terrible blow for you, I'm sure. Lady Shoesmith had children by her first marriage, I think?"

"Yes, there is one boy."

"That would be Richard Eaton, I presume."

"Yes, Richard."

"Have you any reason to suppose, Sir Gideon, that there was any trouble between the boy and his mother?"

24

Sir Gideon lifted his hard eyes to the Superintendent.

"No," he said slowly. "No, they were very fond of each other, I think."

"And Miss Eaton—what were her relations with her sister-in-law?"

"I agreed that she should live with us when we married—it was my wife's wish—and she acts as a housekeeper to a certain extent. She has no money of her own, so it was a kindness on our part—and I must say she's done everything to show her appreciation; we hardly know she's in the flat."

"I see, Sir Gideon. Now do you happen to know a young Jew, thin, with stooping shoulders, wears pince-nez, very polite and well-dressed?"

"I might, a man in my position meets so many people."

"This man has come to your flat?"

"No, don't know him, he hasn't been here."

"Well, he has tonight, and he let himself in. I gather what he told Miss Eaton must have been a blind—I don't doubt he's the man we're looking for."

Sir Gideon sat up suddenly. "Is anything missing—what about my wife's jewels?"

The Superintendent nodded. "I was coming to that, but we've been pretty fully occupied during the twenty minutes we've been here, in a moment we'll ascertain if anything has been taken. Were Lady Shoesmith's jewels valuable, Sir Gideon?"

"They're insured for fifteen thousand—and worth every penny of it," returned the heavy-faced man in the chair.

"Just one more question, sir. What time did you go out?"

"Ten minutes past seven—I attended the annual dinner of the London and Sheffield Commercial Association at the Park Lane Hotel in Piccadilly, and I returned here—to find—" he broke off suddenly, and stretched out a hand for his glass on the mantelpiece.

"All right, sir, thank you," said Marrofat briskly. "Now if you don't mind we'll just look around and see if anything is missing."

"I would rather"—the elderly man looked tired and grim—"rather—not see my wife with strangers—this has been a great shock."

"No, sir, I don't mean that, just the other rooms."

"All right." Sir Gideon heaved himself up out of the arm-chair, took a drink from his glass, then bracing himself led the way out into the passage.

Their first visit was to the bedroom, a spacious room, expensively furnished in the modern style; two doors led out of it, in addition to that from the corridor, one to the bathroom and the other to Sir Gideon's dressing-room.

Upon the wide bed a dress of gold tissue had been carefully laid out, and various feminine garments lay scattered about the room.

"The safe's in my room," said Sir Gideon briefly, and the two police officers followed him into the dressing-room. A brief survey showed them that nothing had been touched, the door of the small, white-painted safe, which served as a pedestal for a square cupboard, was fast shut.

Gartside carefully wrapped his handkerchief round the handle and tried to turn it gently, but it proved to be locked.

"Better see if the contents are all right," suggested Marrofat, "they might have used the lady's keys."

With an effort Sir Gideon knelt down and, producing his key-chain, unlocked the safe. The Inspector turned the handle as before, and the door swung silently open.

Inside there were several packets neatly tied up in brown paper, some bundles of letters, and a thin wad of treasury notes, kept together by a rubber band. Upon the lower shelf was a fair-sized jewel case, securely locked, and quite a number of individual jewel-cases, ranging in sizes from small ones, obviously made to hold a single ring, to others of a considerably larger size for necklaces and pendants.

"No," said Sir Gideon. "Nothing's been disturbed." He opened one or two of the cases, and the jewels sparkled from their velvet cushions. Then he opened a big flat case that lay at the bottom—it was empty, but he did not seem surprised. "Those would be her pearls," he said, "but I expect they're in the bedroom, she always wore them."

He shut the case with a snap, pushed it in, and swung the door of the safe to, locked it, and rose stiffly to his feet.

Marrofat grunted. "Not like a professional job, to leave that lot, and with the keys in the bedroom, too. They'd have a pretty shrewd idea what's in that safe, and know its position to an inch.

That puts me out a bit, I thought I knew that young Jew."

"Yes," Gartside agreed. "I had the same idea, but it would have been out of character for him to have done this job."

Sir Gideon having passed again into the bedroom, the Inspector added in a low voice; "Silky's no killer."

"No, but he might have thought the flat empty," replied his chief, with some asperity. "Plenty of busters have made a killing before now when they've been caught out in the act. You don't need me to tell you that."

The two officers rejoined Sir Gideon in the bedroom, he was standing with lowered head near the bed, looking fixedly at his wife's evening shoes.

Upon the glass top of the elaborate dressing-table were scattered several beautiful rings. The Superintendent recalled Sir Gideon's attention.

"Would you mind seeing if all Lady Shoesmith's things are here, sir?"

The big man turned slowly, walked over to the table, and began idly to finger the rings. "Yes, they're all right," he said slowly. Then, suddenly, becoming alert—"But the pearls—where're the pearls?" And he began to rummage the drawers below.

Marrofat and Gartside went carefully round the room searching with practised fingers any other places that seemed likely, but the pearls were not forthcoming.

"Bathroom," suggested Gartside, in a low voice to his colleague.

"Not there," said the other. "I couldn't have missed them if they'd been about; but you can have a look."

With Sir Gideon he continued to search the bedroom until Gartside returned with a shake of his head.

"Let's go back to the other room," said the Superintendent. And they followed Sir Gideon to the sitting-room. "What were they worth?" he inquired, as he closed the door behind him.

"Seven thousand," replied Sir Gideon, "perhaps more today despite the fall of the market. Old Eaton knew pearls, and they were well bought."

"Well, it's pretty clear," the Superintendent ran his thick fingers through his mop of ginger curls, "it was the pearls he came for. But there's one thing, sir, I think I know our man.

That's a big help, he hasn't got time to get out of the country, and my name's not Marrofat if I don't bring him in."

Sir Gideon sank heavily into his arm-chair once more, but he seemed to have recovered from the first shock, and lit a fresh cigar. "Well," he said firmly, passing the box to the two detectives, "if there is anything which I can do to help you, let me know—money's no object, and I'll spend anything, anything, you understand—to ensure that the man who did this ghastly thing meets with his deserts."

"You can rely on us, sir," Marrofat nodded. "We shan't waste any time, in fact, we'll get right back to the Yard now, if there is nothing further which we can do for you first? Would you care for us to ring up Mr. Eaton, to come round here, or any friend of yours?"

"No—very good of you, Superintendent, but I think I'd rather be alone. Plenty of time for Richard to learn this sad news in the morning."

"Very good, sir, we won't trouble you any more, then. The inquest will be on Monday, and I'm afraid you'll have to attend. It should be purely formal, and I'll let you know the the time."

Sir Gideon made a movement to show the two officers out, but Marrofat stopped him. "I'll take a last look round before I go," he said, "and I expect the doctor's waiting to report. We'll have to lock the bathroom up, of course, and my man will remain on duty, but he won't trouble you, you'll hardly know he's here. Good night, Sir Gideon."

Outside, in the hall, the police surgeon was waiting, a lean Scotsman. In a few brief sentences he stated the cause of death, and his statement bore out De Richleau's view. Lady Shoesmith had died from a number of blows upon the back and base of the cranium, which had rendered her unconscious—she had then slipped underwater.

The Superintendent asked him if he thought the blows alone had brought about her death, and he replied:

"I'd not like to insure the life of ony puir pairson who'd been hit about the heid like that—but—I am of the opeenion that she was still alive when she slippit under water."

"Any idea about the thing she was hit with?" Marrofat inquired. The Scotsman shook his head.

" 'Twas the usual blunt instrument that the papers all haver about, but what that might be I haven't an idea. 'Twas sideways the puir thing was struck, and ye shall have a diagram in the morning, but noo I'll be off to my bed."

"Not a doubt of it," Marrofat said to his junior, when the doctor had gone. "This is Silky's job; he came for the pearls, and he got 'em. Knew that they were only off the woman's body for perhaps a quarter of an hour in the day—and most of the time when they were off her neck Sir Gideon was about. He watched the place for weeks, maybe, and made his run tonight. Then when he got in, the poor lady heard something, or came back into the bedroom to fetch something she'd forgotten—ran right on to him, as like as not—and he coshed her, slipped her back in the bath, and made a bolt for it. That explains his not monkeying with the safe. He was jumpy—jumpy as hell—and he beat it. But what a nerve to stop and talk to the old sister like that. Anyhow, thank God we've got three witnesses to identify—her and the two next door. What a bit of luck, and he hasn't time for a getaway. We'll pull him in before the morning."

"No chance of picking up any prints on the dressing-table, I suppose," suggested Gartside.

"Not a hope." Marrofat shrugged his shoulders. "I let Sammy clear out directly I heard that Silky was wearing white kid gloves."

CHAPTER VI

MR. REX VAN RYN ALSO BECOMES INQUISITIVE

THE Duke de Richleau sat with one of his slim legs crossed over the other in a deep arm-chair. He was beside the fire in the sitting-room of his own flat.

Van Ryn occupied another equally comfortable chair, and upon a small table placed between the two stood a couple of brandies and soda, and a box of cigarettes.

They had just returned from the opposite flat. After Sir Gideon's arrival they had felt that, since they could be of no more use, courtesy required that they should retire; and the

Duke, having assured Miss Eaton that should she or Sir Gideon be in any need of assistance they had only to send across, both had wished the timid, frightened lady good night.

Rex Van Ryn was terribly intrigued that unforeseen circumstances should have made him a witness, at first hand, of a recent murder. From what the Duke had just told him, he no longer doubted that Lady Shoesmith's death was by no means the tragic accident which it had at first appeared. When the Duke suggested that he should have a brandy and talk things over before going on to the dance, he had at once accepted.

"A queer word, murder," the Duke was saying. "Unlike so many other crimes, it expresses such a variety of actions: to kill, from a long hidden desire for revenge, secretly, plotting the death of your enemy—watching him die perhaps—increasing the dose of poison day by day. *That* is murder. Yet equally, if one of us normally reasonable human beings drank four times as much of this brandy as it is likely that we shall, we might become just the slightest bit mentally unbalanced, and on account of some obscure, imagined insult, take such incredible offence that one of us might seize that jewelled crucifix upon the table beside you and dash out the other's brains. *That* would be murder too."

"I'm terribly interested in that case across the hall. Since you've put me wise that it really is murder, I'd give a heap to know who did it—and just how, and when." Van Ryn sat forward eagerly in his chair.

"Yes," the Duke smiled, "murder and sudden death—they are always interesting. It is absurd, because, after all, sooner or later we all have to die. There are hundreds of people dying every minute while we sit here. I myself have never lost the thrill that such a thing always brings upon the spectator, although up and down the world I have seen much death in one form or another. It is perhaps the unexpectedness which holds the mind. We are all so secure in ourselves. We live on, and it is unthinkable to a healthy man that he should not be here next week; then when, without warning, we are brought into contact with death, it is as a writing on the wall, and we are frightened—just a very little frightened—that our own time might come before we are prepared—and it nearly always does!"

Van Ryn nodded. "That's just about it, I'll allow, but

30

I'd certainly like to be that big police boss next door—getting all the dope, and figuring out who did that woman in."

"An opportunity, my dear boy, for you to use your intelligence. Who could have done this thing? There is Miss Eaton, poor creature; there is the housemaid, and that formidable old cook; also we have young Monsieur Richard, and the Jewish young man whose visit has yet to be explained. And then there is a factor which we will call 'X'—an outside personality of whom we have as yet heard nothing, possibly only a burglar after loot."

"I'd say it was the Jew every time. How did he get in, anyway? You know, I can't get out of my mind that I've seen that fellar somewhere before."

"Well, in that case, try and remember where. From what little we know, I agree, a visit so unexplained is most suspicious. But where can you have seen him?"

Van Ryn lay back in the arm-chair, and closed his eyes for a few moments, then he sat up again. "No," he said, "I can't fix it. I'm sure I've seen him some place, and more than once— but where?—that's got me beat. I'll remember maybe in my bath one day next week!"

"Come now," De Richleau urged. "Next week—that is no good. If it was he he will be in Spain or Poland by that time. Think, my friend. Is it in America that you've seen this face?"

"It's right here in London."

"Is it in your office in the city that you've seen him?"

"No."

"Is it in the house of one of your friends here?"

"No, that's not it."

"Is it perhaps at your club?"

"No, it's not that either."

"Is it, then, at a restaurant?"

Rex grinned. "That'll be more like it. There's one thing certain, I'm pretty sure I've never seen him out of evening dress."

"Tell me the places that you go to in London."

"The Embassy quite a bit, the Ritz for luncheon, if I'm in the West End, and the Savoy at times. Listen here," he stood up suddenly, "I've got it—supper at the Berkeley."

"Monsieur Le Coq, I salute you," the Duke waved his slim hand. "But, seriously, this is interesting. Are you quite sure?"

"I certainly am." Rex took a long pull from his glass. "He

31

goes there every night—that is, every night I've been there, anyway—sitting right at the same table in the corner. I knew I'd seen him before some place the very moment I took a look at his face."

For a moment they sat in silence, and then the Duke asked with a little smile: "And are you really eager to follow up this little drama?"

"I am that. I've never been so near mixed up in a murder crime before. I'd certainly like to see the end of it."

"In that case, let's see what we can do. I have an idea, and I will endeavour to arrange something."

"Do you mean you're able to fix it so that we can follow the case from the inside, and get to know just what the police really think, apart from any fool stuff they let get put in the news-sheets?"

"That is what I should like to achieve. Not an easy matter, perhaps. The police have very strong objections to letting outside people participate in any special knowledge which they may secure. And they're right. It's when a criminal thinks himself safe that he is most likely to give himself away. Were they to take every Peter and Paul into their confidence, who knows but what the criminal might learn of their suspicions, and get away? Again, such special knowledge might encourage others to try their hand at detection, and that is the one thing above all others that the police abhor. The amateur does not understand police methods, and by rash enthusiasm may ruin a coup which has cost them weeks of careful work. That's an additional reason why they like to keep their conclusions to themselves."

"How do you figure to fix it, then? Through your pull with the Assistant Commissioner?"

De Richleau laughed. "Oh, no—no, I would not dream of putting my good friend Sir Anthony in the distressing position of having to refuse my request. Which it would most certainly be his duty to do. But are you quite, quite sure that you have made no mistake, and that it was the same young man that passed us on the stairs this evening as you have seen, not once but a number of times, having supper at the Berkeley?"

"Absolutely dead sure!" Van Ryn brought his large hand down with a thump upon the arm-chair.

"And have you seen him there within the last ten days?"

"Yes, I've suppered there three times in the last fortnigh't and I'm pretty sure he was there each time. He was there on Wednesday night for certain. I recall thinking to myself what a pretty girl it was he was hitting it up with. She was a lovely, and no mistake, and a lady too—or I've got her all wrong."

"Excellent, my friend." The Duke rose to his feet. "Excuse me but one moment, and I'll speak to the policemen. Help yourself to another drink."

"Thanks—I will." Rex also rose, and stretched his long legs.

De Richleau returned after only a couple of minutes' absence. "I've left a message," he said, "asking that our big friend the Superintendent will honour us with a few minutes of his time before he leaves the building."

"That's great." Rex sat down again. "I wonder what the motive could have been. That chap was evidently a stranger in the Shoesmith apartment, yet when we were across nobody put it up that there might have been a burglary, and that's how it occurred to me the moment you told me about the woman's head."

"You shouldn't attach too much importance to that, I think. In your own country, I know that robbery with violence is, unfortunately, an everyday affair, but here the professional thief is of meeker temperament. He dislikes, above all things, to kill. To make a robbery, that is his business, and he is prepared to face a certain term of imprisonment if he is caught, but—almost, I think, in the majority of cases—he would rather be caught than kill."

"Well, I'd be interested to know if they find anything missing, all the same."

De Richleau smiled. "If my little plot comes to fruition, your wish will be gratified shortly. If not, we shall have to wait for the newspapers to tell us."

"There didn't seem to be much in that apartment worth going for, I'll allow," Rex admitted. "Expensive sort of furniture, and all that, but not the kind of home where there'd be a stack of old silver or a Van Dyck. Still, there may have been jewels."

"There were jewels—that I can tell you, because I've passed Lady Shoesmith once or twice on the stairs. She was a fine-looking woman—and, if I'm any judge of such things, her jewels must have been of considerable value."

At that moment the Duke's man came in, he stooped a

little beside De Richleau's chair and said, very softly: "Two police officers are asking for Your Excellency."

The Duke nodded. "Show them in." And he rose to greet Superintendent Marrofat and his companion.

"Very nice of you to come over, Superintendent. I wanted a word with you, because my friend and I felt that we might be of some slight assistance to you."

"Very good of you, sir, I'm sure." Marrofat was polite but not encouraging. "In any case, I'd like to take the opportunity of warning you gentlemen that you may be needed for the inquest on Monday. I'll let you know the time."

"I see. Well, we will attend, of course, if you need our evidence. But now, Superintendent, sit down for one moment, and you, Inspector. I won't keep you long, but there are one or two things which it would interest me to know in this strange affair."

"Sorry, sir," the big man shook his head, "I'm afraid we must get back to the Yard."

"Of course, you have a lot to do." The Duke spoke soothingly. "But, as I said, I think my friend and myself may be able to help you."

"Yes, sir, I know you've been of great assistance, but, honestly, we must get along now."

"I think we can offer you a little special information which might interest you, but first you will not object, I think, to satisfying my curiosity as to if my theory of death was correct?"

"There's no harm in that, sir. The police surgeon confirmed your view."

"Good. Then I have by my indiscretion saved you perhaps an hour, thereby enabling you to complete your preliminary investigation already. If you can spare a few moments now, it is at least possible that I may render you still more important service."

The Superintendent shrugged his broad shoulders and sat down. "Any information you've got, sir, will be very welcome, of course."

"Excellent, my dear Superintendent. I felt sure that an officer of your rank would not be so foolish as to resent an offer of assistance just because it came from a civilian source."

"What exactly do you mean, sir?" Marrofat looked puzzled.

"Simply this—my friend and I are interested in this business.

34

Who would not be in the circumstances? We have a very human curiosity, therefore we should like to follow the inside of the affair. I know enough about police methods here to understand that, except for a very special reason, you would not tell us one single thing, and would resent any attempt on our part to interest ourselves in the case. We do not suggest doing so for one moment, but we would enormously appreciate the privilege of being able to formulate our own theories, upon such evidence as you may be able to secure from time to time."

"I'm afraid we couldn't do that, sir."

"Not if we could put you on the track of this murderer—tell you of a certain place which he frequents, where you would most certainly be able to secure some sort of line upon him?"

Marrofat raised one bushy eyebrow. "So you've made up your mind who did the job?"

De Richleau shrugged his slim shoulders. "Perhaps that's saying too much, but there is one strange figure whose presence is not accounted for?"

"You mean the young man that you met on the landing?"

"Exactly. My information is not so up-to-date as yours. Perhaps you know already what he was doing so curiously unannounced in the corridor?"

"No," said the big detective, slowly. "No, but I think I should warn Your Grace that it is your duty to give any information which you may have to the police, and it's no part of our business to tell you what we think."

"My duty! Ah!" The Duke spread out his elegant hands. "A horrid word, but, like many much greater people than myself, I have not always in my life done what appeared to be my duty."

"The withholding of information is a serious matter, sir."

"But I withhold nothing. On the contrary, I am anxious to help you. Come, at least in exchange give us the pleasure of a little excitement at second hand, let us hear tomorrow what you have done tonight."

The Superintendent stood up. "I'm afraid, sir," he said stiffly, "we are wasting each other's time."

"Surely not. If I could tell you of a place where this young man may be, even at this present moment—a place from which there must be many lines of inquiry, one of which might enable you to arrest him in a few hours?"

Marrofat smiled grimly. "I'd be very surprised if you could, sir. And what's more, I'd be very interested to know how a gentleman like Your Grace ever got in tow with an East End crook like 'Silky'."

"You know him, then?"

"Unless I'm very much mistaken, I do, and that's why I'm not going to bring a charge against Your Grace for withholding information. Good night to you, gentlemen." With this parting shot the big man turned on his heel, and walked heavily out of the room, followed by his attendant Inspector.

CHAPTER VII

THE "DARK HAUNT" OF SILKY

Rex Van Ryn threw himself back in the big arm-chair, and positively shook with laughter. "Can you beat it?" he stuttered to the Duke. "Talk about the frozen mitt!" And his wide mouth opened wider to more gusts of laughter.

De Richleau smiled ruefully. "Not a very great success, eh, that little plot of mine?"

"Forgive me," Van Ryn's laughter subsided to a broad grin, "it was great of you to try and get us in on this, but I just couldn't help being tickled by the way that big stiff turned us down."

"We were hardly to know that he had recognized a well-known criminal from our description. That was bad luck. But you realize one thing—do you not?"

Rex looked vague. "No—give it a name."

"That we're no longer under any moral obligation to this marvellous police force. We are, my friend, the stones that the builder rejected. If it should amuse us to do so, we are now quite free to continue the investigation on our own account."

"How?" Rex became suddenly grave. "Just what precisely do you mean, Duke?"

"Simply, that if you're still anxious to follow up the affair—why not? It is not unusual for the really big criminal to have two or more completely separate identities. In this case the police believe our man to be an East End crook, while we have knowledge that he frequents a smart West End hotel. Let's follow up our idea on our own initiative, and seek this young man in a place where obviously the police would never dream of looking."

"By Jove, you're right!"

"Perhaps, at all events, it would provide us with a little mild amusement if luck were with us, and we succeeded in running this 'Silky' to earth before our fat friend."

"Come on," Rex heaved himself to his feet and towered above his elegant host. "Let's get to it right away."

The Duke rose to his feet more gently. "You agree? That's excellent, but let us hasten slowly!" He laid his hand upon Van Ryn's arm. "Let us first settle the details of our campaign."

"We'll go right over and beat up the Berkeley. There isn't a hope in hell he'll be there, but we'll get on to Ferraro, and the hall porter, and all the boys. They're bound to know him. It's ten to one he signs his bills. That'll give us a line, and if he's got an account, they'll have his address."

"And then?" inquired the Duke.

"We'll go right down to his place; if he's at home we'll call the police, if he's not there we'll sit on the mat till he turns up."

De Richleau nodded. "That seems sound, but wait one moment. If we get his address, make our call and if he is at home, how do you propose to keep him till the police arrive? You must remember that he saw us both this evening upon the landing of the flat. The criminal has a trained memory, and whatever excuse we might give for our call he will recognize us instantly and immediately escape."

"Not on your life," Rex laughed aloud. "If I set eyes on that bird, trust me to sit on his head all right."

The Duke smiled grimly. "Delightfully irregular, my dear fellow. Since we have no warrant for his arrest you will most certainly be liable for assault; but I should be completely disappointed in you if you did less. Let us go forth and see if we can catch our man."

As they came downstairs the hall porter ran out to open

the door of De Richleau's car, which was still waiting in the foggy street.

"One moment, Frederick." The Duke called him back into the sheltered hallway.

"Yes, sir?" the ex-soldier saluted respectfully.

"This is a sad business, Frederick, about Lady Shoesmith."

"It is indeed, Your Grace."

"Were you on duty downstairs at the time?"

"I was, sir. I come on at eight o'clock."

"I see—a terrible thing," the Duke went on thoughtfully, "yet one cannot help being interested. Were you here all the time, Frederick?"

"Yes, sir, I was sitting reading my book, and after that the evening paper. I've never moved from here."

"Then you would have been quite certain to have seen any unusual person come in or out?"

"Quite, Your Grace."

"And you saw no one?"

"No one at all, sir, except the young gentleman the police are so interested in. They asked me a lot of questions about him—the time he came, and the time he left, and what he said, and so on."

"I wonder, Frederick, if you would mind giving these particulars to me?"

"Certainly, sir. He came a little after ten, walking he was—not in a car, and he just said to me: 'Sir Gideon Shoesmith?' no more, no less. I told him first floor on the left, so he nods and walks upstairs—in a bit of a hurry he seemed—that would be a little after ten; but he wasn't upstairs no longer than a few minutes, because Your Grace arrived with this gentleman, and you'd hardly gone up when he comes down and asked me, very polite, did I think I could get him a taxi. As luck would have it, one set down only a few doors away, and all I had to do was to beckon the driver up, and the young gentleman gives me a shilling for my trouble."

"And how long do you think he was actually in the flats?"

"Five minutes maybe—not that, I wouldn't think."

"Have you ever seen him before?"

"No, Your Grace, not that I know of."

"Do you know young Mr. Eaton?"

38

"Oh! yes, I know Mr. Eaton, sir, he comes quite frequent to see his mother."

"And do you happen to remember what time he left this evening?"

"It would be before ten, sir."

"You're certain of that?"

"Quite certain, sir. I stood up as he came down into the hall and put me book down—I remember looking at the clock and wondering if I'd be able to finish it before ten; I had just four more pages to go, that's what makes me so certain."

"Thank you, Frederick, thank you, I am much obliged." The Duke turned and, followed by Rex, climbed into the waiting car.

"He didn't exactly go to sleep here, did he?" Rex commented; "five minutes or less."

"Enough," said the Duke quietly, "if he came for her jewels and knew his business. If she was dressing at the time they would probably be in the bedroom, scattered about; perhaps he knew that and chose his time with care."

The big car nosed its way carefully forward through the gloom. "What'll we do," inquired Rex suddenly, "if the people at the Berkeley can't give us any information? That'll pretty well put us up against it!"

The Duke leaned forward for a moment to peer out into the fog, then he settled himself comfortably back, despite the shortness of the journey.

"Don't worry, my dear fellow," he said cheerfully. "If it is as you say, and our quarry is really an *habitué*, we shall find somebody who will be able to tell us something about him. I know Ferraro well, he is a charming fellow, always a table for his old friends, even when the restaurant is crowded to the ceiling—a *maître d'hôtel* of the old type who knows his business, an artist, too—he paints in his spare time, and paints well. He once presented me with a little picture—a charming thing, and when I speak to Ferraro he will tell us what we want to know, even if he has to question every one of his men as to when they have seen this man before. A waiter's fortune lies in his memory, you may be certain that there will be some information for us to go on."

As the Duke finished speaking they arrived before the hotel. In the entrance of the restaurant they found Ferraro: dark,

39

curling hair brushed smoothly back across his high forehead, blue shaven chin, spotless white double-breasted waistcoat. Quick, smiling, authoritative, with but two eyes and two ears, yet seemingly one for every waiter and every guest.

The revolving door had not ceased its turning before he had seen the new arrivals. He did not come forward, but stood near his desk, arms hanging loosely from his broad shoulders, smiling as he made his little bow.

"Monsieur le Duc—you are quite a stranger. Vercini!" he snapped his fingers in the air to one of his lieutenants. "*Numero vingt-cinq*—M. le Duc's old table—What you say? Ah! I am getting old—*numero trente-deux*—it is better, we have redecorated the room since M. le Duc has been to see us. Mr. Van Ryn—good evening, sir, a pleasure to see you 'ere."

M. de Richleau returned the greeting. With one quick glance into the restaurant, he had seen that his favourite table was already occupied, an Indian potentate apparently.

Ferraro caught his glance and knew he knew, and the Duke knew Ferraro knew too, but they were charming to each other, and respected each other for their knowledge.

"My friend," declared the Duke amiably. "we will sup later perhaps—but I come to talk to you a little, a most inconvenient hour I fear, but I will not keep you long. Can we find a quiet corner?"

Ferraro gave one quick glance round the crowded restaurant. The after-theatre rush was over, only a few couples lingered at the tables in the passage; then, muttering a few words to an underling in rapid Italian, he turned and led the way down the corridor.

He took them to the little lounge behind the grill; it was quite deserted and the strains of the band came faint and muted from the distance. The Duke lost no time in describing the young man of whom they were in search.

"But, of course," Ferraro played with something in his waistcoat pocket, "the gentleman M. le Duc seeks is Monsieur Aron—Monsieur Simon Aron. I know him well—he is here this evening."

"Now what have you got to say to that?" Van Ryn exclaimed.

"One moment," said the Duke. "Tell me, Ferraro, how long has this young man been here?"

"Since 'alf past ten—perhaps a bit before. 'E was before the theatre tonight, he told me he expected someone—his friend Mr. Eaton; but Mr. Eaton 'as not come so 'e is alone."

De Richleau nodded to Van Ryn, then he turned again to the Italian. "Have you known this Monsieur Aron long?"

"Oh yes, he is a good customer. Sometimes he do not come for a long time, then all at once he is here, three times—four times—in a week, and if things are bad that is a sure sign Monsieur Aron will come 'ere and spend money; but if things are good or things are bad—it does not matter, always I have a table for Monsieur Aron."

"I understand," the Duke smiled, "yet he is not, what shall I say, one of the young men who have grown up with you since Eton and Sandhurst—what is it you say. The Berkeley Boys! is it not?"

"Ah! no, Monsieur le Duc, quite different, but Monsieur Aron, he understands about good food, and good wine, it is a pleasure to serve such a gentleman—always so quiet, so smiling —and with a knowledge just as to how a dish should be done."

"And does he pay well, this Monsieur Aron?"

Ferraro laughed again. "Does 'e pay! Always—not foolishly, but generous, you understand—and sometimes 'e 'as put me on to things where I make nice money. If Monsieur Aron ask me to len 'im a hundred pounds one night—'e can 'ave it."

"I am most grateful to you," the Duke replied. "I know that you're busy so we will not keep you any longer. We shall, I think, be supping later, my friend and I. In the meantime if Monsieur Aron should show any signs of leaving you might be kind enough to let me know."

"M. le Duc—Monsieur," the ever-smiling Ferraro bowed to them in turn and slipped away.

Once alone the other two faced each other. "Congratulations, my dear Van Ryn," proffered the Duke. "It's our man, without a doubt; you heard he was expecting Eaton to join him for supper?"

"Yes, and that's pretty queer to my mind—why should young Eaton be friends with an East End crook?"

"Possibly they both had a hand in it?"

Rex shook his head. "No, I judge we can cut that idea right out, you're forgetting it's the boy's own mother."

41

"True." The Duke stroked his ascending eyebrows thoughtfully. "Perhaps our friends the police are on the wrong track altogether."

"Maybe—all the more fun for us, but anyway you look at it we've got our man! What'll we do next?"

"Well, the one thing we cannot do is to adhere to our original programme. If I remember, you were to sit on his head until the police arrived."

"We can call the Superintendent on the wire and watch Aron till he turns up!"

"Yes," agreed the Duke with a sigh. "That is, I suppose what we must do, but almost it seems too easy!"

CHAPTER VIII

THE UNOFFICIAL POLICEMEN AND THE UNOFFICIAL CROOK

THE Duke and Van Ryn regarded each other silently, both were turning the situation over in their own minds. There could no longer be any doubt but that they had discovered the whereabouts of that unannounced visitor who had been found in the Shoesmiths' flat. It would be no small triumph to ring up Superintendent Marrofat and inform him politely that they had found his man.

Yet both were a little disappointed that the chase was over so quickly. The Duke's words: "It seems almost too easy," echoed in Van Ryn's ears; he had visions of all sorts of interesting inquiries and questionings, leading eventually perhaps to the visitation of mean streets in the East End, or upon the south side of the river, and finally running their man to earth in the early hours of the morning.

And now the whole business had ended so tamely. Well, there was one consolation Rex felt, at one time it had looked as if he'd have to cut Lady Ingram's dance altogether—now he'd be certain of seeing Felicity. He spoke slowly.

"I suppose you'd better get on to the big boy while I watch the restaurant."

"You're right," the Duke agreed; "at least the Superintendent should show us some consideration for our find."

But it was fated that the evening should not end just like that, for as the Duke de Richleau turned towards the doorway of the little lounge he saw a thin, stooping figure in the entrance—it was Mr. Simon Aron!

"Good evening," said Mr. Aron quietly. He looked full at the Duke, his quick, dark eyes taking in the other thoughtfully. "Ferraro told me that some friends of mine wanted to see me before I left—but I don't think we've met before?"

The Duke smiled. "I fear, Mr. Aron, that for once Ferraro has proved indiscreet. We cannot claim your acquaintance, nor did we send any message. I simply told him that if you left the restaurant he was to let me know."

"I see." Mr. Aron very deliberately removed his pince-nez, put them in their case, and then produced a fat cigarette, which he lit from a gold lighter—but never once did his eyes leave the Duke's face.

"May I—" he inquired hesitatingly, "may I ask why?"

"Certainly," the Duke lied promptly. "My friend"—he waved his hand in the direction of Van Ryn—"and myself are acting on behalf of Scotland Yard."

"Really?" Mr. Aron commented with the faintest suggestion of amusement, but he said no more.

"The police are very anxious to ask you one or two questions, Mr. Aron," the Duke continued. "Perhaps therefore, you would not object to accompanying us to Scotland Yard?"

"I should mind very much," replied the young Jew evenly.

"Nevertheless, it is necessary," said the Duke with some firmness.

"Oh!" the other nodded his bird-like head slowly. "You've got a warrant, of course?"

"No, we have no warrant, but we can procure one with very little delay; I suggest, therefore, that you should spare us that trouble."

"Oh, so you haven't got a warrant? I see, now that's a bit awkward for you, isn't it?" Mr. Aron's voice was sympathetic.

"Don't you worry," Rex remarked with a grim smile, "we'll hold on to you until we get one all right."

43

"Will you?" Mr. Aron brought his head forward to the lower level of his cigarette, his eyes flickered from Van Ryn to the Duke and back. "I'm afraid you've made some mistake," he said evenly. "I'm going home."

Rex had moved a little so as to be just between Aron and the door. "I'll say you're not," he grinned. "You're going to stay right here while the Duke gets the police, and that's all there is to it."

Mr. Aron had also moved a little, so that by an almost unnoticed gesture, his hand rested upon the bell. "I—er—don't know who you are," he said still quite calmly. "Of course, it may be some kind of joke—I don't know—I don't care, really, but if you don't stand away from that door I'm going to ring for Ferraro and have you chucked out."

Monsieur de Richleau realized that they had gone too far; evidently this young man could not be bluffed. He shrugged his shoulders lightly. "Mr. Aron," he temporized, "my friend, you will understand, is from the Uuited States, he has forgotten for the moment that in England things are done differently; but you will realize, I'm sure, that if the police wish to speak to you—they most certainly will—and it is only a question as to if it is to be now or in, perhaps, two hours' time."

Mr. Aron nodded slowly. "Quite—but—er—forgive me if I'm wrong—I don't think you are the—er—police?"

"No, I confess that we are not; but I am quite justified in saying that we are acting on their behalf. It's true that they are very anxious to see you; and may I suggest that even if we are unable to prevent you leaving this hotel you also cannot stop us following you when you go. Neither can you prevent us asking every policeman who we may pass to inform his head-quarters that we have you in view. I am told that what they term the flying squad is of an amazing rapidity. We should all be picked up quite soon."

Mr. Simon Aron's full lips curved into a wide smile. "Yes," he agreed slowly, "that sounds quite reasonable; but may I ask exactly who you—er—are?"

"My name is De Richleau," volunteered the Duke, "my friend is Rex van Ryn."

Mr. Aron nodded his bird-like head to each in turn, his slightly open mouth gave the impression that he was still some-

44

what amused. "And—er," he went on, "just what sort of trouble am I supposed to be in?"

"You will perhaps recall having seen myself and my friend before this evening?" said the Duke.

"Ner," replied Mr. Aron, and he pronounced it just like that, with his mouth still slightly open, and a little sideways shake of the head. "Ner—I don't think so."

"Upon the staircase in Errol House in Curzon Street about ten past ten?"

"Now wait a minute." Mr. Aron drew the hand that held the cigarette across his long receding forehead. "Of course I do, you were coming upstairs as I was going down, that's right."

"Exactly. You had, I think, been to Sir Gideon Shoesmith's flat?"

"Um." Quite unperturbed, Aron nodded his bird-like head in the affirmative once more.

"It's in connexion with your visit to Errol House that the police are so anxious to see you."

"Really?" Mr. Aron seemed to consider, his gaze flickered from the Duke to Van Ryn. "I am afraid I—er don't see why?"

Monsieur de Richleau hesitated. If this man had actually been guilty of the crime committed less than two hours ago he was, in any case, forewarned that the police were on his track. What further harm, then, could be done by speaking of the murder?

"Perhaps," said the Duke, "you do not know that Lady Shoesmith died a few hours ago?"

"What?" Simon Aron scarcely breathed the word, and his wide mouth stood open. "Lady Shoesmith dead?" he said in a quick whisper. "That rather alters things, doesn't it?"

There was silence for a minute in the little lounge. Then he asked suddenly: "How did she die?"

"There is some reason to suppose that she was murdered," replied the Duke quietly.

"Murdered—Really! I say!" said Simon jerkily. "Seems we're n a bit of a muddle here."

"You will appreciate," the Duke continued, "that since the murder, if it was murder, was committed within a few moments, perhaps, of the time at which you visited Errol House this evening—how anxious the authorities are to hear what you have to say."

"Yes, but it doesn't follow that I want to—er—say anything to them, at the moment." Aron gave a nervous little cough into the hand that held the cigarette. "Tell me," he continued jerkily, "what—er—part do you play in all this?"

De Richleau shrugged. "It just happened that my friend and I were present when the alarm was raised, and the tragedy discovered. Also that we chanced to see you on the staircase. Van Ryn remembered that he had seen you before, and *where* —so here we are—it is quite simple."

"Awkward, isn't it, very awkward," said Mr. Aron, with just the suspicion of a smile.

"I should judge it'll be pretty awkward for you to explain just what you were doing in that apartment," remarked Van Ryn, who had remained a silent spectator for some time.

"Yes, and pretty awkward for you when Ferraro has you chucked out on the pavement," suggested Mr. Aron. "But don't let's talk about that!"

For a few moments he puffed slowly at a new cigarette which he had lit from the stub of the last, then he went on carefully, his eyes travelling quickly from one to the other. "Now, I'll tell you, I don't like it, it's much too bad a muddle, and even if you had a warrant I wouldn't answer any questions— not tonight. If I could get hold of my solicitor it would be different, but I can't—not till tomorrow." He paused, and then went on again, shooting out his short, jerky sentences. "But look here, tell me—what exactly are you out to gain—I'll tell you what I think, shall I? You're out for an evening's fun!"

The Duke smiled. "You're perfectly correct. Mr. Aron, we have allowed ourselves the somewhat childish pleasure of endeavouring to forestall the British police, and it so happens that we have succeeded."

"Exactly," Aron nodded. "Now, having found me, are you in a hurry—I mean for an hour or so—to hand me over to Scotland Yard?"

"No, not particularly. All that we wish, Mr. van Ryn and I," the Duke was exceedingly amiable, "is the pleasure of your company till we do."

"I see. Well, that's splendid, because I was just going to put up a little suggestion to you."

46

"By all means," the Duke agreed blandly, "as long as it is not that you should leave us?"

"Ner—oh, ner—I give you my word that I won't run away." For the first time Mr. Aron left his strategic position by the bell. He began to walk up and down the small apartment, one hand in the pocket of his very shapely dress trousers, the other, which held the fat cigarette, constantly going back and forth to his full lips as he talked. He no longer kept his eyes fixed upon either of the others. But, as he went softly to and fro with his head thrust forward, he occasionally gave a rapid sideways glance to see how they were taking his suggestions.

"It's like this," he said jerkily. "If you try to force my hand—I'll get out. Ferraro's an old friend of mine—he wouldn't like to see me arrested, not a little bit. I might, or I might not, go to Scotland Yard later—I don't know—but, in any case, I'd have to talk to my solicitor. But if you're not in a hurry for a bit and cared to join me for—er—a little supper—we could talk things over, and then see how we feel. Is that all right?"

Rex grinned. He was beginning to like Mr. Aron a little better than he had at first. "An armed neutrality while we get better acquainted—eh—Is that the idea?" He turned to the Duke. "What do you say?"

"I?—Oh!" said the Duke de Richleau affably, "I shall be delighted to accept Mr. Aron's very kind invitation. I was just beginning to feel like supper."

CHAPTER IX

MR. SIMON ARON ENTERTAINS

IT was a strange trio that filed into the restaurant a few moments later. The Duke led the way, and it was at him that people turned to look. Even Van Ryn's well-proportioned height and attractive head did not dwarf the distinction of the older man, and De Richleau's fine, sensitive face held many glances as they passed down the long room. Simon Aron brought up the rear of the procession, a position which he had taken naturally as host. Van Ryn had pressed him to go behind the Duke—but Aron had been insistent, and his quick smile flashed out as he caught the American turn to see if he were really following. He knew quite well it was in the other's mind that he might seize the opportunity to slip away.

Once seated at the table Mr. Aron produced his pince-nez, and ran his eye down the long *carte* quickly. However he laid both the glasses and the *carte* aside and turned to his guests.

"Now, I wonder what you'd like? The *croûte* should be very good just now," he suggested hesitantly. "I always used to go to Paris for a few days in November to sample the first one at the Ritz—couldn't go this year—little bit of a muddle one of my friends got into—had to stay in town."

"That'll be fine for me," Van Ryn agreed. And the Duke nodded his concurrence.

"Good, then—what about a *bécasse*?" Mr. Aron went on. "Ferraro does a *bécasse* very well, you know."

"You are, I perceive, a gourmet, Mr. Aron," smiled De Richleau. "The *bécasse* is a bird for which I have a quite exceptional partiality."

"Don't count me in." Rex waved the suggestion aside. "The *foie gras* amd a good long drink will do me well."

"Are you—er—sure?" Simon Aron carefully wiped his pince-nez with his handkerchief, and placed them beside his plate. "We did say that we weren't in any particular hurry, didn't we?"

"That's true," Rex admitted. "All right, I'll have the woodcock, too."

"Splendid. Then after that we shall see? We might manage a peach, perhaps, done with a little Kirsch or something—but we'll see later. Now what would you like to drink?"

"We are, I am sure, quite safe in your hands," said De Richleau amicably.

"Well, personally, I'd say burgundy with the *bécasse*. Ferraro has a little Romanée la Tache, 1906, which is not on the wine list. Nice wine—but perhaps you would prefer champagne?"

"If it's all the same to you," said Rex. "I'd rather drink champagne. Some time before the night's out I'll be going on to a party, and burgundy would send me right off to sleep."

Mr. Aron nodded to Ferraro, who was taking down the order in person. "Better have a magnum of Bollinger put on the ice."

48

"Very good, Mr. Aron, and a little salad with the *bécasse*—eh! salade Japonaise? All right—I send the wine at once. Very good, Mr. Aron."

As Ferraro moved away a rather awkward silence fell upon the three men at the table. It was the Duke who broke the ice. "Is it not curious," he began, "that we three, who to all outward appearance must seem like old friends spending a pleasant evening together—would none of us have known the other two had we lunched here at adjacent tables earlier in the day."

"You didn't know Mr. Van Ryn until this unfortunate business, either?" Simon Aron inquired.

It was Rex who answered. "No, I didn't meet the Duke in exactly that connexion, but I only made his acquaintance tonight. And I'll say he's given me an interesting evening all right!"

"It is to chance you are indebted, not me, my friend," the Duke smiled; "but now we're agreed not to endeavour to procure the arrest of our host until after supper, can't we inquire a little further into this interesting tragedy which has brought us together? What do you think, Mr. Aron?"

Simon Aron's eyes flickered from one to the other. "It all depends," he said non-committally. "What exactly do you want to know?"

De Richleau leant forward. "Mr. Aron, quite frankly we have no shadow of justification for prying into the affairs of other people; it is, in fact, almost an impertinence, but since we have become drawn into this affair we have given way to a quite shameless curiosity. It would interest us greatly to learn just what your association with the Shoesmiths may be? Why you called at Errol House this evening? How long you were there? Who you saw and what you did?"

"I see, well—I promise nothing—you understand? Nothing at all. But I'm quite in the dark as to what happened. If you—er—care to tell me what you know I'll see if I can add anything."

"I wonder"—the Duke raised his well-marked eyebrows—"how far I should be justified in doing that. You will be aware, Mr. Aron, that the police rely very largely upon any admission that may be made by the suspected person in the first examination. The person questioned is in a very difficult situation, because he is quite in the dark as to what the police know, and what they

49

have failed to find out. Now, I think I may say that we know very nearly as much as the police. If I were to tell you what we know, I should therefore, suggesting you were guilty, be enabling you to prepare your defence."

"Defence?" Simon Aron gave the Duke a sharp glance. "You—you're not suggesting that I had anything to do with the actual murder—are you?"

De Richleau smiled grimly. "Having gone so far, I don't think we are, as you say, giving anything away—by admitting that you are the person under suspicion."

Aron gave a quick, nervous chuckle—stooping his bird-like head over his hand. "Dear me," he almost tittered, "we *are* in a muddle. But, seriously," he added gravely, "would you mind if I tried to get hold of my solicitor?"

"Mr. Aron," the Duke fixed his bright eyes on the young man, "under somewhat curious circumstances, we have accepted your hospitality—Mr. Van Ryn and I. But, having done so, we are your guests, and I speak for both of us when I assure you that anything which you may say at this table will be completely forgotten when we leave; or even if the police should enter and arrest you while we are here."

"Thank you," said Simon Aron simply.

There was a long silence; all three spread the delicate pink *paté* upon the thick squares of hot toast, and sipped occasionally at their champagne. Simon Aron was thinking hard. At last he said slowly:

"Look here—it seems to me—this is a bad business. Mind you—if what you say is true, nothing in the world would induce me to talk to the police without my solicitor—and it's not going to be easy to get hold of him till tomorrow."

"I think," said the Duke, "that you are a very wise young man."

"Good, I'm glad you agree about that! Now I'll tell you I was wondering if we can't come to some arrangement—I mean, I don't want to spend the night in Vine Street—but I'm perfectly willing to turn up anywhere you like, at ten o'clock tomorrow morning. Then you can have the fun of handing me over to the police."

Rex grinned. "Come on now, you can't expect to get away with it like that. Just supposing, now, that you were the guy that planned the whole party—what a hope we'd have of seeing you tomorrow."

"Exactly," Simon Aron nodded, "all the same there must be some way we can get round that. I'll stay here for the night, if you like—take a small suite—you can have a man in the sitting-room; or I tell you what—I'll go further. I'm inclined to suffer from insomnia—rotten thing—if you like you can send out for some medinal, give me a dose and send me to bed; then take all my clothes away in a parcel—how's that?"

"Would you agree to the same conditions in my flat?" asked the Duke.

"Um," Aron nodded. "To tell the truth I'm only anxious to avoid a very uncomfortable night, and to have my solicitor with me when I make a statement—that's all."

"If we agree to your suggestion, will you satisfy our quite unjustifiable curiosity?"

"Yes, I don't see why not, providing you tell me just how bad this muddle is."

"What do you say, Van Ryn?" De Richleau asked. "Shall we run the risk of spiking the Superintendent's guns?"

"Why not?" the big American shrugged. "It's not our job to bottle feed the police of this country."

"Then let's make our treaty." The Duke looked fixedly at Mr. Aron. "Upon our part we will tell you what we know of this affair, and we will refrain from informing the police of your whereabouts until ten o'clock tomorrow morning. Upon your part you agree to accept my hospitality till that time, to take the harmless sleeping draught which I shall give you, and surrender your apparel. Also you will tell us that which you know. Is it agreed?"

"And—er," Mr. Aron wriggled his neck with a nervous movement in his collar, "anything which I may say as your host, or your guest, is to be forgotten tomorrow?"

"That is so."

"Um—I'll agree to that."

Rex looked round. "You know, people just wouldn't believe this if they saw it in a play."

Mr. Aron again stooped his head to give his little jerky laugh into the palm of his hand. "Yes," he agreed, "but I'd rather see it on the stage, all the same. I could come out then!

51

But seriously—if you wouldn't mind telling me what happened."

Briefly, and clearly, the Duke outlined the events which had taken place, as far as Van Ryn and he knew them, since they had first seen Simon Aron on the staircase of Errol House so much earlier in the evening.

The young Jew listened intently, his long, almost Chinese eyes narrowing from time to time, as he interrupted to ask a shrewd question until, point by point, he became as fully informed as the other two.

When this recital was finished, Aron nodded his head slowly. "A muddle, eh! A really nasty muddle—" he murmured as if to himself, then he suddenly sat up.

"All right—now I'll tell you what I can. First of all about the Shoesmiths, I only knew them through Richard Eaton. He's a friend of mine. As a matter of fact I've never seen Sir Gideon, I believe Lady Shoesmith only married him a few months ago—and I don't know her very well. I've only met her once or twice at cocktail parties at Richard's flat. The Aunt, Miss Eaton, I've never seen till tonight; so I can't really tell you much about them. Sir Gideon is an accountant, I think, but Lady Shoesmith has plenty of money of her own. Old Eaton had any amount of money, and he left it all to her."

"Who gets the lion's share now?" Van Ryn inquired.

"Richard, I believe."

"Has young Eaton any sort of a job?"

"Yes," Aron nodded slowly, "he's in the book business, runs a private press, you may know it—The Galleon Press, it's called, and he runs the whole show on his own. Richard's clever at types and bindings, he's turned out some quite nice stuff."

"I do know it," the Duke volunteered, "their *Menander* was quite charming."

"I wouldn't judge there to be much money in that sort of lay-out," said the practical American. "Seems to me nobody reads anything but detective fiction these days."

Simon Aron shrugged. "Don't know, still people with money about—who buy good stuff—look at the Nonesuch Press, and the Golden Cockerel, they must have made a packet."

"Let's return to the more interesting subject of your visit to Errol House this evening," suggested the Duke.

52

"Well—I was coming to that. You see I promised to have dinner with my mother this evening, then afterwards I was going to meet Richard here for supper—as a matter of fact we had a little business that we wanted to talk over; then my mother put me off at the last moment, and so it occurred to me that I might go round to Errol House and have a chat with Sir Gideon before I met Richard. So I rang up after dinner, and was told that if I came round at once, Sir Gideon would see me—'' he paused.

"And then?" prompted De Richleau.

"Then when I got there I walked upstairs and I found the door of the flat ajar—so I went in." He paused again. "Then I saw the little grey-haired lady come down the corridor and she turned me out."

A marked silence fell upon the three men at the table. Simon Aron's eyes moved rapidly from one to the other of his guests. 'Sounds a bit thin—doesn't it?" he said with a wry smile, "I was afraid you'd think that!"

"On the contrary," said the Duke quickly, "from what little I've seen of you, Mr. Aron, I would at least pay you the compliment of expecting you to tell a much more artistic story, if you wished to give us anything but the truth. I'm puzzled, that's all."

"Who answered the call?" asked Van Ryn.

"The butler, I should have thought," replied Aron evenly.

De Richleau paused, his slim hand extended to secure another piece of hot toast from beneath the folded napkin. "But surely you must realize that they do not keep a butler in the flat.''

"I know," Simon Aron nodded, "queer—isn't it?"

"Who could it have been that you spoke to, then? Sir Gideon was out, he left at a little after seven to attend the dinner at the Park Lane Hotel, and it was nearly eleven before he returned."

"How about young Eaton?" suggested Van Ryn.

"Ner!" Again Simon gave the curiously pronounced negative 'through half-open lips. "Ner—I talk to him on the telephone two or three times a week—it wasn't Richard."

"Just what gave you the idea it was the butler, anyway?" Rex asked.

"It was the way he spoke."

"Can you recall what he said and what you said too?"

"Oh, yes, I asked—'Is that Sir Gideon Shoesmith's flat?'" and a man's voice said, 'Yes,' then I said, 'This is Simon Aron speaking, I'm a friend of Richard Eaton's—I particularly wanted to have a word with Sir Gideon this evening. I wonder if I could come round now; I'm at my club in Piccadilly'—then there was a little pause, and the voice replied: 'Yes, sir, if you'll hold the line I'll tell Sir Gideon,'—and then I waited for a minute or two, and the voice said: 'Sir Gideon says he can see you if you can come round at once,' then I said: 'Thank you,' and hung up."

"Well, now, can you beat that?" exclaimed Rex. "He had some nerve, I'll say, whoever he was."

"And at what time was this?" asked the Duke.

"Just after ten."

"That must have been about the time it happened," the Duke commented. "Whoever did this thing heard the telephone bell ring, and decided that it was less dangerous to answer than allow it to ring—and disturb the other occupants of the flat."

"That's about it," Rex agreed, "but how do you account for Mr. Aron finding the front door open?"

"Ah, my friend," laughed De Richleau, "he had quick wits, that one, even while Mr. Aron was speaking to him on the telephone, he realized the possibilities of that chance call. Therefore, instead of saying, 'Sir Gideon is out,' he said: 'Come along here now, at once.' Then he finished quickly what he had to do, and went—leaving the door a little open, hoping that Aron would walk in; and you see, Aron did walk in. So that even if Miss Eaton had not discovered him so quickly, he would have rung the bell, and been found by the servants with that door just a little open—therefore suspicion would, in any case, have fallen upon him."

"Exactly." Simon Aron wriggled his shoulders. "So we're in a muddle—in a nasty muddle."

The attentive waiter was clearing the remains of the woodcock from the table.

"Now, what about a peach?" Aron suggested. The others shook their heads.

"Coffee, then—waiter, coffee for three."

54

For a little time they sat smoking over their coffee, not saying much, then Rex remarked:

"Didn't you say you had a date with Richard Eaton tonight for supper? Doesn't it strike you as mighty queer that he hasn't turned up?"

"Oh, Richard!" Simon's dark eyes flickered away from the table, and then with a steady gaze they met Van Ryn's. "Richard's hopeless about appointments, bit of an artist, you know—he's often let me down before. By the way, didn't you say you had a party, or something?"

"By Jove, yes." Rex looked at his watch. "Do you know it's a quarter to one?"

"Don't—er—think I want to hurry you," Aron murmured. "I'm ready to stay up, or go to bed—just as you like."

"Well, if it's all the same to you, I ought to beat it," Rex confessed, "that is, after I've acted as guard of honour for you, back to the Duke's flat."

"You still think—er—that I'm the criminal?" Aron inquired, smiling, as he sent for his bill.

"No, I wouldn't go so far as to say that," Rex replied, regarding the young man curiously, "but I'd be interested to know if you think the police will accept your story?"

Simon Aron laughed again, his queer little nervous laugh into the palm of his hand. " 'Fraid they'll have to," he chuckled. "Anyhow, it seems I've made pretty good arrangements to ensure that it shan't keep me awake!"

CHAPTER X

HOW LADY FELICITY SPENT THE SMALL HOURS OF THE MORNING

It was a little after one when Rex, having seen the Duke and their prisoner safely back to Errol House, walked round the corner to Lady Ingram's in Audley Square.

The dance was in full swing, the whole of the recessed portion of South Audley Street, which forms the so-called square, being

55

filled with lines of cars. Even at this late hour one or two rather bedraggled spectators stood on the pavement by the awning watching the arrival and departure of the guests.

The house was one seething mass of people, and the babel of talk almost drowned the band. Rex shouldered his way through the crush up the staircase; he held a brief, smiling conversation with Irma Ingram, who was still receiving, and, skilfully avoiding the onset of an elderly woman whom he had met at a dinner-party a few nights before, succeeded in reaching the double drawing-room, where dancing was in progress.

His eyes sought only for one small fair head, and his unusual height gave him the advantage of being able to survey the whole room easily from his position by the door. He had soon convinced himself that she was not among the dancers, so he next tried the supper-room, and here he was more fortunate.

"Hallo! Felicity," he grinned, striding eagerly up to her, despite the fact she was apparently in earnest conversation with a sandy-haired young man.

She raised her eyebrows. "Why, if it isn't my big, foolish American," she said gaily.

"Not foolish," he corrected. "Clean, plumb crazy!" And from his smiling glance it was not difficult to tell what he was crazy about!

Lady Felicity Standish looked quickly away. "Have you been here long?" she inquired ingenuously.

"Now, have a heart!" he protested. "Wouldn't I have been around pestering you for dances if I had? I've just this very moment come."

"Isn't that too sad," she smiled demurely. "If I'd known for certain that you were coming I might have saved you a couple. As it is there's not a hope until I don't know when, unless the tenth extra is any use to you?"

"That'll be about four in the morning, and it's no use at all," said Rex firmly. "We'd better go into conference and rearrange the map of Europe." He turned and regarded the sandy-haired young man with a steady stare.

The youth rose awkwardly and looked at Felicity, but she did not proffer an introduction. She just smiled at him sweetly and rather vaguely as she said: "Reggie, dear, wouldn't you like to get yourself a little drink?"

"Think I will," he murmured, and then to Rex, "Here take my place."

"Thanks," said Rex heartily, as he promptly sat down on the vacated chair, "I will."

"Bye-bye, Felicity," said the young man lazily as he moved off, "have a nice time with your big friend."

Felicity turned to Rex, "You *were* rude to poor Reggie."

"Rude?" protested Rex, leaning both arms on the little table. "Not on your sweet life, I just wanted to talk to you—that's all there is to it!"

"Do you get everything you want?" she inquired curiously.

His smile broadened and he nodded. "Most things. That is, if I ask nicely enough! And I want to dance with you so badly that it just gives me a pain."

She considered for a moment, studying him with her fine eyes. "Don't you think," she suggested, "that it's the most frightful cheek, to drift along any old hour? I mean, if you really want to see a girl and know she's going to be at a show, and then expect her to cut dances for you?"

"Ah, Felicity, don't get sore with me. Honest, I couldn't help being late—I couldn't really. I'll tell you all about it. I got all mixed up with the police, you've no idea, it's just terribly thrilling. If it hadn't been for that I'd have been right here on the doormat waiting to see you come!"

She smiled, like a wise mother at a wicked child. "Well, I suppose I'll have to hear what you've been up to, besides—" she looked down at the spray of orchids on her shoulder—"I do owe you something for these divine flowers."

He leaned over the table eagerly. "It was just great to see you wearing those when I came in. Now, what about these dances?"

"It is a little difficult, you know. Every quarter of an hour or so, some young man will be turning up and saying it's his dance!"

Rex beamed at her. "Well, I tell you how we'll fix it, since you seem sort of snowed under, let's cut the whole thing and go some place else."

"Oh! But we couldn't do that."

"Couldn't we?" he grinned again. "Believe you me, we could. What's to stop us? Let's walk right out of here."

57

"I suppose it is the only thing to do if I've got to talk to you, there won't be much chance here!"

"That's marvellous—where'll we go? Embassy or Savoy? Embassy's nearer and time's getting on."

"No, let's go to the Hungaria—the music's such fun. We can dance if we want to, or just sit and watch the queers."

Rex was already on his feet. "That's fine, just slip me your cloakroom check, and we'll start right now." He began to shoulder a way for her through the crush.

A number of the older people were already leaving and they slipped away without comment. The fog was lifting a little and it was not long before they were set down in Lower Regent Street.

"You know, this is the only place in London that has any real atmosphere," Felicity sighed. "Just listen to that band, one might be in Vienna or Budapest."

The dark-haired *maître d'hôtel*, Monsieur Vecchi, hurried forward, smiling his quick recognition. "Oh, good evening, a pleasure to see you 'ere, my Lady—yes, for two—this way, my Lady—please to follow me." He went on ahead of them, turning slightly to see if they followed, and holding his hand high above his head, something after the manner of a Fascist salute, as he led them to a table by the wall.

"What a crowd you've got tonight, Josef," Felicity remarked as they settled themselves.

"Ah, my Lady," he exclaimed. "It is late now, you should have been here an hour ago—but it is the same every night. Where all the people come from, I do not know—but it is the music they like, and we try to make them 'appy. What will you 'ave? A little supper, eh? No—you do not want anything—it is too late, jus' a little fruit and a bottle of wine. Very good, my Lady—you leave it to me," and he hurried away.

"Isn't he a darling?" Felicity smiled. "I adore those great, sad, brown eyes of his, and he's so clever, he always knows just what one wants to eat before one's even had time to think about it."

Rex looked around him. "I've never been to this place before, but I'll say it's a good spot." Then he turned and smiled into her eyes. "Not that I care anyhow, any place would be swell with you around!"

She leant back luxuriously. "You know I'm terribly glad that you took me away from Irma's party—all my friends were there,

58

and they're incredibly nice people really—but they are such crashing bores!"

Rex smiled delightedly, then he sat up. "Listen! That tune they're playing, it's a wonder! Right out of the ark. Say, Felicity, can you dance just like Mother used to? That old-fashioned stuff; come on! Let's." He seized her hand and pushed the table from in front of them. "Come on!" he cried, "you come and dance with me!"

They danced, with only one short interval, until the band stopped for good. The dancers upon the floor grew fewer and the tables emptied, but they danced on. Rex held his slim partner to him with the firmness that is essential to all good dancing; they swayed to the music, and moved as one. They spoke little.

Once he turned his face down to hers, and said softly: "Not tired, Sweet?"

"No," she smiled up at him—using his Christian name for the first time. "No, Rex, let's go on, you dance divinely!"

And at another time: "Felicity?"

"Yes."

"I'm mighty glad I came to England!"

"Are you—why?"

"Felicity—I'm crazy about you—absolutely bats!"

"I don't believe it, but I love to hear you say it!"

"Oh, I mean it! Cross my heart I do."

At last they were compelled to stop. Clapping the departing band in vain for further encores, they sought their table.

Rex settled the bill and gently put Felicity's cloak about her shoulders. "Well?" he asked, with his boyish grin. "What'll we do now?"

"Go home to our little white beds," said Felicity.

"But I don't want to go to bed," he complained. "Can't we go some place? It's just wonderful having you on my own—I don't want to let you go."

"Where can we go? I suppose there are one or two places," Felicity said doubtfully. "But I'll meet all my friends again at the Four Hundred, and the others are just too depressing. Somehow London isn't made for night clubs. Paris is different. I do think bed's the only thing."

"Just as you say, Felicity," he agreed submissively, and he followed her out of the now empty restaurant, where the

59

waiters were already stripping the cloths from the tables and piling the chairs on the table tops.

Outside they secured a taxi; and having settled Felicity inside, Rex leant through the open door.

"Say, Felicity, are you really tired?" he asked.

"No, I'm not tired," she said. "Why?"

"Don't you worry," he laughed, and spoke in a low voice to the driver, then he jumped in beside her.

They crawled down Piccadilly, in the still lingering fog, but as they passed Hyde Park Corner Felicity leant forward and peered out.

"Rex," she said suddenly, "where are we going? I think he's lost his way."

He leant back comfortably. "That's all right, sweet, he'll get us home some way. I never had the chance to tell you why I was so late tonight." And he launched quickly into details regarding the death of Lady Shoesmith, omitting, however, the capture of Simon Aron and the supper at the Berkeley, since it had been agreed between him and De Richleau that not a word should be said regarding this to anybody whatsoever. Felicity was tremendously intrigued. But before she had finished asking questions the cab came to a stop, and she peered out again.

"Rex! Where are we? This isn't Eaton Place!"

"No, but it's home, sweet, my home—Trevor Square. I've got a tiny box of a house here for six months, all on my lonesome."

She sat back. "No, Rex, that's not fair. Take me on to Eaton Place, or tell the taxi to, if you like. I shall be quite all right on my own."

He took one of her hands quickly. "Do you think for one second I'd let you go alone? But listen, Felicity. If we'd stayed at Irma's party, what o'clock would you have got home?"

"Oh, I don't know. Does it matter? Three o'clock—four— perhaps, if I'd been enjoying myself. I've got a key."

"Well then!" She could feel his smile warm about her in the darkness. "It's barely half past two. Step in for a little. There'll be a fire, and drinks, and everything. After all, why not? It's been a marvellous evening up till now, why go and let it finish before it must?"

"My dear, you do want to compromise the girl, don't you?

I shall never hear the end of cutting all those dances and some old trout's bound to have seen me go off with you!"

"No one'll see you here," he urged. "Be a good guy, Felicity, just for half an hour!"

"What would my Victorian mother say?" she mocked. "And she'd be sure to think the worst of her daughter," she added as an afterthought.

"She won't say nothing—'cause she won't know nothing," Rex grinned.

"Idiot! I know she won't. All the same, I suppose you realize that it is definitely 'not done' here in London, for a young unmarried girl to enter alone, at any time a bachelor's apartment?"

"Nor is it in New York, but everybody does it, all the same!"

Felicity's delicious laughter broke the stillness of the silent square. "All right," she agreed, drawing her cloak about her. "After all, why shouldn't we have fun?"

They paid off the taxi, and Rex led her into the small, dark house. Soon they were sitting side by side before the glowing embers of a still warm fire, in the tiny drawing-room that occupied the whole of the first floor.

"Angel face!" said Rex as he kissed her.

"Cad!" said Felicity, as she kissed him back.

At a little after five a taxi came to a halt a few doors from Felicity's home in Eaton Place. Rex handed her out, and accompanied her on tiptoe to her front door. Gently she inserted the key in the lock.

"Good night, sweetheart," he whispered.

She blew him a last kiss from the tips of her fingers. "Good night, my darling," she whispered back.

Rex tip-toed back to the waiting taxi. "Well, I'll say it's been no ordinary evening," he murmured. Then, having paid the man generously, for some quite unaccountable reason he set out to walk all the way home, whistling gaily at that dark and desolate hour of the winter's morning.

61

CHAPTER XI

MR. GRANVILLE SCHATZ ASKS SOME VERY SEARCHING QUESTIONS

"One of the many things which has endeared this country of my exile to me," remarked the Duke de Richleau, "is the English breakfast. Only an Englishman could have the magnificent physique which would enable a man to eat of all these things at such an hour; but it is pleasant for a foreigner, such as myself, to feel that did he by any chance one morning require a kidney, or haddock, a sausage, or the kedgeree, it is there. Monsieur Aron, I beg of you to eat of all these things; you have a tiring day before you!"

As he spoke the Duke waved his hand towards the line of fireproof dishes arranged upon the electric heater, which, together with a York ham, and a cold pie, occupied the best part of the sideboard in the spacious dining-room of his flat.

Simon Aron grunted, it could hardly be said to be more, although it was intended to be a suitable acknowledgment of the Duke's hospitality. He snipped perhaps a dozen grapes from the large bunch which crowned a dish of fruit, and sat down to play with them.

He was never at his best at nine o'clock in the morning, and he was by no means easier for his captivity, silken though its chains might be. Moreover, the Chinese robe of honour which the Duke's man had given him as a dressing-gown, irked him considerably. The weight of its many coloured embroideries bore him down, and the fact that he privately considered the Duke to look a fool, with his neck sticking out of just such another gorgeous garment, was no consolation to Mr. Aron.

"I got on to Granville Schatz," he remarked at length. "He should be here at any moment. Did you—er—do anything about my clothes?"

"Most certainly," De Richleau replied. "I sent my man Max off to your club with the note which you wrote last night, while you were still in your bath. Even now, I expect, he is packing a bag for you."

"Thanks. Did you ever happen to run across Granville Schatz at all?"

"No, I think not," said the Duke.

Simon Aron grunted again. "Clever lawyer, best man in London, I should say." With this he relapsed into silence once more.

After a little time there were voices in the corridor, but it was not Mr. Schatz, as they expected. Instead, Rex Van Ryn made his appearance, looking larger and healthier than ever in a voluminous suit of plus-fours. He showed not a trace of having had barely two hours' sleep.

"Will you join us, or have you already breakfasted?" proffered the Duke.

"Thanks, I've had mine, and I've got a date with a chap at Sunningdale at eleven o'clock, but I just had to come round and get the latest." He grinned at Simon. "How's the prisoner?"

Simon Aron grinned back. "Just—er—waiting for my solicitor to advise me how much in damages I can get out of you two for unwarranted detention!"

"That's the stuff," laughed Rex. "I suppose you've seen the news-sheets?"

Aron nodded. "Not much in them, only about the robbery —that's interesting, though. Point in my favour."

"Why do you say that?" De Richleau inquired.

"Well, I'll tell you. I took a taxi when I left here, the porter can substantiate that. Then the driver can be found. He'll say I never stopped or spoke to anyone on the way, and he took me straight to the Berkeley. If I took the necklace, it must be in the clothes you—er—took away last night. You couldn't hide a thing like that at the Berkeley."

"That's a fact," Rex nodded. "You might have passed it on, though."

"Ner," said Simon Aron, "couldn't have done. Ferraro met me in the hall, and sent my things to the cloakroom. I went straight into the restaurant. Never spoke to a soul until you two arrived."

"You might have slipped it to an accomplice on the sidewalk outside."

63

"Ner, head porter knows me well, he opened the door of my taxi. He'd have seen if I'd spoken to anyone."

At this moment Mr. Granville Schatz was announced. He was a little short, round-faced man, with markedly Jewish features.

Simon Aron introduced him. He shook hands all round with a certain violence, rubbed his palms together briskly, and sat down.

"Now, Mr. Aron, what's the trouble this time?" he questioned genially. "You were very lucky to get me this morning. I'm usually away week-ends."

"Very nice of you to come down, Mr. Schatz," Aron murmured. "Very nice, indeed. As a matter of fact, we are in a very nasty muddle!"

The Duke intervened: "Mr. Aron, I'm sure you will wish to talk to Mr. Schatz alone. If you would care to move into my study, I will give instructions that you're not to be disturbed."

"Oh no! It's very nice of you, but I don't want to say anything private. As a matter of fact, I'd be rather glad if you'd stay."

"You're quite sure?"

"Um—certain." Mr. Aron nodded his head up and down, so that in his robe he had much the appearance of a nodding mandarin.

"In that case, let's all move into the library." De Richleau led the way into the room in which he and Van Ryn had discussed the crime the night before.

"Now let's hear all about it," said Mr. Schatz, producing a very small and very black cigar as he settled himself. "The truth—the whole truth—and as much of the truth as you want the other side to know!" He rolled the stubby cigar between his thick lips and applied a match.

"Perhaps," said Aron, hesitantly, to the Duke, "you—er —wouldn't mind telling Mr. Schatz—just what you told me last night. You see, you were—er—actually there."

"By all means, if you wish," De Richleau agreed. "Van Ryn, you will perhaps assist me if I fail to make any point quite clear?"

Rex nodded, and the Duke related their experiences of the previous night, up to the tracing of Simon Aron to the Berkeley.

"Dear me!" exclaimed Mr. Schatz when the Duke had finished. "I can't handle this, you know. Ring's the man. We must secure Ring before the other side get him. Can I use the telephone?"

"It's on the desk at your elbow," said De Richleau.

"Thanks. Wait a minute, though. It's Sunday. Never mind—try his private house.

He seized the telephone directory and shuffled rapidly through it with his thick fingers. "Here we are—here we are—172, Upper Brook Street, just round the corner, Grosvenor 7970." He gripped the telephone and dialled the number.

"What's that? What's that?" he bellowed a moment later. "Out of town is he? Will he be back tonight? Oh—oh—oh. Tell him Mr. Granville Schatz rang him. S.C.H.A.T.Z. That's it. I'll ring him then." He replaced the receiver and turned to the others. "He'll be back about nine—we must see him first thing tomorrow morning."

"Good," said Simon Aron slowly. "But in the meantime these gentlemen are anxious to produce me at Scotland Yard."

"What's it got to do with them?" said Mr. Granville Schatz bluntly. "They can't stop you walking out of here. Get damages—heavy damages—if they tried!"

"Exactly," Simon nodded. "But, you see, I made an arrangement with them last night."

"Arrangement? What arrangement?" Mr. Schatz snapped, eyeing his client angrily. "You ought to know better than to make arrangements without taking proper advice."

Simon told him of the supper-party and his agreement that he would remain the Duke's guest for the night, and accompany him to Scotland Yard in the morning.

"I see, well—all right. Now you haven't told me your end of this yet." Mr. Schatz eyed the Duke and Van Ryn suspiciously. "Perhaps it would be as well if you reserved what you've got to say till later!"

"Ner," replied Mr. Aron, wriggling his head nervously. "I've got nothing to hide, and our—er—friends know as much as I do already." He then gave an account of his telephone call and his visit to Sir Gideon Shoesmith's flat the previous evening.

"Very queer—very queer indeed," commented Mr. Schatz. "You say the hall porter saw you come and go. That's good—under cross-examination we'll get his time estimate so low that we'd have had no time except to run up the stairs and down again."

"I think this robbery of Lady Shoesmith's pearls should

help things," said Simon slowly. "What do you think? You see every moment of my time from when I left here, till I spoke to Monsieur de Richleau, can be accounted for. I couldn't very well have swallowed the pearls!" he laughed his funny little laugh into the palm of his hand—"In fact," he went on cheerfully, "I'm not feeling quite so bad this morning as I did last night. I don't mind telling you, last night I thought I was in a real muddle!"

"Well," Mr. Schatz opened his round eyes very wide, "I don't wonder—suspicion of complicity—a very nasty case. But I don't think we've got much to be afraid of. The police may have found fresh evidence by now, and be taking up a totally different line of inquiry. We'll have to see them, of course, but we'll prepare a statement first. I think we'll see Ring tomorrow —can't be too careful—but they haven't enough evidence to issue a warrant."

"Well," Simon smiled, "I can't say I'm altogether sorry about that!"

"There are one or two points that I'm not quite clear on," the lawyer continued. "Why exactly did you go to see Sir Gideon?"

Simon Aron's wide mouth curved back into a smile, "There was a little bit of a muddle about Richard Eaton; I thought if I had a word with Sir Gideon we might be able to clear things up."

"I see. But I thought you said you didn't know Sir Gideon?"

"Ner—I don't—all the same I thought he might know my name and see me. It might have helped things."

"What sort of a muddle was this about young Eaton?"

"Well—" Simon hesitated. "To tell you the truth it was about money—Richard was a bit hard up."

"And you thought his stepfather might help him?"

"In a way. You see, Richard hasn't been doing very well in his business—he's a publisher, Galleon Press—you may know his stuff—and his creditors are becoming a bit troublesome."

"Ah, it's been a shocking year for anyone in business," sympathized Mr. Schatz.

"Yes—well, Richard needs the money pretty badly, and when his mother dies—well, she's dead, of course—he comes into a packet. It occurred to us she might help him out. I mean with his present muddle."

"That's reasonable enough. Did the boy get on with his mother?"

"Oh, yes. She was all right—very fond of Richard, I believe. I know he was of her. You see, Richard's father used to allow him five hundred a year, but in 1925 he persuaded his father to put up the capital to buy the Galleon Press for him instead of continuing to give him an allowance. Private press books were a good bet in those days—limited editions signed by the authors, and all that—and Richard made a good thing out of it. By 1927 he was knocking up the best part of a thousand a year, so by going into business he had pretty well doubled his income. Early in 1929, when his father died, books were still booming, so I suppose the old man considered that Richard was quite adequately provided for. Anyhow, Richard didn't benefit by a penny under his will. So, when the slump set in and the business started to go downhill, Richard's income dwindled to practically vanishing point with it."

"I see. And his mother came into all the old man's money. Is that the case?"

"Um. She got the family place, Cardinal's Folly, down in Warwickshire, with the income on old Eaton's fortune for life. Richard comes into the lot by her death, but that didn't help him in his business muddle, and he wanted her to let him have a thousand or so to help him out; but the trouble was that most of her money was tied up in trust."

"They could have got an Order of the Court if he was the beneficiary."

Simon nodded. "I thought of that, but for some reason it couldn't be done. Special clause in the will. Anyhow, if Richard was to have the money it meant selling some property at Slough —property outside the Trust—and Sir Gideon didn't like the idea."

"Why? What had it to do with him?"

"Nothing really, but I think he was trying to prevent Lady Shoesmith selling the property. He had some idea it would grow into much greater value in a few years' time."

"I see. Wanted to keep it in his own nest, eh? But how did you propose to influence him?"

Mr. Aron turned his head from side to side uncomfortably, and his smile was a little sheepish. "Well, quite honestly—

between ourselves—I think you'll agree, Mr. Schatz, such a situation could never arise among our people. It seemed pretty hard on Richard—and it occurred to me that I might shame him into it!"

"How do you mean, Mr. Aron?"

"I thought if I suggested lending money to Richard myself —Sir Gideon's a public man in a way—I thought perhaps he wouldn't exactly care for it to be known that a Jew had lent his stepson money, without security or interest, when he and his wife had refused. I'll tell you, I was quite prepared to go through with it, but I hoped he'd think it over, and advise her to sell the property."

"Say now, that was damn decent," said Rex.

"Very fond of Richard," murmured Simon Aron, in his quiet way.

With a rapid movement of his tongue Mr. Granville Schatz switched the butt of his small black cigar from one corner of his mouth to the other. "I suppose you realize," he said suddenly, "that all this makes a very strong case against Richard Eaton?"

Simon Aron stroked his chin with his long fingers, and regarded his lawyer thoughtfully. "I know," he said at last. "Mind you, I don't believe for one moment that he did it—but it's just possible. I saw that at once. I'm very fond of Richard; the least I could do was to give him time to get out of the country!" A wide smile spread over Simon Aron's face. "That's why I didn't fancy being questioned last night!"

CHAPTER XII

SUPERINTENDENT MARROFAT ADMITS TEMPORARY DEFEAT

"HAVE you made any attempt to get in touch with Eaton?" Mr. Schatz inquired.

"Ner," Simon Aron shook his head.

"Very wise," said the other, "very sound. I quite understand your sympathy for your friend, Mr. Aron—but you must keep out of this."

De Richleau leant forward. "It would be interesting—extremely interesting—to know if Richard Eaton spent the night at his home, or if on the other hand he did not. I'm not, of course, suggesting that we should involve Mr. Aron in any way, but I take it that you would have no objection to my endeavouring to ascertain?"

"Not at all—not at all." Mr. Schatz pushed the telephone across the desk to the Duke.

"You could, perhaps, give us Richard Eaton's number?" De Richleau suggested to Simon.

"Yes—Park 9903."

"Thank you." After a little time the Duke got a reply. "Is that Park 9903?—Yes, I would like to speak to Mr. Richard Eaton—oh—I see—can you perhaps tell me at what time he went out?—Oh, dear me—No, I'm afraid I can't help you—I'm just a friend." He replaced the receiver quickly and turned to the others.

"That, I imagine, must have been some kind of servant. She seemed distressed, and is apparently awaiting Eaton's return. She thought that I was one of his friends, and it's quite clear that he has not been home all night. His dress clothes are still on the bed, and the poor woman is anxious as to what has become of him."

"Richard's charwoman," volunteered Simon. "He can only afford a tiny flat now and has a woman who comes in daily." He flung himself back suddenly in his arm-chair, and exclaimed: "Oh, this is a rotten muddle!"

"Looks pretty black against Eaton," remarked Rex.

"You thought it looked pretty black against me last night," Aron replied. "His not having been home doesn't mean anything. Richard's nervous—worried out of his wits—he probably got tight, and spent the night out somewhere."

"Yet you yourself suspected this," suggested the Duke.

"Well, in a way," admitted Simon. "But then I'm funny. I like to meet trouble half-way—if I can!" He laughed nervously, and added: "What are we going to do about it?"

"We'll see the police," Mr. Schatz replied, "but first we'll prepare a statement, and we'll take it with us. You can sign it at Scotland Yard—but we'll take a copy, then there can be no mistakes!" He turned to De Richleau. "May I use your table?"

69

"Certainly, paper you will find here"—the Duke pulled out a drawer—"Ah, I see you have a fountain-pen. In the meantime you will not mind if I inform Superintendent Marrofat of our intended visit?"

"Thanks. I see, you're coming, too?" Granville Schatz looked at the Duke doubtfully.

De Richleau smiled. "But certainly—surely you would not wish to rob me of my little triumph? Besides," he added with a laugh, "how do we know that Mr. Aron and yourself are not, after all, confederates, and that you apparently take him to the police, but actually—as they say in the United States—you make the perfect get-away? No, I will order my car, and you will permit me to give you a lift to Scotland Yard."

"Just as you like," nodded Mr. Schatz shortly. "Now, Aron, we'll make this statement as short as possible. Everything of importance has got to go in, but there's no need to make a novel of it. Young Eaton's financial affairs are no business of yours. That's so, isn't it?"

"Yes," Aron nodded.

"All right, let's make a start, then. 'I, Simon Nathaniel Aron, of'—what's your address now?'"—Mr. Schatz began to write in a thin angular script while Simon Aron leant over his shoulder, supporting himself by one hand on the desk.

In the meantime, De Richleau had arranged himself comfortably with the telephone, and had just succeeded in getting through to Scotland Yard. "I wish to speak to Superintendent Marrofat," he said decisively. "No, it does not matter what my business is, and no one else will do." There was a long pause.

At last he spoke again. "Ah, good morning, Superintendent, how do you do this morning? What?—am I?—I am Monsieur de Richleau—yes—Oh—all that I wish to know is if you have found your friend Silky yet? You have?—good—accept my congratulations. Tell me now, quite honestly, are you satisfied with your examination of this man Silky? You are not. Ah, you have no idea how my respect for you is increased by that admission. You will remember last night I said I might be able to be of service to you. What?—you were coming round to see me about that—but that is excellent—come round by all means. My friend, Van Ryn, and I have a little surprise for you."

He rang off and turned to Rex. "Our friend is a little more

reasonable this morning. He has the honesty to admit that he brought in the wrong man last night. And although he's still not overwhelmed with the idea of making us a party to his dread official secrets, he says he's quite prepared to be grateful if we can assist him to find Mr. Aron."

"That's great," Rex exclaimed in a low tone. He was anxious not to disturb Mr. Aron and Mr. Schatz, who were still busy compiling the statement, so he led the Duke to the other end of the long room. "You know this murder business gives me a colossal kick. I suppose it's the hunter's instinct coming out; but I'd certainly give a whole heap to know just what did take place in that flat last night. Do you reckon it was Eaton?"

De Richleau raised his slanting eyebrows. "Who can say, my friend, matricide is not unknown, but it is rare. It's just conceivable that if this young man was of a certain temperament he might lose all control when he was thwarted and strike his mother. If that happened she may have recovered consciousness again, sufficient at least to stagger into the bathroom, only finally to collapse afterwards."

Rex shook his head sceptically. "She wouldn't have been lying in the bath that way!"

"No," the Duke shrugged, "the floor would have been the more likely place, but it's not impossible that she should have recovered enough to go to her bath, hoping that it would revive her. You must remember that the human brain is so constructed that if she had sustained concussion her body would probably carry out the plans made for it by that brain before she received the blows. Being, in fact, unconscious, she may have again collapsed and slipped under water. She died as much from drowning, I think, as from the blows upon her head."

"You don't figure that Aron may have done it after all?"

De Richleau shot a quick glance in the direction of that young man, who was still bent over the shoulder of his solicitor.

"I hardly think so. After all." He spread out his slim hands. "What possible motive could he have? If it is correct that he is a partner in the Foreign Issue house of Schröchild Brothers he must be very rich. Even if he were in temporary difficulties he's not the type to steal a pearl necklace however valuable. He would use other ways if he was criminally inclined—a little forgery perhaps —or the manipulation of his company's stocks and bonds."

71

"That's true, I allow. Besides, he went directly to the Berkeley afterwards—at least, so he says—and he must be wise to it that the police'll check up on all he does say. So if he did do the job—what happened to the pearls? No, I think we can count Aron out of this from now on. Young Eaton must have stayed behind, and it'ud be he that answered Aron on the wire and left the hall door open."

"If that were so, why should Eaton seek to involve his friend by bringing him to the house at such a time?"

"Ah, there you are." Van Ryn's mouth took a grim line. "Chap who'd do in his own mother wouldn't think twice about giving the works to a friend."

"I see, you credit Eaton with the double degree of cunning. You suggest that the very idea of bringing his friend into this would appeal to him as being an extra precaution to divert suspicion from himself?"

"That'll be about the size of it. Don't forget this chap's a bookman—maybe he's read a deal about crimes and psychology. If so it's all in keeping."

"Perhaps you're right; yet I feel that Aron is no mean psychologist. He is Eaton's friend and must know him well. He seems quite positive that Eaton is incapable of such a thing."

"Maybe now, but what about last night? Did he tip us off about Eaton's financial jam? No, he did not. Believe you me, he thinks it's his pal all right; but he was mighty clever, I'll say. He managed to keep us amused like a couple of village kids, just to give Eaton the wind to quit the country."

"You're quite right there. It's plain that was his intention and I admire him for it."

"It's pretty near aiding and abetting murder!"

"True, perfectly true," the Duke smiled. "I'm afraid I am an unregenerate person; always, you know, I have held life cheaply. I have never made what is termed 'the safety of society' my especial care. In fact friendship and personal honour have always appeared to me to be of far greater importance than, shall we say, 'making the world safe for Lady Shoesmith.' I am, I fear, as much out of tune with the mental theories that govern democracy as I should be with its governing physical theories if I walked out into the street neatly painted with woad! It would have given me the greatest pleasure to have been in

72

Simon Aron's shoes last night. Had I suspected one of my own friends I should have enjoyed intensely the feeling that every hour with which I delayed a full inquiry I was giving my friend a better chance of reaching safety. And how skilfully he handled the situation! I tell you, Van Ryn, I like this young man, and if he desires it he may count upon my friendship."

"Your way of thinking's mighty unmoral, from everything I've been taught, but I get the idea all right. I've a feeling I'd act just that way myself if it was a friend of mine when it came to a show-down; all the same I wish we'd known about Eaton last night!"

"What would you have done?"

"Done?—why we might have had the satisfaction of getting the right man after all. Eaton's not our boy-friend. We could have tipped off Marrofat, and he'd have had every port in England watched. It's too late now, he'll have gotten clean away on one of the morning boats."

De Richleau shook his head. "In these days it's not so easy to get clear away. He has a few hours' start, but that is all. The wireless will begin to twitter soon enough, and then every policeman in Europe will be watching for this young man. That was the tragedy of the Roman world. Every known civilized country was under the dominion of the Empire. There was no place outside it in which those who had committed one fatal blunder might seek refuge. Without, all was savagery and darkness. It was for that reason that the Romans committed suicide— there was no possibility of escape! It is the same today since the new civilization has once more knit the world together; there is hardly a dark forest or an isolated valley where police organization does not penetrate. And the further afield this poor young man goes the more obviously a stranger he will become in the foreign communities with which he mixes, and therefore the more easily recognizable."

"That's interesting, and it's true," Rex agreed. "Tell me, what 'ud you do if you had to get out—quick?"

De Richleau smiled. "I should be sorely tempted to take the Roman way. It would be infinitely preferable to battling for existence among the lower orders at my age, and at any age, better than the ignominy of prolonged imprisonment or possibly a far less pleasant mode of death. Yet I should pray

73

for courage to resist the temptation, because I know that suicide is an act of cowardice, and I feel convinced that help would be given to overcome it."

"And say you had a packet tucked away?"

"Then I think I should seek a rather dingy boarding-house in Bloomsbury. I should not let a word of any language except German—in which I happen to have a fair fluency—pass my lips, leaving people to understand my meaning as best they could and I should settle down to spend at least six months conscientiously studying Egyptian archæology at the British Museum. Then possibly, but not before, I might attempt to leave the country. If I was successful so far I would, I think, make for one of the great South American cities by a roundabout way, where living is cheap and even the poor find consolation in the sunshine. What would you do?"

Rex shuddered. "I couldn't stand for six months not knowing but what I might be spotted any hour of the day. If I had to beat it, I guess I'd pinch an air-plane from Heston or Hanley!"

"And then?" the Duke asked, smiling. "An aeroplane, remember, has its limit of flight—particularly a light plane such as you might handle alone."

"Three hops and I'd be in Russia—you can always buy gas if you've got the dough. I wouldn't think those Soviet Kommissars are extra friendly with the British police, and I'd get a job there easy, teaching flying-school."

"I fear the prospect does not attract me," sighed the Duke. "I am too old to view life as it is lived in Soviet Russia with anything but a purely academic interest."

De Richleau's man entered silently and stooped beside his chair. "Superintendent Marrofat and another officer are waiting upon Your Excellency," he said in a low voice.

"Ah, let them come in," said the Duke, rising to his feet. "Let them come in!"

CHAPTER XIII

MR. SIMON ARON HIMSELF BECOMES INQUISITIVE

"My dear Superintendent," the Duke advanced with outstretched hand, "and our friend Inspector Gartside. Good morning, gentlemen."

"Morning, sir, I hope we're not disturbing you." The big Superintendent eyed the Duke's Chinese robe of honour with some surprise, but even as he did so his glance slid over De Richleau's shoulder to the two figures by the desk. With a quick motion of his left hand he signalled to Gartside to remain near the door.

"Mr. Van Ryn you have already met," the Duke continued, "and you will doubtless be acquainted with the legal reputation of Mr. Granville Schatz. My other friend, however, I believe you do not know."

"I'll be very interested to make his acquaintance," said the Superintendent briefly.

Simon Aron came forward, smiling slightly, a queer figure in his Chinese satin robe, embroidered with birds, dragons and butterflies in every colour of the rainbow.

"It gives me great pleasure to present you," the Duke waved his elegant hand between them. "Mr. Simon Aron— Superintendent Marrofat of New Scotland Yard."

"How d'ye do?" said Simon quietly.

"Am I to understand that you are the person who was found by Miss Winifred Eaton in the hall of Sir Gideon Shoesmith's flat at about ten o'clock last night?"

"That's right." Simon admitted.

"In that case I have a warrant for your apprehension. I must warn you that anything you say may be in evidence against you."

Simon Aron said nothing. Instead, Mr. Schatz came forward. "Superintendent, I'm Mr. Aron's solicitor; you may know my firm, Bildermann, Schatz and Bildermann, of Northumberland

Avenue. I'd like to have a sight of that warrant." He held out his stubby hand.

"You may, sir—and here it is." The Superintendent drew a paper from his inner pocket and handed it over.

"Ha! I thought as much," nodded Mr. Schatz, handing the paper back after one quick glance. "You needn't worry, Aron, I'll have you out on bail tomorrow. That warrant's not for murder, it's only for being unlawfully upon enclosed premises. It's the old trick of holding a suspected person on a lesser charge while the greater is investigated."

He turned to the police officers. "Mr. Aron has already made a statement to me regarding his movements last night. After you have seen it I hope you will withdraw your warrant and spare my client any unnecessary inconvenience."

The Superintendent took the paper which the lawyer held out, he turned it over, "It isn't signed," he commented suspiciously.

"Oh no!" Mr. Schatz agreed blandly. "We thought you might like to be present when it was. I am a commissioner for oaths, so this can be attested at once if you like."

Superintendent Marrofat proceeded to read the declaration in a deep voice. *"I, Simon Nathaniel Aron, aged 26, Company Director, and partner in Schröchild Brothers, resident at the National Club, Piccadilly, W. 1, do hereby solemnly declare that at or about ten minutes after ten o'clock upon the evening of the 22nd of November, 1931, I did call at the flat of Sir Gideon and Lady Shoesmith, situate in Errol House, Curzon Street, Mayfair, my purpose in so doing being to discuss with Sir Gideon certain family arrangements of a financial nature which were contemplated between Lady Shoesmith and her son by her first marriage, Mr. Richard Eaton. I had no interest of any kind in these arrangements other than my friendship for Richard Eaton, and my sole object was to endeavour to persuade Sir Gideon, as one business man to another, of the wisdom of allowing these arrangement to be completed, since I was strongly of the opinion that Sir Gideon was antagonistic to the settlement. I had no previous acquaintance with Sir Gideon and have never yet seen him to my knowledge. I felt, however, that he would know my name as a friend of Richard Eaton's. I therefore rang up his flat at a few minutes after ten o'clock. I was answered by a male voice which I took to be a servant's.*

Having stated my name and requested an interview I was told, after a short interval, that Sir Gideon would see me if I could come round at once. This I did, walking the short distance between the National Club and Errol House. Upon arrival I inquired of the hall porter for Sir Gideon's flat as I had not previously visited his residence, and upon being informed that it was on the first floor I walked upstairs. Having reached the landing, I found to my surprise that the front door of his flat was slightly open. I walked into the passage, thinking that I should find somebody in the hall, but it was empty. I was just about to go out again and ring when a lady appeared who I now understand to be Miss Eaton. She questioned me upon my business, and on my informing her of it she said there must be some mistake as Sir Gideon had been out all the evening. I therefore left at once and walked down the stairs, passing two gentlemen, whom I later learnt to be Monsieur le Duc de Richleau and Mr. Rex Van Ryn. The porter secured a taxi for me at the entrance of Errol House and I drove direct to the Berkeley Restaurant.

"Immediately upon my arrival I spoke to M. Ferraro, the manager. He sent my coat to the cloak-room, and I occupied a table in the restaurant till about half past eleven. When I was leaving. M. Ferraro informed me that two gentlemen wished to speak with me. On going to the small lounge I found the Duc de Richleau and Mr. Van Ryn. It seems that the latter knew me by sight and had come on to the Berkeley in the hope of finding me. These gentlemen accepted my invitation to supper, and later I agreed to remain in their company until I could consult my solicitor as to if it was my duty to visit the police. I returned, therefore, with the Duke to his flat, where I passed the night and have there remained until the arrival of my solicitor this morning. I hereby take oath that the foregoing is a full, true and accurate statement in every particular, in witness whereof I place my hand this 23rd day of November, 1931."

The Superintendent paused for breath, then looked up. *"IF it was your duty to visit the police indeed!* I should have thought anybody might have known that."

"Really?" Simon Aron shook his head with a little nervous jerk, he seemed just mildly interested.

Marrofat's ruddy face lit up suddenly with a bright smile. "Come on now, Mr. Aron—what else do you know about this job?"

"Nothing," Simon regarded him evenly. "You've got my statement."

"Nothing, eh? All right—I'll hold you. If you don't mind we'll step along to the Yard."

"Look a bit silly, tomorrow, won't you?" Simon suggested quietly. "What about the papers?—'*Wrongful arrest of partner in Schöchild Brothers!*' We can trace that 'phone call at my club; somebody must have answered it, and I can prove knowing Lady Shoesmith and her son. Why shouldn't I call? The door happened to be open. Is that all the evidence you're going to bring that I was unlawfully upon enclosed premises? If you're not careful you'll be in a muddle—or do you—er—enjoy giving stories to the Press?"

The Superintendent pursed his lips together. "Yes. I'd like to be left alone on a desert island with some of those newspaper chaps for a bit," he glowered. "It's a wonder we ever get anybody with them about. All the same, that won't stop me holding you—if I've a mind to!"

"I don't think Mr. Aron would mind answering any reasonable questions, Superintendent." Mr. Schatz tactfully bridged the gulf.

"Oh, not at all," Simon agreed.

"That's better." Marrofat sat down on the arm of an easy-chair. "Let's have that conversation of yours on the telephone in detail—as near as you can."

Simon complied.

"Now, about your visit to the flat. Did you see anybody other than Miss Eaton, or see anyone coming in or out, or hear any suspicious noises?"

"Ner—not a thing."

"Right. Now you're a friend of Mr. Eaton's, aren't you? Just what was the financial business you were so interested in?"

"Oh, no, *I* wasn't interested." Simon shook his head.

"Well, let's hear about it, anyhow."

"It's this way. Lady Shoesmith thought of selling some property to assist Richard in his business."

"I see. Why?—is he hard up?"

"Don't know; most businesses are doing pretty badly these days—shouldn't think he's an exception!"

"And why did you choose this time of night to go and see a man you'd never seen before—on business?"

"Well—er—it wasn't my business. I work pretty hard

78

during the day—so does Sir Gideon, I believe. As a matter of fact I was fixed to dine with my mother last night, but she put me off, so I thought it was rather an opportunity to drop in and see him."

Marrofat nodded his mop of ginger curls. "Now do you mind telling me just what your reason was for not coming down to the Yard last night. You could have saved us a lot of trouble."

"Really? I'm so sorry." Simon was meekness itself. "You see, I didn't feel I could tell you anything—so I just didn't—that's all!"

"You're a very clever gentleman, aren't you?" said the Superintendent with a shade of bitterness. "Not feeling you could tell us anything, and then turning up with your solicitor as a sort of keeper!"

"Ner—I'll tell you," Simon smiled. "I'm just careful—that's all. You see, I didn't have anything to do with this business and—er—I want to keep out of it!"

"Well, I suppose I can't blame you," the Superintendent spoke in a more cordial tone, "but it would make crime detection a sight easier if the public would come forward at once and help the police by telling them what they know. We never give names to the papers when we can possibly avoid it—it's just because they're bone lazy most of the time."

"I'm sorry," said Aron again sweetly. "I hope I haven't put you to a lot of trouble?"

"Well, in a way you have, sir. I had six of my men out all night, getting a line on a chap we thought was you, and when they brought him in early this morning we find he's all snug and warm now—going straight for the time being, that is. He was playing the flute at the Excelsior Electric in a job he's got between six o'clock and midnight. Talk about injured innocence—my hat!" He laughed suddenly. "He was great, wasn't he, Gartside?"

The Inspector grinned. "You're right there, sir. As good as a play, Silky was, when we brought him in. You gentlemen should have seen him. He did the real high horse about spoiling his Sunday in the bosom of his family. Going to complain, he was —to the Society for the Protection of Reformed Criminals—and I don't know what else!"

"Well, anyhow," Marrofat turned to the Duke. "It was

very much my own fault. If I'd taken your tip last night, sir, I understand we should have had this gentleman's story a long time ago. We shan't hold him, of course, but I take it, Mr. Aron, you'll be available any time? I expect we shall want to see you again."

"Of course, Superintendent," Simon nodded. "You can always get me at my office or the club."

"If you'll sign the statement then, sir, we won't trouble you any more for the time being." He handed the paper back to Mr. Schatz, who went over with Simon to the desk, where the latter made the usual declaration and appended his signature.

"May one ask what your next move is to be, Superintendent?" the Duke inquired casually.

The big man made a grimace. "Now that's a question, sir, but I'll tell you one thing, I'm not proud. If Your Grace has any more pointers, I'd be glad to hear them this time."

"That's very nice of you, Superintendent, but I fear I can't help you very much. You will yourself have seen the necessity of hearing what Richard Eaton has to say."

"Richard Eaton? Yes—he was the last person to see his mother alive. I sent Gartside down to his flat last night to get his statement, but he wasn't in—hasn't been in all night."

"So I understand. I telephoned to his flat a little over half an hour ago, and he had not then returned. Tell me, Superintendent, did your fingerprints prove of any interest?"

"Not a thing—Lady Shoesmith's, Sir Gideon's, Miss Eaton's —I took impressions of all three last night before I left, in order that we might eliminate them, and be able to pick out any strange markings this morning; but so far we've had no luck."

"The hall porter?" suggested the Duke. "Naturally, you questioned him. I take it he saw no other person who might be implicated in this matter?"

"No, he seems a sensible sort of chap. He was in his chair in the hall reading from eight o'clock till we came on the scene. He'd taken one or two people up in the lift before nine, but afterwards is a quiet time. He remembers Eaton leaving, and is pretty positive about the time he left; and he confirms Aron's statement in every particular as far as he is concerned. There was nobody else about at that time. He's certain of that. The gentleman in Flat Six came down with a lady in the lift, and the housemaid from No. Four went out to the post; but apart from that—nothing."

"And was there no sign of burglary?" the Duke inquired.

"You heard, of course, that Lady Shoesmith's pearls had gone. You'll have seen that in the paper. They're said to be worth £7,000 too."

"Yes, of that I was aware; but I was thinking of actual signs of housebreaking. If Aron is ruled out, and for the time being Eaton also—because after all he is the dead woman's son—and the porter tells us that no one went upstairs, surely it suggests that somebody must have broken in or come down from the roof perhaps?"

"No, I've been into that pretty thoroughly. There wasn't a sign. The bedroom and dressing-room windows were both locked on the inside. There's a sheer drop below them of twenty feet, and no access to the roof. This wasn't a cat burglar business."

"Have you considered the fire escapes on the other side of the building?"

"Yes, but you know yourself how they work. A series of galleries under the windows of each floor, with iron gates at the end of each before you come to the ladder. Those gates have got spring locks, which are worked from inside the building, rather like the area gates they used to have to protect basements. There'd be a switch in each flat, and a main switch down in the hall that would release the lot in case of fire. Of course a man who knew his job could get past one of those gates. He could pick the lock easy on a foggy night, and very little likelihood of being spotted from the mews at the back. But I've examined the whole system and there's not a sign of anything having been tampered with."

"You don't think it possible that our suspect managed to gain this roof from another, then lowered himself from gallery to gallery?"

"No, I was up early this morning, and after I'd had my talk with Silky, I came along here to have a thorough look round. I went over every gate and gallery in the building, but they're all in perfect order."

The Duke spread out his slim hands. "In that case it doesn't seem that there's much else to be done. I take it that you're perfectly satisfied as regards the servants?"

"Quite—they couldn't have passed the sewing-room where Miss Eaton was sitting, without her seeing them. She sits with her door open, it seems, in case Lady Shoesmith calls her. And then, they were together at the time. It's very improbable that they'd both be in it; the housemaid was devoted to the lady, too, been with her twenty years; I'm afraid it looks to me like the young man."

Van Ryn, Schatz and Simon had been listening with silent interest, but now the latter spoke—quietly but seriously, with his head cocked on one side. "You're wrong, Superintendent, I know Richard Eaton. He's one of the most normal men I've ever met. I shouldn't think he's ever lost control of himself in his life. You can take it from me, it isn't Richard."

"It would be a particularly atrocious crime if it were," said the Duke. "But I fear, Mr. Aron, that your friend's situation will prove a very difficult one. There can be no doubt that the murder was committed between the time when Miss Eaton left Richard with his mother and the time that Miss Eaton discovered the body. Who else except Richard Eaton was present at that time? In addition, there is his strange disappearance. Even if we accept your theory that he spent the night 'on the tiles', as you sometimes say, surely he would have returned home by half past ten in the morning?"

"I don't know about that!" Rex laughed. "A fellow doesn't go making whoopee all on his own if he has a sweetie. Maybe she's handing him his morning tea at this moment. After all it's Sunday—and we know he's got his day clothes on."

"My dear fellow," urged the Duke, "you forget that he had an appointment with Aron for supper last night, and failed to turn up—and it should have been a meeting of some importance, I understand?"

"You didn't mention this, Mr. Aron," said Marrofat quickly.

"Didn't I?" Simon looked up. "Sorry. Yes Richard was to meet me at the Berkeley at eleven. He never turned up."

"And why was the appointment an important one?" Marrofat asked with an air of persistency.

"Oh, only that we were to talk over the final arrangements between him and his mother—that was why I was anxious to see Sir Gideon first, really."

"You seem to have been, very interested, Mr. Aron!"

"Well, you see, I think Richard valued my advice, in a way." Simon spoke deprecatingly.

"And he never turned up for his supper party, eh?" The Superintendent rose to his feet. "I think I understand now, why you didn't feel you could tell us anything last night, Mr. Aron. It won't be your fault if Richard Eaton's not out of the country by now—will it? But it's not as easy as all that," he spoke with unaccustomed harshness. "We'll bring him back, don't you worry."

Simon smiled again. "I'm afraid you've been reading some of Mr. Edgar Wallace's detective novels, where people smuggle one another out of England. I'll tell you—I couldn't do that sort of thing if I tried, and honestly, I think you're wrong about Richard."

"Well—we'll see." Marrofat turned to the Duke. "I'm very grateful, sir, for all you've done for us. We'll be getting along now. The inquest will be at eleven o'clock tomorrow. You'll receive official notices in the morning. I'd like both yourself and Mr. Van Ryn to attend. We needn't trouble you, Mr. Aron, but I expect we shall see each other again before the case is finished. Good morning, gentlemen."

Amid a chorus of polite "good mornings" the police officers made their exit, and the Duke sank back once more in his big arm-chair, his embroidered robe like a flowing cascade of colour about him.

"D'you know!" said Simon, with his jerky little laugh, "he doesn't like me—I don't believe he likes me one little bit!"

Mr. Schatz laughed for once. "He couldn't hold us," he said triumphantly, "and what a time we'd have had tomorrow if he'd tried!"

"I think all the same," De Richleau remarked, "that you're fortunate, in that it's the police of Britain with whom you have to deal, Mr. Aron. Abroad they treat these things somewhat differently. They lack that marvellous sense of the liberty of the individual from which you have so benefited today."

Simon nodded vigorously. "I know, abroad I'd have been terribly scared of this muddle. As things are here, I wouldn't even mind about a few days in prison, as a matter of fact; I'm only worried as to what's become of Richard."

"Yes, that seems to be the key to the mystery now."

"I wonder." Simon looked down at his dragon-covered garment. "I wonder if you'd mind if I dressed now? I think I'd like to make a few inquiries about Richard, on my own."

"By all means," De Richleau pressed the bell. "Have Mr. Aron's clothes arrived from his club?" he asked his man, who appeared as silently as usual.

"Yes, Your Excellency, the chauffeur got back with them a little time ago. I did not like to disturb you while those—er—gentlemen were here, but the chauffeur brought a message for Mr. Aron."

"Indeed, please give it to Mr. Aron then."

The discreet valet turned to Simon. "The chauffeur was asked to say, sir, that there is a gentleman who is waiting to see you at your club. He said, sir, that the matter was urgent, and he would wait there until you could come."

"Did he say anything else?" asked Simon quickly.

"No, nothing else, sir, except the gentleman's name. It was Mr. Richard Eaton."

CHAPTER XIV

A PAGE FROM THE LIFE OF RICHARD EATON

LESS than half an hour afterwards, Simon Aron led the way into his club. Owing to the manner in which he had learnt of Richard's arrival there, it had been impossible for him to conceal it from the Duke, Van Ryn, and Mr. Schatz, even if he had wished to do so. In consequence he and the Duke had dressed with all speed, and it had been agreed that since Richard Eaton's situation could not be made worse by the presence of the others, and Mr. Schatz, at least, might prove useful, the whole party should accompany Aron round to the National.

At this hour of Sunday morning, the club, was almost deserted. They found Richard Eaton all alone in the big, cheerless, guests' waiting-room. Simon went forward to greet him, and the others remained in a little group near the door.

"Hallo, Richard!" Simon Aron's rather toneless voice did not altogether hide his suppressed emotion. He held out his hand. "I'm awfully pleased to see you."

84

Eaton took it quickly. He was a young man of medium height, with rather an attractive smile, but his smile was a little tired as he said: "I'm in a muddle, my boy, in fact I'm in the hell of a mess!"

"Um—I know," Simon nodded quickly.

A puzzled expression crossed Eaton's face. "How can you? Oh, of course, you've seen about Mother in the papers."

"Yes," Simon nodded again.

"It's pretty ghastly, isn't it? I was terribly fond of her, though it hasn't had time to sink in yet, and I shall feel it frightfully later on, I know. But as a matter of fact, when I said I was in a muddle—I didn't just mean that I was cut up by her death. This is a special muddle that I've got myself into by going round to see her last night."

"I know," said Simon Aron once again.

"My dear fellow, how can you know?" said Richard Eaton, almost sharply.

"Well—er—I happen to know a bit about it, anyhow," affirmed Simon. "But I'd like to introduce you to these friends of mine." He jerked his head in the direction of the others, who at his glance had moved over to join him. "This is Mr. Granville Schatz, my solicitor—the Duke de Richleau—Mr. Van Ryn——er—Mr. Eaton."

Richard Eaton gave a pleasant nod to each in turn. He was polite, but obviously found it difficult to restrain his annoyance at their presence. He turned to Simon: "Look here, you don't think me rude, old chap, but what I want to talk to you about is rather urgent. Can you spare me five minutes alone?"

"Yes, if you like, of course, but give me a chance to explain who these gentlemen are; I take it you want to talk over last night's business? If I'm right, it would be rather useful to have Mr. Schatz with us, don't you think?"

"Yes, perhaps you're right."

"Now the Duke de Richleau and Mr. Van Ryn are also in this, in a way—it was they who—er—found your mother. As a matter of fact I spent the night with them because of this business; that's why the Duke's chauffeur came to the Club for my things. They were both with me when I got your message."

"I see," Richard looked dubious.

"Mind you," Simon put his hand on his friend's arm "don"t

85

think I want you to discuss anything in front of anybody, if you'd rather not, but they do know all about this muddle, and sometimes four heads are better than two."

"Mr. Eaton," the Duke stepped forward. "I must quite frankly apologize for what must seem to you the entirely vulgar curiosity of myself and my friend; but having been drawn into this very tragic affair, we should consider it the greatest privilege if you would allow us to remain and hear your version of what took place last night."

Richard looked into De Richleau's bright, intelligent eyes, and suddenly he smiled. "Simon's right," he said. "Simon's always right, four heads are better than two—if you're friends of his by all means stay."

"Splendid," Simon nodded his bird-like head. "Now let's sit down and talk things over."

"Yes, let's—but for God's sake give me a decent cigarette. I haven't had time to go back to my flat this morning, and I hate the shop Turkish that you buy on railway stations."

Simon produced his case. "Here you are, old chap, have an Al Rashid, same as you smoke yourself."

"How curious," remarked De Richleau, "that you should smoke Al Rashids. I smoke them, also, when I smoke a cigarette at all, but mine are longer than that—about three and a half inches long."

"This is the ordinary size, but I've had the long ones. I think they're the best in London." Simon turned to Richard. "Now let's hear where you've been all night."

Richard blew a ring of blue smoke. "I caught the 11.52 to Dover," he confessed, "and I was going to cross by this morning's boat to Calais, but I saw this awful news about my mother in the paper, so I came hareing back to town by the 8.26 this morning."

"Um," Simon nodded. "And you thought you'd like to have a chat with me before you saw the police, eh?"

"Saw the police! What the devil for?"

There was a sudden silence in the long, heavy room. It was De Richleau who said quietly:

"I fear, Mr. Eaton, that you are not, perhaps, very fully informed regarding the present situation."

"How do you mean?" Richard inquired.

86

"You—er—wouldn't know, for instance," Simon said with his jerky laugh, "that I was—er—very nearly arrested for the murder of your mother last night?"

"Good lord, no! But why— What in the world made them suspect you?"

"You remember that we were to meet at the Berkeley for supper?"

"Yes, I tried to let you know that I didn't mean to turn up. I thought you were dining with your mother, so I telephoned, but you weren't there."

"No, she put me off—so, I had plenty of time on my hands, it occurred to me that a little chat with Sir Gideon wouldn't do any harm; thought I might persuade him to advise your mother differently."

"My dear fellow, how awfully nice of you—I'll bet you couldn't, though. I had a ghastly row with the old man in the afternoon."

"As a matter of fact I never saw him, but it must have been just about the time that I called that—well," Simon wriggled his neck quickly, "the police thought it was me!"

"Simon, how awful! But from what you say, I gather they're chasing someone else by now?"

"Um," agreed Simon briefly.

"What's the latest idea, do you know?"

"Yes, they're looking for the last person to leave the flat before I arrived."

"And who was that?"

"Well, Richard, as a matter of fact it was—er—you."

"What?" Richard Eaton's face expressed blank surprise. "Me!" he ejaculated suddenly. "Simon, you're joking!"

Simon shook his head. " 'Fraid not, we've just this moment left the man who's in charge of the case. Rotten, isn't it?"

"But it's impossible," Richard burst out. "What nonsense! Although—I don't know—" he added more gently. "No wonder you all looked so queerly at me when you turned up here. This is a ghastly mess!"

" 'Tis a muddle, isn't it? Still, I'm awfully glad to see you, Richard. The moment I heard you were at the Club, I knew for certain that you hadn't done it—but I don't mind telling you that there was a time, last night, when I thought you had!"

87

"You really thought for a moment that I—"

"Um," Simon interrupted. "I did—I knew you were in a muddle, you've been living on the edge of a nervous breakdown for weeks. You might have got tight—gone off your head—anything—I didn't know. The very nicest people are capable of all sorts of things if they're abnormal at the time."

"You certainly ought to know, Mr. Eaton," Rex remarked, "that, rather than let suspicion fall on you, Mr. Aron wouldn't come across with a single thing until this morning. Just to give you a chance to make a getaway."

"That was awfully decent of you, Simon," Rex smiled gratefully, "but just like you—I understand, too, what you mean by anybody being liable to go off their head for a bit, and do the most incredible things. It seems absurd when applied to oneself, but I quite understand how you feel about it."

Simon shook his head. "Mr. Van Ryn's exaggerating. All I said was—that I wouldn't talk to the police till I had my solicitor with me, a very normal sort of precaution that, and we couldn't get hold of Mr. Schatz till the morning."

"No, I know you too well to believe it was only that. You deliberately held the fort to give me a sporting chance to get out of the country. It was damn decent of you, Simon."

"My dear old chap, don't be silly."

"It was. But I say—look here—" A sudden frown overspread Richard Eaton's face. "Until a moment ago I hadn't an idea that the police suspected me. I was only worried about what I did last night, and now, by George, that very thing's going to make it a thousand times worse."

"'Fraid they do suspect you, old chap. You see, there's no trace of anybody but you and I having been near the place. And after all, your movements last night are—er—a bit difficult to explain."

"I know. Give me another cigarette. Thanks." Richard sat smoking in silence for a moment, then he said: "Look here, I'd better tell you the whole thing from the beginning. This is actually what happened.

"After lunch yesterday I thought I'd have another go at old Gideon. So I went round to the flat. As you know, up till now he's been as nice as pie—butter wouldn't melt in the old brute's mouth. It's always been: 'Well, Richard, I'll have another talk with your mother. We'll see what we can do to help you,' and then he puts me off by asking for more figures, and more figures, and more figures.

"You know, Simon. It's been going on for months now, and every week my wretched creditors get more and more pressing."

"Yes, I know," Simon nodded. "You've had a jolly rough time; most people would have had a breakdown long ago."

"It has been pretty bad. My bank's been very decent to me, but naturally they've got their limit, and I had no securities or anything of that kind that I could lodge with them for cover against a larger overdraft, and I had to keep the Press going or else the whole show would have blown up. They said I was a fool to try and carry on, anyhow, and I dare say there's something in that. Beautifully printed books and limited editions have simply gone to blazes in the last eighteen months, and there was never enough capital behind the business to stand a bad patch like this. I was quite prepared to wind it up, if that could have been done decently. Mother's never cared about 'Cardinal's Folly,' and it's been shut up practically ever since my father died, but I love the old place, and I was quite willing to go down and rusticate in one wing if Mother would have made me an allowance of a couple of hundred a year, but I insisted that the business must be wound up first, and I was determined that I wouldn't let my creditors in.

"Whenever I saw Mother she was awfully sympathetic, but I simply couldn't get her to do anything; all she would say was that she was quite willing to help me, but Gideon was to advise how it was to be done. Well, I had six writs in last week. I managed to scrape the cash together to settle four, but there are two big debts, and even if I was lucky Monday, and Tuesday, and had much more money than I could hope for in the post, I might manage one, but I couldn't possibly do both. If either of them is allowed to get a judgement against me, I'm done. It was no longer a matter as to the manner in which I was to be helped, it was a case of getting a thousand pounds from somewhere, or going under. So I saw Gideon after lunch yesterday and put it to him straight. What do you think the old devil said?"

"Don't know," Simon murmured.

89

"He advised me to go bankrupt! Can you believe it? Go bankrupt, and let everybody in!"

"I'll say that's a bad show," Rex agreed sympathetically.

"Well, he did. I tried to point out to him that it was commercial suicide, that I'd never be able to be a partner or director in anything, or even get a job in a decent firm again. 'Oh, it's not as bad as all that,' he said. 'You haven't done anything dishonest; you'll get your discharge in six months—much better file your petition. You can settle your creditors at six bob in the pound—you'll be clear then, and your mother will see what she can do to help you later on.' Jolly, wasn't it?"

"Pretty thick," Simon grinned. "Lot of help you'd have got later on, if it had depended on him."

"Yes, I expect his next bright idea would have been to ship me off to the Colonies, and you know about how much use I'd be out there!"

"The great open spaces where men are men . . ." laughed Rex.

"Well, I don't mind telling you, Richard." Simon half closed his eyes. "I knew you couldn't go on much longer unless something was done. That's—er—why I thought I'd go and have a chat with Sir Gideon myself. Did you decide anything?"

"Yes, I told him that I had no intention of filing my petition, and that if I couldn't find any other way out, I'd call my creditors together, put the whole situation before them, and abide by their decision."

"Certainly, proper thing to do," said Mr. Schatz.

"Um," agreed Simon. "I don't believe they'd have made you bankrupt; probably they'd have let you carry on with a creditor's committee. We do, if we can; we don't believe in smashing people."

"Well, anyhow, the old man said that all he wanted to do was to advise me for the best, so I left it at that, and cleared out. Pretty sick I was, too."

"What time was this?" Mr. Schatz inquired.

"About four o'clock. I tried to get you, Simon, at your Club, but you were out, so I went back to the office. It was shut, of course being Saturday afternoon, but I always carry a set of keys, so I dug myself in there. I started to make out a list of the creditors, and to prepare, as far as I could, an approximate statement of the position to date. I was there for about four hours, then I decided to have a last cut at Mother. I knew Gideon was dining out, so I'd be able to get her on my own.

"I got to Errol House about half past eight, I think. She was just finishing dinner with old Winnie. I had some coffee and kümmel. I couldn't have eaten anything if I'd been paid. I told her I had dined—although, of course, I hadn't. I suppose for three-quarters of an hour we just made conversation. At least, I did. I didn't want to talk about business with Winifred there; but Mother was full of the plays she had seen and all sorts of other things, so I just let her run on, occasionally saying 'Really!' 'How nice!' 'What fun' and so on. I was waiting till Winifred cleared out, although, as a matter of fact, I was dying to launch the fresh arguments that I'd been turning over in my mind on the way there. Anyhow, at about a quarter past nine, Mother said she must dress because she was going out to supper with Gideon. I went into her bedroom with her." Richard paused suddenly, swallowed, and looked away. Aron patted his arm.

"What's the matter, old chap? Feeling rotten?"

Richard half-laughed, and swallowed quickly again. "Silly of me," he said. "So sorry. But ever since I've been a small boy I've sat and talked to Mother while she changed for dinner, in an arm-chair by her dressing-table. It seems queer to think that I shall never do that again."

"You have my very deep sympathy, Mr. Eaton," said the Duke in a low voice.

"Thanks. Well, as I was saying, directly we got in the bedroom I opened up at once. I told her about my talk with Gideon that afternoon, and I asked if she couldn't possibly see her way to selling the Slough property, even if Gideon didn't approve, and guaranteeing a loan for me at my bank in the meantime. She was awfully nice about it, but quite firm; she said that even if she let me have the thousand that I wanted for this week, how did she know that I wouldn't be wanting another thousand next—or two, or four—or ten? She never had pretended to know anything about business, but she really thought Gideon's idea was best. Let the business go altogether, and then she'd see about utilizing the money which should go to my creditors, to doing something for me instead.

"I tried to explain what an awful thing it was for a young man like myself to go bankrupt, and that even if one paid up everybody in full afterwards, other people never knew that, and the stigma clung to one all one's life. I pointed out that it would absolutely ruin my chances of getting another job. But all she would say was 'Gideon says lots of people do it in these days. Gideon is a business man, he ought to know;' and she was quite certain he would never suggest anything that was dishonourable. So what the devil could I say? It was like trying to explain the differential calculus to a child of three. She simply didn't understand." He paused.

"And what happened then?" Rex prompted him.

"Well, after we'd been arguing for about half an hour, she said she simply must have her bath or she'd be late, so 'I must run along now, and mind and let her know how I was getting on!' So I kissed her good night and she went into the bathroom. Then, just as I was passing her dressing-table to leave the room—I saw the pearls."

"Good God!" Simon Aron sat up with a jerk in his arm-chair "It was you who pinched the pearls?"

CHAPTER XV

"HERE'S TO THE CRIME"

RICHARD gave a wry grin. "Yes," he said, "I took the pearls.

"I suppose I stood looking at them for about ten seconds. Not more. By that time I had the whole thing cut and dried. I knew that the governor had paid seven thousand pounds for those three strings, and they're worth more today. I reckoned I'd pawn them over the week-end for two thousand at least, if not two-five. That was more than enough to see me through my troubles for the time being, especially with Christmas coming on. Christmas is always a good time with me, so I should have ample breathing space to make new arrangements—take a partner, amalgamate or sell the business and retire to grow cabbages at Cardinal's Folly. At all events, avoid bankruptcy somehow, I knew Mother would never prosecute, and she adored her pearls, so she'd sell the Slough property to get them back. I don't suggest for a moment that it was the right thing to do—but, to a certain extent, by seizing the initiative, I was only forcing her to do what she would have done months ago of her own free will if she hadn't married Gideon."

Simon grinned. "You know, Richard, this is a muddle; we're in a real muddle."

"I know. It's pretty ghastly, isn't it?"

"How did you mean to unload the pearls?"

"Well, I was taking a bit of a chance about that, but I know the man in Paris from whom Father bought them. He comes over here once or twice a year, and occasionally he looks me up. He's interested in fine books, that's why he comes to see me. Anyhow, I thought I'd say that Mother was in difficulties and wanted to raise money on them, so she'd sent me over to arrange a loan, as it was a question of great urgency. You see, he knew the pearls, and he knew me. I thought there was a pretty good chance of getting him to play."

"Bit risky, wasn't it?" hazarded Simon. "I mean, you hadn't a letter from her, or anything."

"Of course it was, the whole thing was a forlorn hope, but I meant to save the business if I could, and with any luck I'd have got away with it."

Simon nodded. "Then you saw the papers this morning and came straight back. Of course, you're out of all your worries now, you're a rich man by your mother's death."

Again a sudden silence fell upon the little circle, but Richard did not seem to notice it. He spoke again quite naturally. "Yes, when I'd seen the paper my first thought was to get back at once. I didn't know what to make of Mother's death, of course—but then, the paper didn't give any details. It never occurred to me that the police might suspect me. I just wanted to talk the whole thing over with you, Simon, and see if we couldn't hit upon some plan to get the pearls back into the flat so that someone would come across them, and people would think they'd never really been missing at all."

"This is a bad business, Mr. Eaton," said Mr. Schatz suddenly. "Of course, I'm only watching Mr. Aron's interests. But, all the same, it's a very delicate matter. As a professional man, you understand, I could not advise my client to be a party to an attempt to mislead the police, by restoring the necklace under a subterfuge."

93

"Where is the necklace?" Simon asked.

"Here you are." From his inside pocket Richard drew the long strips of satin-smooth beads, and handed them across.

For a moment Simon let them dangle from his fingers, then he passed them to Schatz. "I think perhaps you'd better take charge of these for the moment. Now, Richard, I'm afraid you'll have to go to the police. I don't see anything else for it."

"Yes, what do you think they'll do?"

"Well, they'll want a statement, of course, and they may try to detain you on some charge. If they do, don't you worry, we'll get you out on bail tomorrow—er—how about a solicitor? Have you got a good man?"

Richard shrugged. "There are the family people—Rathbone, Lobin and Rudd."

"Are they any good at this kind of thing?"

"About as much as a sick headache, I should think. I always call them 'Muggins, Juggins, and Grubb'—sort of people who always take a fortnight to give you an appointment, if you want to see them, because the only surviving partner is away in the country visiting his still more aged aunt!"

"Well, now, I'll tell you, Richard," said Simon earnestly. "I do think it's awfully important that you should have a good man."

"Whom do you suggest?"

"I—er—think, if we could persuade Mr. Schatz to act for you—we should have done a good morning's work."

Richard looked towards the little round-faced solicitor. "I've the very greatest confidence in Mr. Aron's judgement," he said. "I'm afraid I've got myself into a pretty serious mess, and I'm quite sure my family solicitors can't cope with this sort of thing. If you care to look after me, Mr. Schatz, I shall be very grateful."

A slow smile lightened Mr. Schatz's heavy features. "I've made my reputation out of muddles, Mr. Eaton," he said. "A good muddle and a good cigar are all I need to keep me happy, so I'll take your case, if you like. But I must warn you of two things. First, in the ordinary way I don't touch criminal law. Doesn't pay. Secondly, my bill will be a pretty stiff one. I don't charge six and eightpence for an interview and three and fourpence for a telephone call, plus the fifty per cent that the Government allow. I've saved people thousands of pounds on one interview before now, and, on the other hand, I've put in whole days at nothing at all. For example, this little job this morning is going to cost Mr. Aron fifteen guineas. Either you'll get a bill if I'm any good to you, or you won't get a bill at all."

Richard smiled. "Righto. Thank goodness I needn't worry about money any more. I'll settle your account and send you a nice cabinet of cigars into the bargain, if you can only get me out of this. But can you handle it if you don't touch criminal law?"

"The law, Mr. Eaton, is a matter of common sense—and knowing how to use a very good library of reference books. After that it's a matter of briefing the right counsel. And we're lucky there; I've already left a message for Ring. I thought we might need him for Aron, but now we'll brief him for you."

"All right, Mr. Schatz. In that case, I'll leave everything to you."

"Then I think the sooner we make our position clear to Scotland Yard the better. As Aron says, they may decide to detain you on a minor charge, but on what, I don't quite see. They can hardly say that you were unlawfully upon enclosed premises in your mother's flat—whereas with Aron that might, have held water. Still, if they do try something of the kind there should be no difficulty about getting bail tomorrow."

"Can't they charge me with murder if they want to?"

"They can, and of course if they do, we can't get bail; but they don't like to charge for murder if they can avoid it— that is, unless they're certain of their ground."

Rex stood up and stretched himself. "Do you fellows realize that it's just on one o'clock? Pretty soon we'll have to be thinking about a spot of lunch. I don't know what you think, Mr. Schatz, but if they're maybe going to put Mr. Eaton behind the bars, a square meal and a bottle of wine beforehand wouldn't exactly do him any harm."

"Yes," Mr. Schatz agreed. "I see no harm in that at all. I could ring up the Superintendent and tell him that Mr. Eaton has placed himself in my hands, and that we'll be round to see him about three o'clock."

"In that case," said the Duke, "I should be delighted if you care to return and lunch with me."

95

"Not on your life," Van Ryn interrupted. "This is my party. Besides, if we went back to Errol House as like as not Mr. Eaton here would be recognized and taken off as before we'd fed. I got a little box of a house in Trevor Square, down Knightsbridge way; and the dear old dame who keeps house for me just loves a party. If you don't mind a picnic, come right along with me."

Van Ryn's invitation was generally accepted; so the whole party filed out and stowed themselves into the Duke's big Hispano.

The house that Rex had taken for his stay in England was indeed the tiniest affair. The street door opened direct into the dining-room which, with the stairs, occupied the whole of the ground floor. The drawing-room where he had entertained Felicity in the early hours of the morning took up the whole of the first floor, and on the second was his bedroom and bath. The tall American had to stoop his head to go through the doorways, but the tiny house had quite a number of small but charming pieces of furniture, and was as bright and comfortable as any bachelor could desire.

Immediately they arrived Rex yelled at the top of his voice for Mrs. Bottom, and a small, plump, middle-aged woman appeared from the basement.

"Come on," he commanded, "We're five great hungry guys here for luncheon. What 'uv you got in that pantry of yours?"

She evidently adored Rex, and smiled indulgently at him through her spectacles. "Oh, Mr. Rex—and I thought you were safe away getting your golf at Sunningdale!"

"You did, eh?" he teased her. "Leaving you here to hit it up with all your boy friends! I know you!"

"What things you do say!" she reproached him. "The idea—at my time of life—but what we're going to give these gentlemen, I don't know. There's the venison I jugged for you yesterday, and you never came home to eat. I could soon hot that up—and we could send Annie round to the Hyde Park for some smoked salmon, same as you done before when we was in a hurry; though it's a wicked extravagance buying food from them hotels. There's plenty of fruit and cream in the house. Then there's the best part of a York 'am, and the Stilton."

96

Rex laughed. "That's marvellous, Mrs. Bottom. You send Annie round to the Hyde Park for that salmon. Tell her to ask for Peter, same as before—and say it's for Mr. Van Ryn—they'll know. You cut along downstairs, we'll lay up for ourselves."

"All right, Mr. Rex." Mrs. Bottom turned to descend once more into the lower regions, casting over her shoulder as she did so. "And don't you go and forget about them cork mats. Last time you laid up you burnt the table something shocking!"

"Come on, Eaton." Rex pulled open a drawer in the sideboard. "We're going to just forget all about last night for the next hour or so—lend a hand with these knives and forks and things, while I just see if I've forgotten how to shake a cocktail since yesterday."

"An excellent idea," said the Duke. "Mr. Schatz shall make his telephone call to Scotland Yard if you don't mind, then we'll forget for a little this thing that has brought us all together. For my part, if the good Mrs. Bottom will permit me to invade her larder, I propose to make a salad. It is an accomplishment of which I am somewhat proud."

"Perfect. You come right down with me, the old dear just loves a party. I'm going to get the ice. Schatz—the 'phone's in that locker by the stairs." Rex and the Duke disappeared below.

Richard and Simon began to lay the table, and Mr. Schatz sat down to the telephone. He got his number, spoke for a moment in a low voice, then joined the others. "The Superintendent's not there," he said, "but I've left a message that we'll be round about three."

Rex reappeared with a dish of crushed ice, and an outsize in cocktail shakers. Into the latter he began to shoot varying proportions of liquor from half a dozen bottles that stood ready on a side table. "Come on, now! Atta Boy!" He laughed as he wrapped the big shaker in a napkin and began to swing it up and down from between his knees to within an inch of the ceiling. Then, with a sudden twist, he removed the metal cap and poured the foaming amber liquid into the waiting glasses.

The Duke returned at that moment, and his smile seemed to denote that his foray into Mrs. Bottom's larder had proved successful. He set down the big bowl which he was carrying, and they all took up their glasses.

"Well, here's to crime," cried Rex cheerfully, lifting his

to his lips. Then, suddenly realizing, he added: "Sorry, Eaton, I certainly didn't mean that." But his change of expression was so sudden that the whole party roared with laughter. After that the strained and serious atmosphere which had been upon them all the morning melted completely away. Even Mr. Schatz, who was busy with the electric toaster, became almost gay!

"Cocktails," said Rex, as he poured the third round from the seemingly inexhaustible shaker, "were made to be swallowed, not tasted. Never give a guy a large cocktail—but plenty of 'em—make 'em dry, and drink 'em quick. Come on, boys, it takes a fourth to make an appetite! Here's to crime. Oh, hell, I forgot again. Well, never mind—here's to cocktails!" He suited the action to the word and threw his head back.

As he did so the front door-bell rang. "Who the lord can that be?" he exclaimed. "D'you mind, Aron?" Rex indicated the door near which Simon was standing. "Tell 'em I'm dead, or going to be married!"

Simon slipped back the catch, but he had no time to say anything. The bulky figure of Superintendent Marrofat pushed past him into the room.

"Oh—sweetie—look who's here?" groaned Rex.

They did look. A purposeful smile lurked about the corners of the big man's mouth, but it was not the kind of smile that is conducive to general gaiety. "Glad to see you all enjoying yourselves, gentlemen," he said, with heavy humour, as his quick eye took in the array of glasses, and the preparations for the feast.

"Come right on in, big boy," Rex invited. "I'm throwing a little party, and yours is the one little honey-face in all the world I wanted most to see."

Any trace of humour that might have been there before vanished from the Superintendent's face. "I'm not here for joking, Mr. Van Ryn. I think this gentleman"—he turned to Richard—"is Mr. Eaton. I must trouble you, sir, to come with me."

Mr. Schatz endeavoured to intervene. "I spoke to your office a few moments ago on the telephone. I informed your people that Mr. Eaton had placed himself in my hands, and that we would be with you by three o'clock."

The Superintendent did not seem impressed. "Really?

98

Very good of you, I'm sure; but I'm glad to say that we're not altogether dependent on the efforts of you gentlemen, at the Yard. Mr. Eaton, I must warn you that anything you say may be used in evidence against you."

"Superintendent," Mr. Schatz intervened again. "I shall prepare a statement on Mr. Eaton's behalf, but we have not yet had time to draft it."

Marrofat's baleful glance fell upon the solicitor. "Mr. Eaton is entitled to the presence of his lawyer, so if you care to accompany him, you can. But if there are any more statements to be prepared—we'll prepare them at the Yard."

"Aw, Hell," said Rex. "What fool said big men make happy mothers?"

CHAPTER XVI

THE SENSITIVE FINGERS OF THE DUKE

Two hours later the Duke, Simon Aron and Rex Van Ryn were still seated at the table in the little house in Trevor Square. They had adhered to their host's suggestion, and no reference had been made to the tragedy of the night before, since Richard Eaton and Mr. Schatz had been so abruptly carried off by the Superintendent.

After their departure the party had lost much of its previous gaiety, but they all, none the less, enjoyed what proved to be a most excellent meal; for despite the fact they had been strangers to each other the day before and their apparent diversity, they had actually many interests in common.

Aron and Van Ryn knew and respected each other's houses in the City. The Duke and Simon both proved to be collectors of books and old coloured prints, while Rex and De Richleau were equally keen fishermen; and all found that they had many acquaintances in common.

The time therefore passed quickly, and they were still cracking nuts and circulating the port when Mr. Schatz rejoined them.

Rex offered him a belated luncheon, but the lawyer refused.

"No. Very good of you, Mr. Van Ryn, but it's too late to think of lunch at this time of day. I'll rob you of some of that Stilton and a biscuit, though, if I may—and just one glass of port."

"That's swell, take off that top-coat, and sit right down." Rex indicated a vacant place at the table. "Now give us the late wire."

"Not very much that's good, I fear." Mr. Schatz helped himself liberally to butter.

"They've kept Richard, I take it," said Simon. "Else he'd come back here. What—er—charge are they holding him on?"

"The worst. We had to admit to having taken the pearls, of course. It would have been most unwise to attempt to conceal that. I couldn't do it—and when the Superintendent heard that, he went the whole hog and had a warrant drawn for murder."

"That means we can't get bail, doesn't it?" Simon asked.

"Yes, bail is never given in a charge of murder—rotten for the boy—he was pretty cheerful when I left, though, considering all things."

Simon nodded. "Tell me, how did they find out about Richard? When you 'phoned you didn't say where you were talking from, only—er—that he had placed himself in your hands, and you'd be at the Yard about three."

"They checked back the call?" suggested Rex.

"Ner—even if they did, Marrofat wasn't in when Schatz rang up. They couldn't have traced the call, found Marrofat, told him all about it, and left time for him to get down here from Westminster, all in ten minutes—couldn't be done."

"It is conceivable," said the Duke, "that he was on a flying squad car in the neighbourhood. These cars are fitted with wireless now, in which case it would have been possible. But I confess I should be interested to learn how he managed it."

Mr. Schatz smiled. "Well, I can enlighten you. I expect they traced the call as a matter of routine—the police are nothing if not thorough—but the Superintendent didn't learn where Eaton was in that way. When we got to Scotland Yard he was handed my message, and that made him a little more amiable. He realized then that we were on the level, and he was just a bit pleased himself by this little *coup*. I asked him how he did it, because I had been wondering myself on the way there, and this is what happened.

100

"He had about a dozen men out looking for Eaton; one at Eaton's flat, one at his office, one at Errol House, and so on —anywhere that Eaton might be likely to go for advice or assistance if he was still in London. He sent them out directly he left us this morning, having made up his mind pretty definitely that Eaton must have done it. Of course, he's got on to Eaton's financial difficulties already; even I was surprised how much he'd found out. He had particulars of all the writs on his desk there. Well, he didn't forget that Aron was one of Eaton's best friends, so there was a man watching the National by the time we arrived there, and the moment Eaton came out with us he was recognized from his description. Naturally the detective followed us here, and reported immediately; so Marrofat came straight down. He must have been already on his way when I rang up."

"Neat bit of work," Rex commented. "I'll say I wouldn't care to get up against your police, they know their game all right."

"Um," Simon agreed. "They're not exactly mental gymnasts, but their system's thorough; but I'll tell you, the one thing I don't like about them is that if they think they've got the man who did the job, and it's a pretty good case, they just won't look at any other line of inquiry."

"That's the danger here," said Mr. Schatz. "They've definitely got a case against this boy. Marrofat admitted that he'd pretty well settled it in his own mind after his talk with Aron this morning, and when they learnt about the pearls—that finished it— they hadn't a doubt he did it. But now we come to it, what other line of inquiry is there?"

"I—er—take it we're agreed that it wasn't Richard?" Simon looked round the table.

"No more than it was myself," the Duke replied immediately. "His whole story has the ring of truth. His position, as a young man faced with bankruptcy, must have been made doubly distressing by the knowledge that his mother had ample means, as well as the wish to save him—and would have done so but for the adverse influence of his stepfather. One can well understand and sympathize with his sudden decision to attempt to avert catastrophe by taking the law into his own hands. Besides, anyone with the slightest knowledge of psychology can see that

101

he is neither the weak-brained abnormal who might commit such a crime upon a sudden impulse, nor the utterly callous criminal capable of killing his own mother for gain. I have not a shadow of doubt regarding Richard Eaton's innocence."

"Nor I," Rex agreed. "Having seen the way he acted when he first sat in to talk it over, and having had him come across with his story, I don't believe he did it for one second. But I'll say he's in a jam all right."

"In that case let's analyse the position," Mr. Schatz suggested. "As far as I'm concerned I wouldn't have touched the case, if I'd thought he'd done it—I've got all the work I want, but I'm sorry for that young man."

"Well, now," Simon jerked his head sharply, "I'm going to suggest that we go right over the affair from the beginning—see if there's any point we've overlooked."

Mr. Schatz pushed his plate from in front of him and produced his notes. "Now this is the position as I see it." He looked round, "Any of you stop me if I go wrong."

"At eight-thirty, on the evening of Saturday the 22nd, Eaton called upon his mother at Errol House. I don't think we need go further back than that, at any rate for the moment. He was seen to enter by the porter, let in by the maid, Brent, and admits this himself. He found his mother and aunt just finishing a light dinner, he took coffee and a liqueur in their company and sat talking trivialities for some time. At nine-fifteen, or thereabouts, Miss Eaton went in to the sewing-room at the kitchen end of the flat, while Eaton accompanied his mother to her bedroom. He then approached the business that he had come upon, and after a protracted discussion in which his mother refused to agree with his suggestions, she, at about ten minutes to ten, terminated the interview and went into her bathroom. Eaton, succumbing to a sudden and unpremeditated thought, took the pearls from the dressing-table and left the flat. The hall porter saw him go, and gives the time with definite conviction as some minutes before ten o'clock; at about the same time as Eaton left Errol House, Aron rang up from his club."

"Ner—wait a moment," Simon interrupted. "It must have been after ten when I rang up. I remember noticing the clock in the hall as I left the Club; it was well past ten."

"Sure about that?" Mr. Schatz asked quickly. "It may make a lot of difference to us."

"Quite sure," Aron nodded.

"How long interval would there be between the time you 'phoned and the time you left the club?"

"None. I took my hat and coat and walked round to Errol House—mind you, I don't say the clock at the club wasn't fast, but that's unlikely."

Mr. Schatz looked round. "You see my point?"

"Sure," Rex grinned. "If Eaton left before ten it couldn't have been he who answered Aron's call."

"Exactly. Mind you, we mustn't count on this until we've checked the time that call was made. We should be able to do that, and if we can, our case is that a man unknown was in the flat after Richard Eaton left. If we can bring evidence to show that Aron didn't leave his club until after ten, and was seen going out, having come straight from the telephone boxes, it would strengthen our case enormously."

"There should, I imagine, be no difficulty in tracing the original call," remarked De Richleau.

"Club operators keep a record of calls," Simon nodded. "I'm certain of that."

"You think we're pretty safe there?" said Mr. Schatz. "Good, then we'll go on. Aron's call was answered by a man who, from his manner, Aron assumed to be a servant. After inquiring if Sir Gideon was in, and could he see him, there was an interval—he was then told that if he came round at once Sir Gideon would see him. Aron therefore left his Club and walked round to Errol House, arriving a little after ten—about eight to ten past, eh?"

"That's right," Simon agreed.

"Right. Upon being told by the porter that the flat was on the first floor, Aron walked up—found the front door open, and stepped inside. Before he had time to go out again and ring, Miss Eaton appeared and turned him out. On the landing, as he went downstairs, he met the Duke and Mr. Van Ryn. We have their evidence, and the hall porter's, to show that Aron must have left the building at ten minutes past ten, or very shortly after. . . . Now at what stage did you come into the proceedings?" The lawyer looked at De Richleau.

103

"Van Ryn could not have stayed in my flat for longer than five minutes, he only came up in order that I might give him one or two addresses; he admired some of the trifles, but I should say about five minutes at the outside."

"That gets us to a quarter past ten, then. As he was leaving you both saw the maid, Brent, come out from the Shoesmith's flat in a semi-hysterical condition and a moment later discovered Miss Eaton sitting beside the dead woman in the bathroom. That is so, isn't it?"

"That's all O.K.," Van Ryn assented.

"Well, I'm afraid we haven't established much that's new. We know that Lady Shoesmith met her death between nine-fifteen, when Eaton accompanied her to the bedroom, and ten-fifteen when you people met the parlourmaid. If we allow that Eaton was innocent, then it must have been between nine-fifty when he had left the flat, and ten-fifteen. We hoped to confirm the time of Aron's 'phone call as a minute or two after ten, and if we can do that we can definitely establish that whoever answered that call, it was not Richard Eaton. Therefore, there was some person unknown on the premises at the time, *and*, during the twenty-five minutes in which the murder must have taken place."

"If only Richard hadn't taken those pearls." Simon shook his head. "That's what'll make the police so certain he did it."

"The pearls! Good gracious me!" exclaimed Mr. Schatz, clasping his hand to his breast-pocket with a sudden look of consternation. "I completely forgot to hand them over to the Superintendent." As he spoke, he drew forth the three long strings and laid them upon the mahogany table. "I'll take them to the Yard later on. I don't want to be left with valuable things like this longer than necessary."

The Duke picked up the pearls. "I can quite understand that," he smiled. "How did it occur that you forgot to hand over—what, I suppose, will be termed 'exhibit number one'?"

"I can't think, most unusual for me to forget anything so important. I was, of course, intent at the time in preventing Eaton from saying too much. It's quite extraordinary how chance remarks, which seem quite innocent at the time, may be construed against one later on. I was trying to keep him to the bare facts without antagonizing the Superintendent."

"Well, I guess the pearls belong to Eaton anyhow, now his mother's dead," Rex submitted.

"I don't know, I'm sure," said Mr. Schatz. "In any case they will have to be handed over to the police for the time being."

"It may interest you to know," remarked the Duke, who had been letting the necklaces slide through his fingers, "that these pearls are false!"

CHAPTER XVII

THERE INQUISITIVE PEOPLE PLAN THEIR CAMPAIGN

"May I look?" Simon leant forward eagerly.

"By all means." De Richleau pushed the pearls across the table. "However, I'm quite certain of what I say, my fingers cannot be deceived in such a matter."

Simon took the necklace quickly and drew one of the strings across his wide mouth. For a moment he held one of the largest of the pearls between his teeth, and touched it gently with the tip of his tongue, then he nodded vigorously.

"You're right; but they're a wonderful fake, aren't they? Just sufficiently uneven to make them appear a well-matched string, the real thing."

"Eaton could not have been aware of this," said Mr. Schatz.

Rex laughed. "Poor feller, wouldn't he have been real mad if he'd got to Paris and found he'd had all his trouble for just nothing at all?"

"Now. How will this affect Richard's case?" said Simon slowly.

"Not at all," the lawyer replied promptly. "How can it? We've admitted that he took this necklace; that is the vital point. He may have believed the pearls to have been real at the time—but he took them, and many a man's gone to prison before now for stealing what turned out to be a handful of paste. It doesn't affect his case in the slightest degree."

"Um." Simon pulled slowly at his fat Al Rashid. "Wonder where the real necklace is? This must be a copy."

105

"All her other jewels were intact," remarked De Richleau. "I ascertained that from our friend the Superintendent this morning before we saw Eaton, and he would have mentioned it, I feel sure, if a duplicate necklace had been discovered—at least—if a necklace of this description had been found at all, there would never have been any suggestion that anything was ever missing."

"Maybe the original has been sold," suggested Rex.

"That's possible, but why?" Simon looked round the table with half-closed eyes. "Lady Shoesmith was a rich woman, Sir Gideon was a rich man. Most women think a lot of times before they sell their pearls, that's the last thing as a rule. If you remember, Richard said this morning that his mother would be certain to sell the Slough property to get them back."

"It is conceivable," submitted the Duke, "that the real pearls may have been stolen years ago and these excellent copies substituted; such profitable exchanges are known to have been made by clever thieves on many occasions without arousing the least suspicion in the owner."

"Ner!" Simon shook his head. "Don't agree. I agree with you about diamonds, emeralds, pictures, old furniture, works of art, if you like, but not pearls. Pearls have to be restrung at least twice a year if they're worn every day as these were. Lady Shoesmith's jewellers would have spoken to her about it for their own protection."

De Richleau smiled. "You are correct, Mr. Aron. I hadn't thought of that. Then it's clear that if any theft or substitution has taken place unknown to Lady Shoesmith, it has occurred within the last few months."

"Her jeweller ought to be able to give us a line," said Rex. "Either he strung the real goods last time or he can tell us if it was the duds, and in the last case he'll be able to put us wise as to when the duds came to town."

"Van Ryn is right," said the Duke. "Did you by any chance, Aron, happen to hear Eaton mention who his mother's jeweller was?"

"Ner. Sorry, I don't know."

"Perhaps Mr. Schatz could procure that information for us; if he could, and further give me a line of authorization stating that I am acting on behalf of Eaton's solicitor. I will

106

undertake the inquiry. It was doubtless one of the big people in the West End, and I am tolerably well acquainted with them all. I feel they may answer even an authorized inquiry more freely if it is made by someone with whom they have had dealings before."

"I can get the name from Eaton," Mr. Schatz agreed, "when I see him in the morning before the inquest, but I don't see this leads us anywhere. The knowledge that Lady Shoesmith sold her pearls five years ago, or that they were stolen from her last week, doesn't strengthen our position in any way."

De Richleau shrugged his elegant shoulders. "Possibly you're right; but in this case we have so little to go upon, that even the points which have no direct bearing should, I feel, be followed up, in the hope that further information may come to light."

"In that case," Simon picked up the necklace again, "don't you think it would be worth while to try and find out who made this?"

"The fake—sure," Rex nodded. "That's the other half of the same question."

"If Lady Shoesmith pawned, or sold her pearls, or even has the originals put away somewhere for safe keeping, the copy will, I expect, have been made to the order of her jeweller," the Duke pointed out.

"But if we find the maker," suggested Simon, "and he was not instructed by the jeweller, or Lady Shoesmith herself, then he was probably instructed by the thief. D'you mind if I take them." As he spoke he slipped the necklace into his pocket.

Mr. Schatz looked highly disapproving. "I don't quite think . . ." he began. "You know I ought to take them along to the Yard right away."

"Oh—I see." Simon narrowed his eyes and smiled. "D'you think so? I'll give you a receipt for them if you like. As a matter of fact Richard gave them to me—I think you saw him do so at the Club—I passed them on to you for safe keeping, now I'm relieving you of them again."

"We ought to hand it in, Aron, but if you've any special purpose in retaining possession of it"—Mr. Schatz spread out his plump hands—"well, I've got my client to think of."

"In a way I have. You see, I know a lot of funny people."

Simon stooped his head and laughed nervously into the palm of his hand. "I'd like to show this to one or two of them, just on the off chance, you know."

"All right, in that case I think we'd better forget you ever gave it to me at all." Mr. Schatz looked round the table. "But I don't see the point in all this, I think you're both wasting time."

"If the real necklace was stolen we might have a bit of luck and trace the thief," Simon replied. "But I feel with the Duke that we shouldn't neglect any line of inquiry."

"I cannot possibly see how anything which you may find out can have anything to do with the murder," said Mr. Schatz almost crossly, "but it's your time not mine."

"Exactly," agreed Simon calmly. "Is there anything else you think we might do?"

"No, I'm afraid there's very little *to* do. The only thing we really have in our favour is that Richard Eaton could not possibly have been at Errol House at the time you say you rang up, and it is important to check that call."

"What about the house-girl and the cook?" suggested Rex. "Couldn't one of them have let in a boy-friend? Say that had happened, and he gave Lady Shoesmith the works, he might just have got through with it and been going to have a crack at the safe when he heard Aron come in, got scared, hidden for a bit, and then done a fade out directly the coast was clear."

"The maids were together all the time," Schatz objected. "And even if they were both in it neither could have passed Miss Eaton's room to let a man in without her seeing them."

"Well, what about one of them slipping the boy-friend a door key; they wouldn't have to worry about letting him in then?"

"And if they did, what about the hall porter? He's prepared to declare on oath that nobody went in or out except Eaton and Aron between a quarter to ten and ten past ten."

"Maybe the porter's in the same racket," Rex persisted.

"Let us consider Van Ryn's theory," the Duke intervened. "Even without the maids, let's assume that the porter was a member of the gang. He could probably have supplied a duplicate key to the flat. He would not have allowed his accomplice to enter until Eaton had left, then probably he would have some

108

prearranged signal whereby to warn his confederate in the event of Sir Gideon arriving home unexpectedly, or any other unseen emergency. Upon Aron's arrival he would use that signal. The confederate, then having committed the murder but not having had time to secure the jewels, would abandon the attempt immediately leaving the front door open behind him. Instead of going downstairs and meeting the unexpected arrival face to face, he would run up to the next landing above, wait for a moment until he saw Aron enter the flat, and make his dash downstairs while Aron was talking to Miss Eaton. This does seem to me to be a quite possible solution, although I should regret to lose Frederick, a polite, pleasant man."

"Don't agree," Simon differed. "I look at it this way, if the porter were in it he would have lied about the time Eaton left, or the time that I arrived, in order to protect his accomplice."

"That's sound," said Mr. Schatz quickly. "All the same we'll get the private inquiry people to look into things tonight; there may be something in Mr. Van Ryn's idea. We'll have the porter, the housemaid and the cook watched all next week, and I think you'll be surprised at the details of their family history that I shall be able to lay on the table in a few days' time. We'll soon know if there's anything fishy about any of them."

"I'm not quite happy in my mind about the roof and the fire escapes," said De Richleau thoughtfully. "I concede Aron's point about Frederick, it's unlikely that he would adhere so strictly to the time of Eaton's departure and Aron's arrival if he were involved in any way. In fact his evidence is at present our one hope that we may be able to clear Eaton of this terrible charge. But we must all admit that some unknown person did get into that flat, and if not by the main entrance past the porter—how?"

"The Superintendent said the fire escapes were quite impracticable," Mr. Schatz tapped the table with his fat forefinger, "and," he added, "that was before he had settled on Eaton. He ought to know."

"Don't you believe it." Van Ryn's eyes shone brightly. "I've yet got to find the fire-ladder that'll get me beat, and I'm telling you; I'll take a look at Errol House myself, just to show those boys at Scotland Yard."

"For God's sake don't you go and get yourself locked up," Simon expostulated.

"Not on your life. The Duke's got a flat in the block. What's easier than for him to take me round the back, and I'm telling you, I'm with the Duke all the time. A guy's got into that flat somehow, and if the porter's not a crook the killer must have come down off the roof or up from the yard."

"No harm in making a thorough examination of the premises ourselves," Mr. Schatz allowed. "I think, too, we should have a detailed account of the occupants of the other flats and as far as possible their movements during the time concerned."

"That should not be difficult," said De Richleau. "From certain observations which I have made I've come to the conclusion that my man is upon somewhat more than friendly terms with the unfortunate Frederick's wife. I'll speak to him tonight and I don't doubt that we shall receive quite a mass of information regarding the other occupants of Errol House; and there are, after all, only ten flats."

There was a short silence, then Simon Aron said with his habitual hesitation: "I wonder now if any of you have thought about Miss Eaton?"

"What, that poor old dame!" Rex sat back at the end of the table and roared with laughter. "Don't be silly. She just wouldn't know how to begin."

"You remember," Simon went on, "she could have seen the maids go down the passage past her room, but they couldn't see if she left her room—and she found the body."

De Richleau shrugged. "How is it possible? Blows like that can only be given by a strong man. You've seen her, a frail little woman; I shouldn't think she weighs more than eighty to eighty-five pounds. No, that idea is absurd, my friend."

"Now are there any other suggestions," Mr. Schatz inquired, "because I don't know if you realize it, but it's nearly five o'clock? I want to get home."

"Ner." Simon Aron shook his head; the others said nothing.

"All right, I'll get hold of Ring tonight, and I'll put the agency people on right away, to find out what they can about the porter, the parlourmaid, and the cook. I shall see Eaton tomorrow morning, with Ring, of course, and I'll let you know," he looked at De Richleau; "that is if Eaton can tell us, his mother's jeweller. I shall have to attend the inquest. That reminds me" —he turned again to the Duke—"the Superintendent asked me to tell you that you and Van Ryn will not be required; only evidence of identity will be taken and they will ask for a postponement. However, I think I ought to be there just in case they play us any tricks. After that I'll see the family lawyer. What was his name? Gubbins was it, or Mudd? and get a sight of the will; I can get their address from Eaton in the morning."

"I'll—er—find out about that telephone call at the Club," Simon volunteered, "and I'll talk to one or two people about the pearls."

"For our part," said the Duke, "Van Ryn and I will make a thorough examination of all the approaches to the flat, also I will visit Lady Shoesmith's jeweller—if Mr. Schatz is sufficiently fortunate as to secure the name—and I will employ my man to secure from his *chère-amie* an extensive account of all the inhabitants of Errol House. And, gentlemen, if you're agreeable, I suggest that you should join me for dinner tomorrow night, which will give us all an opportunity of listening to any news of interest which any one of us may have secured during the day."

"That's awfully nice of you," said Simon. "I was going to suggest that you all dined with me, but the Club's too public, it would have meant a private room somewhere."

"What this case is going to cost young Eaton, with me working on Sundays and dining out at night, I don't like to think. But I'll be there," Mr. Schatz smiled.

De Richleau stood up. "I am enchanted," he said. "Shall we say, eight o'clock, and black tie?"

The smile on Mr. Schatz's face broadened to a grin as he said: "So I've got to dress, eh? Well, that'll be another tenner on Richard Eaton's bill!"

Simon put his hand on the little man's shoulder. "That's it," he said. "And if Richard couldn't afford it you'd be briefing Ring out of your own pocket, wouldn't you?" At which they all laughed.

"Well," said Rex, "you've ruined my Sunday golf, and now, for your party, I've got to high hat a date with the prettiest girl in England. Still, I'll do that cat burglar on the Duke's iron ladder all right—and a lot more, too, if need be, to get Eaton out." He moved over to the side table. "And now, boys, would you believe it, it's cocktail time again!"

111

CHAPTER XVIII

NEWS OUT OF HATTON GARDEN

At dinner the following evening the same rule was observed as at the Sunday luncheon, and by mutual agreement the subject of the murder was banned throughout the meal.

It was a longish affair, since the Duke prided himself upon his table and disliked the modern fashion of snatching a few brief courses between cocktails and the play; but the time slipped away rapidly, as they skimmed from one topic to another, and almost before they were aware of it dinner was over and coffee upon the table.

"A cigar, my friends, then we will get to business." As the Duke spoke his man carried round a long cedar cabinet offering it to each in turn.

"Now that's what I call a cigar," remarked Mr. Schatz appreciatively, taking one of the long golden-brown cylinders from the box and holding it under his nose. "Look at the oil in that leaf."

"I am happy that you should like them," said his host. "I always think that Hoyo de Monterray is the finest factory in Havana, and these Anillo d'Oros are of their best."

"Um," Simon Aron nodded. "I think you're right, Hoyo's are the best cigars in the world."

The Duke carefully put out his match and waved the lighted end of the cigar quickly beneath his aquiline nose, savouring the fragrant scent of the burning tobacco. "May I suggest," he said "that Mr. Schatz should be the first to give us an account of his activities."

"By all means," the lawyer leaned forward with both arms on the table. "Well, first I secured Ring. I regarded that as very important. I spoke to him on the telephone last night and he agreed to see me at his private house this morning. I had a long talk with him and there's no doubt he's by far the best man we could have. I took him straight down to see Eaton and he was very impressed with the boy. Eaton liked him, too, I could see that, and at a time like this it is very essential he should have every confidence in his advisers; after that I had to go to the coroner's court.

"As we expected, only formal evidence was taken, and they've got an adjournment until next Monday; then I went on to Rathbone, Lobin & Rudd. I'd 'phoned them earlier to say that I should want a sight of the will. I saw old Rudd. I gathered he had only just finished with Sir Gideon. A nice old gentleman, he looked very much over his spectacles at me though; said 'he didn't think he had the pleasure of knowing my firm, but then of course they never touched police court work.' I agreed, and added that 'we never went in for the Chancery side.' He didn't quite know how to take that.

"However, to come to the point, there's no doubt that Richard Eaton is the principal beneficiary. The late Mr. Eaton left everything in trust, with income to his wife for life. At her death a sum of five thousand pounds was to be utilized in the purchase of an annuity for Miss Winifred Eaton, and remainder absolutely to young Richard.

"Now, as regards Lady Shoesmith's will, you realize, of course, that her own estate is quite a separate matter, apart altogether from the trust in which she only had interest for life. She leaves a number of bequests, of which the principal are—five hundred pounds to a nephew, who is a lieutenant in the navy, and two hundred and fifty to Susan Brent, if still remaining in her service; after that there are a number of charities mentioned for sums of fifty and a hundred pounds, and a few gifts of jewellery to friends—the residue of her estate then goes to Sir Gideon."

"Of what—er—does her estate consist?" asked Simon.

"There are certain securities and personal effects, but the principal item will, of course, be the Slough property, which the late Mr. Eaton made over to her absolutely in her lifetime."

"When was this will drawn, d'you know?"

"Last April, upon Lady Shoesmith marrying again; that, as you know, is usual."

"Tell me," Simon inquired again, "is Richard mentioned in his mother's will?"

"Yes and no," Mr. Schatz replied quickly. "Neither he nor Miss Eaton benefit, but in one clause Lady Shoesmith says: 'Knowing my son Richard Elmsdale Eaton and my sister-in-law

113

Winifred Lucy Eaton both to be adequately provided for under the will of my first husband, etc., etc.,' then she goes on to make various dispositions of her property."

"Are there any other beneficiaries under the late Mr. Eaton's trust?" asked the Duke.

"No, none whatever. The five thousand to purchase an annuity for Miss Eaton and remainder to his son. Had Richard predeceased his mother, upon her death the whole would have gone to Miss Eaton, and in the event of her also having predeceased Lady Shoesmith, the money would have gone in equal portions to three distant relatives. It was, of course, for that reason that it would have been impossible for Eaton to have got an order of the Court enabling him to participate."

"What do you figure Eaton'll come into under this trust?" Rex inquired.

"Rudd tells me not less than three hundred and fifty thousand pounds."

"And what's he reckon Lady Shoesmith's personal estate will pan out at?"

"Eighteen thousand, if the Slough property sells at a reasonable figure; that is, after the various legacies are paid and exclusive of the pearls."

"Then to sum up, as it were," Simon carefully laid the long ash from his cigar in the onyx ash-tray at his side, "by Lady Shoesmith's death Richard stands to gain, £350,000, Sir Gideon £18,000, Miss Eaton £5,000, the nephew £500, and the maid £250. Go on, Mr. Schatz, did you get anything else out of old Rudd?"

"No, nothing. I gathered that the old chap was deeply shocked about the whole affair. It seems he's very fond of Richard Eaton, known him since he was a boy, and considers him quite incapable of such a thing. He expressed approval when I told him we'd secured Ring, and offered to help in any way that he could; but I fancy Rudd's very glad he hasn't got to act in this affair. It's a bit out of his depth." Mr. Schatz drew with an air of satisfaction at his Hoyo. "And now I'd like to hear what you people have been up to all day?"

"Mr. Aron," the Duke proffered.

"Ner—I haven't done much—you go ahead."

"As you wish—I can speak for myself and Van Ryn, since

we have been together most of the day. When we received Mr. Schatz's message over the telephone we went round to Collingwood's in Conduit Street and discussed the matter of the pearls with the manager there. It seems that Lady Shoesmith has not had her pearls restrung since the beginning of August."

"Did she—er—take them in herself?" Simon interrupted.

"No, Sir Gideon brought them in. The man remembered the occasion because they usually take two days to restring such a large necklace, and Sir Gideon was most insistent that they should be ready the following day, because the day after that he and his wife were going to Deauville."

"What—er—date was this?"

"August 9th, and at that date there is no doubt whatever but that she was still in possession of the genuine pearls. Collingwood's are quite positive that they have never restrung any imitation pearls on her behalf, neither have they at any time had copies made of the originals on her instructions."

"Then she must have had the copies made elsewhere or else the imitations have been substituted without her knowledge, during the last four months," said Mr. Schatz.

"That is precisely the situation," agreed De Richleau. "We then returned here and carried out a most exhaustive examination of the fire escapes and galleries at the back of these flats. Perhaps Van Ryn would like to report to you upon that, personally."

"No," Rex shook his head. "Go right on, you know all there is to it."

"Just as you wish. The escapes then are definitely constructed with a view to making burglary difficult, if not impossible, controlled from the inside as they are. This in no way interferes with their use in time of emergency. If the lever is put over in the main hall or in any individual flat, the gates open outward with the greatest ease, and as they open a section of the steel ladder falls automatically into position; therefore, if you approach from below, not only are the gates locked against you, but it would be difficult even to reach the lock for the purpose of attempting to pick or force it. Given the height and the muscles of our friend Van Ryn, an escalade is admittedly possible, but it would be difficult even for him, and we both regard it as beyond the powers of any ordinary individual. And, of course, as you will recall, no trace of any such attempt was discovered by the police."

"Saying there was someone inside," said Simon, "someone who switched the gates open, could it be done then?"

"Undoubtedly," De Richleau nodded. "We tested that by releasing the spring in this flat. If that is done, it becomes the essence of simplicity; the person who desires to come up seizes the lowest rung of the ladder with the crook of a stick or umbrella and pulls it towards him, the short length of ladder will slide down into place and the gate of the gallery swings open at the same time; they are worked by one movement."

"And that brings us right back to the porter, the house-girl and the cook," said Rex.

"Yes," Mr. Schatz nodded. "Well, I've put the inquiry people on to them. I shall get a first report tomorrow, I expect, just giving general information, previous situations, family history and so on."

"It also raises the question of the other occupants of Errol House," the Duke went on. "Max, my man, an intelligent fellow whom I have had with me for a number of years, had a long conversation with his *chère-amie*, the porter's wife, last night, thereby supplementing the original knowledge which I do not doubt he possessed, and he gives me the following particulars as to the occupants of these flats.

"No. 1—myself and my staff; No. 2—Sir Gideon Shoesmith; No. 3—Mr. and Mrs. Vidal—French people, I believe—an old couple who have been here since the flats were built. He is over seventy and his butler is said to be as old as his master, if not older; No. 4—the Dowager Lady Lancastle, she has no male staff; No. 5 is empty; No. 6—Captain Cedric Brockenberg, the racing motorist. He has a manservant, age about forty years; in No. 7 there is Miss Fayette de Lancy, she has no male servants, but for the purpose of our inquiry I think we should include a certain Mr. Shuster who is said to pay the rent of her flat; he can be considered as half resident; No. 8 is again unoccupied; No. 9— Mr. and Mrs. Julian Hazelwode, young people quite recently married. He is Lord Notary's son, they employ only maids; and lastly, No. 10—Sascha Marrowitz, the portrait painter."

Simon ticked them off on his fingers. "Captain Brockenberg, his valet, Miss de Lancy's friend, Julian Hazelwode and Sascha Marrowitz; that's five. Has Marrowitz got a man?"

116

"No, he is what you term 'a queer', he took the flat because it was at the top of the building and he largely replaced the roof with glass to form a studio; he lives completely alone. But, in any case, I learn that he is at present in Germany."

"Did you get any information regarding the movements of the others on Saturday night?" asked Mr. Schatz.

"Frederick's wife made certain further inquiries during the course of today and was able to furnish Max with some particulars before we met this evening." The Duke smiled.

"Miss de Lancy, as you may know, delights a certain section of the public by her art each evening at the Palladium. She never returns home, therefore, until a little before midnight and Mr. Schuster has never been known to visit her flat when she is absent, although he often brings her home. The Julian Hazelwodes entertained friends to dinner on Saturday, six or eight young people, our informant thinks. They arrived in the neighbourhood of eight-fifteen, and all went out together a little before eleven, including the host and hostess, to dance somewhere, perhaps—possibly to the Ingram party that Van Ryn attended later. This little dinner also accounts for the movements of Captain Brockenberg's man. It seems that the Hazelwodes have a friendly understanding with his master by which they borrow him when they entertain; he must therefore have been fully occupied during the period under review."

"And Brockenberg?" asked Simon.

"Since his man was with the Hazelwodes, it's probable that he dined out late. Frederick reports that he came down in the lift with a lady a little after nine."

"Then that leaves—er—only your own man," Simon suggested tentatively.

"My two men," the Duke corrected. "I keep a chef; but, as it happens, since I dined out that evening he was at liberty and did not return until past eleven; Max, my valet, has been with me for many years and is devoted to me. In fact I have to thank him upon more than one occasion for my life. We have travelled in queer places together, Max and I; quite honestly I believe that no leisured respectability would compensate him for my death. He is that fine type of personal servant for whom there is no recompense except the appreciation and friendship of his master. With Max, in this matter, we shall not be concerned."

117

"This doesn't seem to get us much further," said Mr. Schatz, pursing his lips. "We'll get the inquiry people to find out, too, just how old and shaky Mr. Vidal and his butler are, but I don't think much is likely to come of that. You don't mention the women in these flats, are they quite out of the question?"

"Quite," De Richleau nodded his head. "The base of the skull was badly fractured. It would have to have been a strong man to have dealt such blows. But let us hear now if the time of that all-important telephone-call has been settled." He turned to Aron.

"Yes," Simon nodded. "I saw the people at the Club. They keep a record, we traced the number, and the call was put through at 10.3."

"Three minutes past ten," Mr. Schatz repeated. "Now that is something definite to go on, a very fine point in our favour. I suppose you didn't find out anything about the pearls?"

"Well, as a matter of fact, I did."

"Come on, then," laughed Rex. "Spill the beans."

Simon grinned. "I had a talk with one or two people I know in Hatton Garden, then I had a little bit of luck. I ran across the the chap that made them."

"But what good fortune," the Duke smiled. "And may one inquire *when* he made them?"

"Early in August. Must have been just before Lady Shoesmith went to Deauville."

"This is most interesting. And did she give him instructions herself, or was it as we suggested, a thief who had them made for substitution?"

"Ner—" Simon was thoroughly enjoying himself, he looked round the table, smiling broadly. "It's very interesting, this— he was ordered to make the copies by Sir Gideon Shoesmith."

CHAPTER XIX

SIMON ARON MAKES INSINUATIONS

"So the old man fixed it," said Rex.

"Interesting, isn't it?" Simon murmured, as he leaned back, both hands thrust into his trouser pockets.

"And," said the Duke, studying him fixedly, "may I inquire what you infer from that?"

118

"All depends—perhaps he was acting on her behalf; curious, though, that it should have been just at the same time that the real pearls were restrung."

"How do the dates compare? I understand that Collingwood's restrung the real pearls on August 9th. Sir Gideon left them in the afternoon and called for them on the following day."

"Then the dates do compare rather well, really." Simon smiled. "He left them in Hatton Garden to be copied on the 8th. As it happens he was in no end of a hurry there as well—said he couldn't leave them for more than twenty-four hours. Now, I don't mind telling you, in the ordinary way they'd take a week to do the selecting of the false pearls from stock on a job like that, but this chap sat up matching all night; I bet it cost Sir Gideon something—those sort of people don't work for nothing."

"We may assume then that Sir Gideon took them first to your man to be copied, and immediately he got them back he took them to Collingwood's to be restrung. It's certainly curious that on previous occasions the jewellers had always been allowed two days, and on this they were only given one."

"In other words," said Mr. Schatz abruptly, "you infer that the pearls had been entrusted to Sir Gideon for restringing and he took the opportunity to have them copied as well?"

Simon's head nodded like a Chinese mandarin's. "Exactly. D'you know, directly I heard he'd been in such a hurry, I thought there must be something fishy about it."

"You are assuming, of course, that Lady Shoesmith had no knowledge of the transaction?" asked Mr. Schatz.

"Um!" Simon leant forward eagerly. "Let's assume for a moment that Sir Gideon, for some purpose, never mind what, wanted to have Lady Shoesmith's pearls copied without her knowledge. How could he do it? She always wore them. It would be a difficult job. He couldn't just go to the safe and borrow them for a week, and he couldn't have a copy made without handing over the original—not a good enough copy to deceive Lady Shoesmith, anyhow. His only chance would be when she had them restrung. He could offer to take them to Collingwood's for her and take them to Hatton Garden instead."

"He'd have been in a nasty jam if she'd stepped into Collingwood's to collect them when the other guy had the goods," said Rex quickly.

"Ner." Simon shook his head. "Ner, I think he was clever there. He knew she wouldn't call on Collingwood's on the 8th because they always took two days. If she called on the 9th it didn't matter—he'd say he'd forgotten to take them round the day before. If he'd had them restrung first, and copied afterwards, he might have been in a muddle—a very nasty muddle—if Collingwood's had told her he'd collected them and he couldn't produce the goods, but he avoided that."

"It certainly looks as if he'd done it without her knowledge."

"Um, otherwise why was he in such a hurry?" Simon pressed his point. "If Lady Shoesmith didn't mind being without her pearls for a couple of days when they were restrung, surely she wouldn't have minded being without them for a day or two more to have them really well copied."

"I still don't see," Mr. Schatz drummed upon the table with his podgy fingers, "how this can in any way affect Eaton's case. He confesses to having taken the pearls and whether they are real or false is quite immaterial."

"You don't see?" Simon looked at the lawyer with half-closed eyes. "But surely, there can only have been one reason for his wanting to have them copied—without Lady Shoesmith's knowledge, I mean?"

"Presumably he wished to pledge or sell the real ones."

"Exactly!"

"You mean he must have been hard up?"

"Exactly!"

"I see your point. We have hitherto regarded Sir Gideon as a rich man, if that were not so, there might be some motive. . . ."

"Exactly! Apart from the legacies, he comes into Lady Shoesmith's personal estate."

Rex laughed. "Oh, have a heart, Aron, it couldn't have been Sir Gideon. He was out all the evening."

"I didn't say he wasn't." Simon chuckled into the palm of his hand. "All the same, if he was sufficiently hard-up in August to risk copying the pearls to raise about three thousand —well, eighteen thousand might come in pretty handy in November. I don't know—I'm just wondering, that's all."

"Have you by any chance any accurate information about Sir Gideon's financial situation?" the Duke inquired.

"Ner," Simon shook his head, still smiling. "He's supposed

to be a big man in Sheffield, I believe. He's a chartered accountant. There's a lot of money to be made by a clever chartered accountant; he sees the insides of so many people's books."

Rex grinned. "Yes, they get the low-down there, all right, play the market in other people's stocks. It's a great game as long as you don't come up against the unexpected—tariff wall, or prohibition or something of that kind—if you do, you take the air just as badly as the fellow who owns the books."

"Then—er—there's the question of the Slough property," Simon went on slowly. "Sir Gideon didn't want Lady Shoesmith to sell that to help Richard—he didn't want that a little bit."

Mr. Schatz looked up sharply. "D'you suggest that he wanted his wife to sell it to help him?"

"I don't know," said Simon innocently. "I'm only wondering. He might have thought it would come in useful if he wanted help himself later. On the other hand, the same thing may have happened to Slough as happened to the pearls."

"Say, that's going a bit far!" argued Rex. "He couldn't cash in that property without her knowledge."

"Don't know—don't say he has. Thanks," Simon carefully selected another long Hoyo from the big box that the Duke pushed towards him. "But lots of husbands and wives have their accounts at the same bank, and the wife lets the husband act for her. Some women'll sign anything you put in front of 'em, you know."

"Yes," said Mr. Schatz. "Had a case myself only last month. Man transferred a whole block of securities from his wife's account to his own to cover a loan account. Did it years ago, she never knew a thing about it till he died, but she signed the papers at the time; and now, poor woman, she's practically penniless—dreadful case."

"And you think, Aron, that something of the sort has taken place here." De Richleau looked thoughtful. "If it had, of course, it then becomes an immediate explanation as to why Sir Gideon was so anxious to prevent Lady Shoesmith from helping her son. Had she decided to sell, the title deeds would have had to be produced; that would have meant immediate exposure for Sir Gideon. If we have any evidence to show that it was her intention to sell against Sir Gideon's advice, that would provide a very strong motive for the murder."

121

"Exactly!" Simon's bird-like head went up and down. "He would have been in a terrible muddle."

"I think you are allowing yourselves to be carried away to an almost fantastic degree of speculation," said Mr. Schatz with a shake of his head. "To begin with there's no proof that the pearls were not copied with Lady Shoesmith's knowledge and at her request. As far as the Slough property is concerned, we know quite definitely that she had not the least intention of selling it without Sir Gideon's approval, and your suggestion about him having lodged the deeds to cover an overdraft has not the slightest foundation. Above all, there is no single factor which might suggest that Sir Gideon was in the flat between seven o'clock and a little before eleven. He is miles outside our proved time limits, and not only was he not there, but we know that he was at a public banquet, where every moment of his time can be accounted for."

"I've forgotten for the moment what that banquet was," remarked De Richleau.

"The London and Yorkshire Commercial Association at the Park Lane Hotel—only half a block from Aron's Club," Rex volunteered.

The Duke nodded. "Yes, of course, I remember now. But I confess I agree with Mr. Schatz. We have no real grounds for suspecting Sir Gideon personally. At the same time our inquiry about the pearls has not proved altogether fruitless. Thanks principally to Aron, we've secured some very interesting information, and I feel that we might well follow the matter up. Could you, for instance, Mr. Schatz, ascertain from Lady Shoesmith's solicitors the present whereabouts of these valuable deeds?"

"Certainly. I'll make a point of it tomorrow."

"And could you, Van Ryn, through your banking interests over here, perhaps, secure some information regarding Sir Gideon's financial stability, and more particularly the state of his accounts in recent months? I take it that in your position you would be able to press for a much more detailed statement than would be forthcoming through an ordinary banker's inquiry?"

"That is so," Rex agreed. "Most times they're close as oysters about personal accounts, but I'll turn the inquiry over to the special branch, they get the dope all right."

"Admirable—and Aron, you perhaps could fill in any gaps that may appear in Van Ryn's report by making a similar inquiry through Schröchild Brothers?"

Simon gave his jerky little laugh into the palm of his hand. "I think we can manage that."

"And in addition," De Richleau smiled, "if you could manage to have a further talk with some of your friends in Hatton Garden, we might learn if the real pearls have come on the market."

"Ner—I don't think so. As a matter of fact I did have a chat with one or two people today, but they couldn't tell me anything. I'll tell you, it's not easy; still I'll see what I can do."

Mr. Schatz pushed back his chair and stood up. "Well, we can't have too much information," he declared. "But I don't think you can seriously consider Sir Gideon. The pearls and the deeds have no bearing on the case, nor would the fact of his being hard up, if you found it to be true. He could not possibly have been the person concerned."

"No," said the Duke slowly. "But if the motive was sufficiently strong, it is just possible that he employed some other person to act for him."

CHAPTER XX

HOW THE DUKE WILED AWAY THE HOURS BETWEEN TWELVE-THIRTY AND THREE

Two days later the Duke de Richleau stood admiring the ducks on the lake in St. James's Park, many of which are said to be the lineal descendants of those placed there by Charles II.

Earlier in the morning the Duke had sent a message to Simon Aron, carefully explaining the exact point in the park at which he proposed to be at twelve-thirty, and suggesting that Simon should join him there and, afterwards, for luncheon.

De Richleau had carefully refrained from speaking to Aron upon the telephone, as he might easily have done, since he had felt that Simon being a very busy young man, might suggest that they should confine their meeting to lunch. For the same reason he had omitted to mention where the luncheon was to be, in order to give Simon no opportunity of keeping the latter appointment only.

It was one of those rare mornings in November when London has a peculiar loveliness of its own; a pale but pleasant sunshine upon the falling leaves, and a nip in the air without the slightest malice. The Duke had decided that it was definitely a morning to walk in the park, and his only problem had been to choose an interesting companion. It was a problem which had come to worry him more and more in recent years. It seemed to him that only a little while ago nobody he knew had done anything at all. They might be in the army or the Diplomatic Corps; write monographs on Chinese art; or play some part in the government of a nation. In fact, they had all been busy people in their way, but it had been a charming, leisurely business. But now all that seemed changed. Everybody worked; only the old, the dull, the uninteresting, still had leisure, the rest were frantically active, keeping a million telephone transmitters buzzing with their conversations, and causing their secretaries to fill countless thousands of note-books with the high speed hieroglyphics of their dictation. They arrived late for luncheon, and abandoned their coffee with muttered excuses of having to get back to their offices. An infinitely pathetic world in the eyes of Monseigneur le Duc de Richleau.

It had occurred to the Duke, therefore, that morning when he had been seated at breakfast in his Chinese robe, that it would be an interesting experiment to see if Aron's curiosity regarding the Shoesmith affair would be sufficient to drag him from his office in the city, in the middle of the morning. If Aron turned up, as the Duke thought he would, the problem of spending the hours between twelve-thirty and three in a pleasant and interesting manner would have been solved; and De Richleau never disguised the fact from himself or his friends that the principal object of his life was to pass it in a pleasant and interesting manner.

The Duke turned from his contemplation of the ducks, thinking how suitable it was that the royal birds should have had such numerous progeny, when Charles himself had been responsible for half the aristocracy who had used the park in after generations, and saw hurrying towards him down one of the gravel paths the slim figure of Simon Aron.

124

Tightly buttoned into a smart blue overcoat that made his shoulders seem narrower than ever, with short quick steps Simon came hastening along. He waved his stick in greeting when he realized that the Duke had seen him.

De Richleau sauntered to meet him, a smile playing about his thin lips. "Good morning, Aron," he said lightly. "Why do you hurry so, you will be out of breath, my friend?"

"Thought I was late—man kept me at the office."

"It would not have mattered in the least if you had been," the Duke smiled. "It only occurred to me at breakfast that it would be a delightful morning for a walk in the park, and I thought you might care to join me."

"Good God!" Simon ejaculated. "I wish I'd known that. I thought it was something important. I've got an awfully busy day on."

"Dear me!" De Richleau's eyebrows went up, and he appeared to be most concerned. "That fool of a man could not have given you my message clearly. Just to think that I have brought you all this way from your office. I am indeed sorry."

Simon glanced to right and left, and then quickly at his watch. The Duke chuckled inwardly, thinking of the White Rabbit in *Alice in Wonderland* and, in truth, Simon's arc of nose lent colour to the likeness. "Can't be done," he said at last, resignedly, thrusting back his watch. "Well, anyhow, here we are."

"Yes," said the Duke sweetly. "Here we are, let us walk a little." And he began to stroll gently along the bank of the lake. "Tell me, Aron, do you come often to this charming park?"

"I?—Ner—" Simon fell into step beside him. "To tell the truth, I don't think I've ever been in it before in my life."

"Now, that I think is quite amazing, for you are a great lover of beauty, are you not? And this little park, when the flowers are out, is quite charming. Even as you see today, when the flowers are no longer here—providing there is a little sunshine —it is a very pleasant place in which to be."

"Don't know how it is, but I never seem to have time."

"Ah, I know, it is so sad that lack of time. I am a fortunate person, incurably lazy; and I would not be cured of my laziness if I could. It enables me to enjoy so many pleasant things that other people have not the time to do."

125

"Do you come here every day?" Simon inquired.

"Oh, no, only if the weather is propitious, and not always then. Sometimes I take the car out into the country and walk for a little in the woods—there are so many lovely places near London —which are quite deserted on a weekday, where one can idle away an hour and yet be back in time for lunch in town. If I had thought, we might have gone this morning."

Simon shook his head. "Very nice, but difficult for me to get away. I've got a lot on just now."

"Indeed!" De Richleau smiled slightly. "Have you ever stopped to consider, Aron, how many years it will be before the day arrives when you will not have a 'lot on'?"

"You're quite right," Simon laughed into his gloved hand. "We're awful fools to work as we do, I suppose; but I get abroad a bit now and again."

"And where do you go to when you go abroad?"

"France mostly. Touquet, Deauville, Monté; but I never get away for very long."

"France, eh? But that is not France, my friend. France is the wooded meadowlands about Poictiers, the sun-baked olive groves of Provence, the forests of Navarre, where one can still hunt the boar. How I should love to see them all again."

"Well—I mean, why don't you, if you're so free?"

"Yes—I shall go again, but it is always a danger for me. I have to take my precautions before I set foot in France, it is my misfortune to be an exile."

"Really." Simon was interested, but he did not like to ask why.

"Yes," the Duke went on. "I am an exile for many years. Perhaps you may not even know it, but there is still a King of France, that is to say, for us who have preserved the loyalties of our birth. He is known to the world as the Duke de Guise. When I was a young man there were hopes of restoring the monarchy, a hope which I fear is now for ever dead, but in those days it was quite a serious possibility. I was deeply implicated in a political conspiracy to bring about a *coup d'état*, and I do not grumble at the penalty; it only makes me a little sad at times that I cannot return freely to the places which I love."

"That's a rotten muddle," Simon murmured sympathetically.

"It might have been infinitely worse," said De Richleau

philosophically. "For myself it was not so bad as for some of the other young men who were implicated with me. Such property as my family saved from the Revolution has been in London ever since, so my income was in no way jeopardized by my participation, and that has served to make life tolerable."

"You do—er—sometimes go back, though?"

"Yes, at long intervals, but it is a risk which I am not prepared to take so readily now that I am an older man. A few months inside a French fortress would make havoc of my constitution; besides, it is impossible for me to stay in the houses of my friends without bringing a certain risk upon them, too. And in the public places where my own world gathers, I should be recognized immediately."

"That's rotten, but I suppose you go abroad to other places."

"Yes, indeed," the Duke smiled. "I think I would almost as soon face a French fortress as live in London all the year. I have a villa in Italy, and an old castle in Austria, but I do not care to go to Austria much now. Since the war all my friends there have lost their money. Oh, it is pathetic, all those dear, charming people, so gay, so hospitable, that I used to know; they never thought of money, and now that they have none— they think of nothing else."

Simon nodded. "Things are pretty bad out there. I went to Vienna last summer. Of course, I knew they were in a muddle, but I didn't realize how bad it was, no life in the place, and every other shop to let."

"Ah, my friend, you should have been in Vienna before the war—a lovely town—be careful—" The Duke's exclamation was caused by Simon very nearly stepping in front of a taxi-cab as they crossed the Mall. Having safely negotiated the crossing, Simon asked:

"By the by, did Van Ryn get that report on Sir Gideon, do you know?"

"Yes, he came in to see me last night. It seems that Shoe-smith's resources are extremely slender. His accountancy house does very little regular business, only six clerks are employed. But he acts for several big men in a private capacity, men who don't wish their business accountants to know about their personal dealings. It's probable that in this way he has secured the pickings in certain big deals which would be equal in value on the regular profits upon auditing the accounts of a far larger number of firms than he handles in the ordinary way."

Simon shook his head. "Much more precarious, though. All right in a boom period—but not much fun now."

"Exactly. I gather from Van Ryn that a good portion of Shoesmith's time is occupied with the Sheffield and Kingslade Estate Development Company. It seems he is chairman. It is not a big company, only two hundred thousand pounds. They were paying good dividends up to a year ago, but they passed their last dividend, and they paid nothing in the interim either. What results have your inquiries had?"

"Much about the same. I can tell you one thing, though. The S. and K. are under-capitalized. They're in a muddle, Gideon's had to take up a lot of shares since last spring, otherwise they wouldn't have been able to carry on."

"That," said the Duke, is very interesting. "Did you find out any more about the pearls?"

"Ner—nothing. Weren't sold in this country, else I think I would have heard something. But I wonder . . . ?"

"What?" inquired De Richleau curiously.

"You remember he went to Deauville in August? Well, I wonder if he unloaded them there. It would be nice and easy afterwards to explain a big payment into his bank by a run of luck at the tables."

"That is most certainly a possibility. Have you any news of the deeds?"

"Schatz 'phoned me—they're at the bank."

"I see. We were wrong there, then. All we can say is that Sir Gideon is not quite the solid man of wealth which we had at first assumed him to be; and that, in fact, he had actually been called upon to finance his Development Company to a considerable amount during the last eight months."

By this time they had arrived at the Piccadilly side of the Green Park, and as they came out on to the pavement the Duke pointed with his stick across the road.

"The Park Lane Hotel, my friend. If it is agreeable to you, it's there today that I propose to give you luncheon."

"Very nice of you. It's a place I never go in to the ordinary way—why, I don't know."

De Richleau smiled. "Then, I will tell you. It is because it's a comparatively new place, and you prefer to go to your old haunts, where you can be quite certain that the *maître d'hôtel* and waiters know all your little idiosyncrasies. Am I right?"

Simon laughed his little jerky laugh into his hand. "Absolutely. How did you know?"

"Because I've never yet been there myself for that very reason. However, today we will experiment. Maybe we shall find the food and service admirable. In which case we can add to our list with confidence for future occasions."

They crossed the road and passed through the swing doors of the Park Lane Hotel. Having deposited their coats, the Duke led the way to a small table in the lounge. "Would you care to join me in a cocktail?" he inquired. "Or would you prefer to take a chance upon the sherry here?"

"Cocktail, I think, and something with rum in it. I enjoyed the little walk, but I'm a bit chilly." Simon rubbed his thin hands together.

"A Baccardi, perhaps?" the Duke suggested.

"Ner—I'd rather have Jamaica rum, if you don't mind, with one third lemon juice and a dash of curaçao."

De Richleau beckoned a waiter and gave his order.

"Tell me," he added to the man, "who is the *maître d'hôtel* here now?"

"Mr. Pirelli, sir."

"Ah, indeed, well, tell them to keep a table for two near the *caisse* for luncheon." He turned to Simon. "Pirelli . . . I do not know the name, do you?"

Simon shook his head. "Ner—I may know him when I see him, but I don't think so."

"I want to find somebody here that I know, without going to the management. It occurred to me that at a table near the desk we should be able to see all the waiters in turn. I shall be very surprised if there is not one among them who has worked in some place where I have been an *habitué* in the past."

"Good plan that," Simon commented. And so it proved, for they had scarcely taken their seats some quarter of an hour later, when De Richleau tapped Simon's arm.

"I know that face," he said, indicating a small, fat waiter who stood some distance away with a large wine *carte* under his arm.

129

In another minute the waiter caught sight of them and came hurrying over. "*Altesse!*" he exclaimed, beaming. "What a pleasure to see you 'ere in London. You have not come here before; Monsieur Pirelli, 'e will be so pleased. We will make you so 'appy 'ere, you go nowhere else."

The Duke smiled and nodded. "It is a long time since I have seen you."

"Yes, *Altesse*, I am Jacoby, you remember the Preisling Palais in Munich, 1929. Ah, that was a restaurant. What wines, what food! But it is all very nice 'ere," he added hastily. "You 'ave order your lunch?"

"Yes, we have ordered our lunch, but I would choose a wine—a hock I think—it's too cold for a Moselle."

"I have no old wine, *Altesse*—we cannot get them 'ere in London—but I 'ave still some good '21, the Löwengrin Furstenberg, 1921. That is a fine wine, a name not much known perhaps but good, very good."

"Very well, bring a bottle, and later you shall recommend some cognac for us to drink, after we've had our luncheon."

The fat little man retired full of smiles, and with marked deference; very soon Pirelli himself came hastening over to see that they were receiving every attention.

When luncheon was over and Jacoby carefully warming the glasses in which he was about to serve the brandy, De Richleau began to question him.

"Tell me, Jacoby, in addition to the Restaurant and the Grill, you have private parties here, do you not? Dances and banquets?"

"But, yes, *Altesse*, afterwards, if you permit, it would be a pleasure to show you our *grande suite*. Reception-room, dining-room, ballroom, we can seat two hundred and fifty persons; and if the dance room is not needed the wall between is made to fall back, then we can seat four hundred and fifty—and we have smaller suites for parties more *intime*, very comfortable, and everything most modern."

"Delightful," murmured the Duke, cutting short the flow. "I believe a friend of mine was at a dinner here last Saturday."

"Saturday, let me remember," Jacoby cast back his head. "No, impossible, *Altesse*. Thursday, perhaps, that was the

130

Corinthian Club dinner, but Saturday that was a dinner only for business men—I do not think . . ."

"This was a business dinner, Jacoby, to which I refer. Could you, I wonder, produce for me a table plan of the gathering which took place on Saturday?"

"Certainly, *Altesse*, the office of Monsieur Pirelli will 'ave a copy. You will excuse—" Jacoby hurried away to return a few moments later with the required plan.

De Richleau studied it in silence for a moment, then he leant towards Simon. "Here you will observe at the top table is our friend Shoesmith, between Sir William Juddkins and Mr. James Ritherdon."

Simon nodded silently.

"Jacoby," De Richleau spoke in a low voice, "the waiters who were on duty at this dinner, were they hirelings or a part of your regular staff?"

"The regular brigade, *Altesse*, we have dinners or dances five nights out of six. The Imperial Room it is booked now for every night till Christmas."

"Good. Now listen carefully. You see this name, Sir Gideon Shoesmith, I wish all the information you can get about him. What time did he come? What time did he go? What did he eat? What did he drink? And particularly remember this, did he receive any message during the dinner, or did he leave the room for any length of time? Did he make a telephone call from the hotel? Did he seem cheerful and normal after dinner, or did he seem excited and upset? Question every one of these waiters who attended at the banquet, also the hall porter, the cloak-room attendant, and the young woman at the telephone. Neglect nothing. Here is a photograph—taken, it is true, from the papers of a few days ago, but it is a good likeness. I will leave it with you. Come to my flat—Errol House in Curzon Street—tomorrow afternoon at four o'clock; that is a good time for you, is it not?"

"A very good time, *Altesse*."

"Excellent. Come, then, at that hour and tell me what you have learnt." The Duke thrust a crinkly paper into the ready hand of the stooping waiter. "There will be another like that," he added, "if you can tell me what I want to know."

Jacoby bowed almost to the table. "Leave it to me, *Altesse*, all that there is to know you shall 'ave it." He bowed again and slipped away.

"We have been fortunate." De Richleau turned to Simon. "Jacoby is a capable man. If Shoesmith employed an agent in this business, as our latest theory leads us to speculate, he would be almost certain to receive information before he went home that the thing had been done. I think now we may be certain to hear of it, if he received a message or talked to anybody on the telephone."

"Um," Aron nodded enthusiastically. "Congratulations upon your staff work."

"Thank you." De Richleau laughed as he paid his bill. "And now," he suggested, "what about another stroll in the park?"

"Good God!" Simon exclaimed aghast. "I don't know if you know it, but I've got some work to do." And with murmured thanks he hurried away with his head well down, while the Duke lingered to assure the smiling Monsieur Pirelli that his restaurant was excellent and that he would most certainly honour the Park Lane Hotel again.

CHAPTER XXI

THE DUKE DE RICHLEAU DABBLES IN FINANCE

UPON the following morning the Duke de Richleau drove into the City of London. Unlike the previous day the weather was cold and dreary, with more than a suspicion of fog, which threatened to bring a premature night upon the narrow streets by midday.

Only upon very rare occasions did the Duke go east of Temple Bar. The atmosphere of the commercial world was uncongenial to him, and such business as he had occasion to transact could usually be accomplished by telephone or meetings arranged at his own flat. He felt, however, that on this occasion he had no reasonable excuse for asking the people whom he wished to see to come to him, and therefore, since he urgently wished to secure certain information, he must face the irritation of traffic blocks and the depressing atmosphere of the gloomy streets.

He knew little or nothing of the four men whom he hoped to see, only that all of them had sat either next, or next but one, to Sir Gideon Shoesmith on the previous Saturday night at the London and Sheffield Commercial Association dinner. He had carefully taken a note of their names from the plan which he had seen with Aron at the Park Lane the day before, and in the evening, after some little time spent with various reference books, he had traced their addresses in the city.

His first call was upon James Ritherdon, who had sat upon Sir Gideon's right. That Ritherdon was a stockbroker De Richleau knew, also he fancied that he had heard his name in connexion with the Turf. He was endeavouring to recall the exact circumstances when the car drew up before a block of offices in Austin Friars.

The Duke gave his name to a smart and civil commissionaire, who led him to a comfortable waiting-room with a bright fire, but he had only had time to glance at the first few pages of the current *Punch* when, rather to his regret, an exceptionally good-looking secretary arrived and smilingly ushered him into Ritherdon's private office.

The stockbroker proved to be a big cheerful-looking man. He rose quickly, shook hands with vigour, and pulled up a comfortable chair for the Duke beside his impressive mahogany desk.

"Now, Your Grace," he said genially, "what can I do for you?"

"I come upon a rather delicate mission," the Duke admitted, "and I trust you will accept my word for it that the inquiries I wish to make are not dictated by idle curiosity. I need hardly say that any information which you may be kind enough to give me will be treated with the strictest confidence."

"Quite so," said the stockbroker. "Quite so," but he looked a shade worried. "Of course, you will understand that I can give you no information regarding the accounts of any of my clients."

"Indeed, no," De Richleau protested smiling, "this is quite a simple, personal matter. I believe you were at the London and Sheffield dinner last Saturday night?"

133

Mr. Ritherdon's face cleared. "Oh yes, and a rotten show it was. I hate functions, lot of prosy old men and Saturday night, too. Why they can't hold them on a weekday, beats me. I suppose it's for the sake of the provincial people. Yes, I was there."

"You sat next to Sir Gideon Shoesmith, I think?"

"Yes, poor chap, the very night his wife was killed, too. Awful thing, must have happened while we were sitting there, as I was saying to my wife afterwards. Is it anything to do with the case?"

"My inquiries might have some bearing upon it. I may say that I am acting for young Richard Eaton, who, as I dare say you know, has been arrested in connexion with the crime."

"Pretty clear case against him, isn't it? At least, from what I've heard the boy was up to his ears in debt, and I'm told he confesses to having gone off with the pearls."

De Richleau accepted a cigar from the box that the stockbroker pushed towards him. "There is, of course, a case against Eaton," he admitted, "but it is by no means conclusive. I happen to have been privileged to hear his story from his own lips, and I personally am quite convinced of his innocence. It's in the hope of bringing fresh evidence to light that I'm making these inquiries."

"Well, if he didn't do it, it must be a ghastly thing for a chap to be accused of murdering his own mother; but I don't see how I can help you?"

"Do you happen to remember at what time you left the Park Lane Hotel?"

"Yes, I cleared off just as soon as I could with decency. I was joining a party at the Savoy afterwards, and I wanted to dance, not sit there listening to those old fossils throwing bouquets at each other. I must have slipped out at about ten minutes to ten.

"And can you recall if Sir Gideon was still there when you went?"

Mr. Ritherdon looked De Richleau full in the eyes. "I don't remember," he said firmly.

"Surely!" the Duke protested. "Since Shoesmith was actually seated beside you, with a little effort you could recall if you said good night to him before leaving?"

The stockbroker smiled. "As it happens, I didn't, but you

know what these shows are. Once the King's been drunk people start circulating a bit, move round and sit with a friend, if they can find a place, while the speeches and the music go on."

De Richleau had a very shrewd idea that Ritherdon feared to be more definite in case he should be drawn into the affair. He therefore stood up to take his leave.

"Mr. Ritherdon," he extended his hand, "I must thank you for the exceedingly kind way in which you have received me, and it's unlikely that I shall have to trouble you again, but I would like to ask you one more question. In the event of it proving necessary, in fact, if it was found that your evidence was needed to corroborate certain points upon which a man's life may hang, do you think you might search your memory and make some more definite statement regarding the dinner last Saturday?"

The stockbroker looked into the Duke's bright grey eyes. "I don't quite know what you're driving at," he said slowly. "I can't see what the dinner's got to do with the murder, anyway, and as you've spotted for yourself, I don't want to be drawn into this sort of business if I can help it; but if a man's life is involved I should, of course, be prepared to answer any questions; and my memory's pretty good."

"Thank you." De Richleau smiled. "That is all that I want to know, and now I will not take up any more of your time."

Ritherdon led his visitor to the door. "Ever do anything on the Stock Exchange?" he inquired casually.

"Occasionally," said the Duke. "What are Sheffield and Kingslade Development Company standing at today?"

"Ten and six—eleven bob—there aren't many dealings, it's almost a private concern."

"You can sell five thousand forward down to nine shillings for delivery next month, on my account, if you wish."

Ritherdon gave him a quick look. "All right, very pleased, I'm sure. You know, I suppose, that Shoesmith's interested?"

"Yes, on the board, I believe. I will be quite frank with you. In my opinion he did not behave at all well to that stepson of his. When the case comes on I think his reputation may suffer considerably. I don't suggest for one moment that his conduct has not been all that it should be with regard to his companies,

135

but the British public is nothing if not sentimental. I think there may be heavy selling in those concerns in which he's interested."

The stockbroker nodded. "I see your point. Of course, it's a gamble. Fact he's been hard on his stepson doesn't alter the company's assets, but the public do get funny sometimes. Maybe you're on a good thing."

"Fortunately, I can afford a little gamble sometimes," the Duke smiled. "Good day to you, Mr. Ritherdon."

As he went down in the lift De Richleau made rapid calculations. He had the advantage over Ritherdon in that the latter did not know the story of the pearls being copied. That was bound to come out at the trial. The Duke de Richleau meant to see that it did; he meant to see also that Shoesmith's advice to his stepson as to filing his own petition without any thought of his unfortunate creditors should be made public. Sir Gideon's credit would be in a pretty poor way by the time the affair was ended. Those shares would fall to five shillings the Duke reckoned. "Five thousand at four shillings profit per share, twenty thousand shillings, fifty pounds to the thousand, that makes one thousand pounds—well, well, perhaps, after all, it had been worth coming to the city this morning."

His next call was to be upon Sir William Juddkins, O.B.E., and his car soon took him to Moorpath House, in a narrow turning off Moorgate Street. It was a shabby, old-fashioned building, and upon the lift he found a large placard, "out of order." He had, therefore, to climb the seven flights of stone stairs, and paused, breathless, before the glazed door which bore the legend, "Juddkins & Co., Estate Agents."

One of the few things which really put the Duke into a thoroughly evil temper was to lose his breath. Under no circumstances had he ever been known to run, but climbing seven double flights of stairs, however slowly accomplished, had defeated his care. The unusual exertion had drawn the blood from his brain, and his momentary loss of the power of thought absolutely infuriated him. He waited for a few moments on the landing to recover his composure.

At length, feeling somewhat recovered, he pushed the door and stepped through into a small confined space shut in with partitions. In the one opposite the door there was a sliding

136

panel upon which in faded lettering could be read the one word "Inquiries."

The Duke knocked; there was a slight slithering of papers, and the panel slid back to reveal the head of a pimply-faced and sulky-looking youth.

"My name is De Richleau," said the Duke. "Does Sir William happen to be in?"

"Who from?" asked the youth, gazing at him stolidly.

"I am not *from* anybody," answered the Duke with some asperity. "If your master is in kindly inform him that I wish to see him."

The youth slammed the sliding door to with a bang and De Richleau heard him rustling with his papers on the other side of the partition. After a little the sound ceased and the panel was suddenly thrust open again.

"Sir William says, what's yer business?"

"It is of a private nature," replied the Duke, exercising some restraint. Again the panel was slammed to, only to be thrust open again a minute later.

"Sir William says will you wait."—Slam!

De Richleau frowned, but he took comfort from the fact that the cigar which he was smoking was a good one. Ritherdon evidently understood cigars; the Duke had noticed when he took it that it was a Punch, and the condition was excellent.

Five minutes, ten minutes, at length the panel did open once more.

"Sir William says will yer come this way," and the pimply-faced youth thrust open a door in the partition.

The outer office proved to be far from inviting. High desks with two or three stools, from one of which the horse-hair stuffing was trying to escape, windows black with the grime of generations, rows of battered ledgers, and letter-files thick with dust.

The inner office was scarcely less depressing: an enormous iron safe, a jumble of papers, a number of land development charts yellow with age, and a little ferret-like man with pale blue eyes, apparently Sir William, seated at an open roll-topped desk.

He did not rise as De Richleau entered, but motioned with a pen to a sagging arm-chair. He seemed to be a man of few words.

"Sit down. What can I do for you? I don't think I know you, do I?"

The Duke smiled, the idea of his knowing this person appealed to his sense of humour. "No," he said mildly. "No, I don't think we have ever met."

"Well, what's your business? I dare say you know I'm a very busy man."

"Indeed—well—I will endeavour not to detain you more than a few moments. I am making a few inquiries, and I should be grateful for your assistance. I may say that these inquiries are not merely idle curiosity upon my part, and they are strictly confidential."

"Do you come from an agency?" asked Juddkins suspiciously.

"No—no, I fear I am completely unsponsored. I must ask you to take my word for it that the result of my inquiries is of some importance. I believe you were at the London and Sheffield dinner on Saturday night?"

"Well, what's it got to do with you if I was?" Juddkins gave the Duke a furtive look. "By the way, you're a foreigner, aren't you?"

"I am a Frenchman by birth," agreed the Duke, "but I cannot quite see what that has to do with—"

Juddkins cut him short. "Well, I don't see why I should discuss my private affairs with you."

The Duke shrugged his shoulders. "My dear Mr. Juddkins," he began amiably. . . .

"Sir William Juddkins," snapped the little man. "Sir William Juddkins, that's my name."

"Ah, yes." De Richleau rose slowly to his feet. "Sir William Juddkins," he repeated, "you are then a knight?"

"I am," declared the ferret, "and what's more I was among the first batch of O.B.E.'s in the War."

"Let me then recommend to you, Sir William, a book called *Morte d'Arthur*, by Sir Thomas Malory. You will, I trust, enjoy the contrast between the knighthood of yesterday and the knighthood of today. I find it exceeding strange."

Sir William Juddkins also rose to his feet. "I don't quite know what you mean," he began angrily.

"No? Oh, no, I didn't suppose that you would," the Duke replied as he replaced his hat at a somewhat rakish angle on his head and prodded the swing-door open with his cane. "Only, my good Juddkins, to use one of your excellent British sayings— it is utterly impossible to make a silk purse out of a sow's ear."

De Richleau walked out in an atmosphere heavy with the pregnant silence of baffled rage.

His next call was upon Mr. Sidney Keiling, a wholesale cutler in Mark Lane, and in a comparatively short time, although it seemed a lengthy journey, he was set down before Keiling, Son & Keiling's office. Here he was unlucky. A Mr. Keiling junior received him, a very pleasant young man, who regretted to inform De Richleau that his father was at the works in Sheffield in fact, it seemed that Mr. Keiling senior rarely came to London except on business or for an occasional function.

The last name upon De Richleau's list was that of Christopher Deacon, also seemingly engaged in the cutlery trade. His office was on the third floor of a block in Cannon Street and the Duke was more fortunate on this occasion.

Most of the people with whom he came in contact were aware of his title, and it was not his custom to announce himself by it; but having met with such a discourteous reception at the Juddkins office, and feeling that the Juddkinses of this world and their satellites would be more suitably impressed for his present purpose, he had announced himself boldly at Keiling's, and with such success that here again he adopted similar tactics.

"If Mr. Christopher Deacon is in would you be good enough to tell him that the Duke de Richleau would be glad of a few words with him."

The girl who had received him hurried away and a moment later a small, spectacled man of middle age came hastening out to him. "Good morning. I'm—er—I'm Deacon," he said a little nervously.

"And I am the Duke de Richleau. Can you spare me a few moments of your time?"

"Oh, yes, of course, won't you come in, my—er—sir." He had almost said "My Lord," and the Duke repressed a smile as Mr. Deacon held open the swing gate.

"Thank you." De Richleau walked through the counting-house to a small but neat office.

Mr. Deacon dragged forward the only arm-chair from his desk. "Do—er—won't you sit down?"

"Thank you," the Duke smiled, "but don't let me rob you of your chair."

"No, no—Go on—do," Deacon urged anxiously.

Without further protest the Duke lowered himself into Mr. Deacon's swivel chair, while its owner stood before him, like a rather nervous, but expectant schoolboy.

"Mr. Deacon," the Duke began, "you were present I believe, at the London and Sheffield dinner on Saturday night?"

"Oh, yes." Mr. Deacon brightened perceptibly. "It was a wonderful gathering. Lord Stallworth took the chair."

"Indeed," the Duke smiled amiably. "I am very anxious to obtain certain information regarding this dinner, and I think you can help me."

"Oh, anything I can do," said Mr. Deacon eagerly.

"I believe you sat next to James Ritherdon, did you not?"

"Yes, I was very well placed, and Mr. Ritherdon told me about his horse, Tea Cup. He says it's a certainty for the Lincoln. Of course, I never bet in the ordinary way, but I think I must have a little on, having met the owner, you know."

"Quite," said the Duke genially. "Having had the tip from you I almost feel that I must have a little on myself. Do you by any chance remember the time that Mr. Ritherdon left?"

"Yes, he left very early. We had only had one song. I was so sorry, but he had to catch a train to the country."

"I see, and so I suppose you moved up next to Sir Gideon Shoesmith?"

"No—er—I don't really know Sir Gideon Shoesmith very well; I've been introduced to him, of course. What a terrible thing that was about his wife."

"Yes, a tragedy. I suppose he was busy talking to his other neighbour, Sir William Juddkins?"

"Oh, no, Sir Gideon left the table before Ritherdon."

"That was early to leave so pleasant a party."

"Sir Gideon hadn't gone home. I saw him again later on, as a matter of fact he wished me good night at about twenty to eleven as the last guests were leaving."

"I suppose you could not tell me who Sir Gideon was talking to in between? I have a very special reason for wanting to know."

"I don't think I saw him until he came back to the table after the speeches were over."

"You were perhaps engaged with your other neighbour?" De Richleau suggested.

"No—er—" Mr. Deacon flushed slightly—"to tell you the truth I haven't been in London from Sheffield very long and I don't know many people. The gentleman on my other side moved down the table to talk to some friends soon after Ritherdon left, so in a way I was sitting all alone through most of the speeches."

"Then you would have had an excellent opportunity to observe the company; most interesting, I don't doubt. Can you not recall where Sir Gideon was sitting during that time?"

"Well, of course, I was very interested in the people, so many names that I know in business, or at home, you know; and I'm pretty certain that Sir Gideon Shoesmith was not there. In fact I'm pretty sure about it—I—er—amused myself by referring to each person by my table plan, to see as far as possible who they were."

"That," said the Duke, "is exceedingly interesting; but where do you think Sir Gideon could have gone?"

"I really don't know. He may have gone to the cloakroom or been talking to somebody in the lounge of the hotel; he must have missed all the speeches, and they were so good."

De Richleau stood up. "I am extremely grateful to you, Mr. Deacon, for having given me so much of your time."

"Won't you—er—have a cigarette? I'm afraid they're only gaspers." He tentatively offered the box upon his desk.

"Thank you." The Duke took one and lit it. "Thank you very much. I must be going now or I shall be late for luncheon. I am exceedingly obliged to you, Mr. Deacon, and if I can be of any service to you at any time, pray command me."

"Oh—er—thanks awfully—not at all." Mr. Deacon rescued the Duke's stick from the floor, colliding with him in his nervous endeavour both to show him the way out and allow him to go first, and finally escorted him to his car.

De Richleau drove to the Belgian Embassy, where he was engaged to lunch. On the way he was deep in thought, and even at luncheon it was remarked that he was a little distrait.

Once back in his flat, he waited impatiently for Jacoby to arrive, and when at length the wine waiter from the Park Lane had kept his appointment and delivered his report which occupied

141

more than half an hour, the Duke himself let him out. He then went to the telephone.

After some minutes he got through to James Ritherdon. "Is that you, Ritherdon?" he inquired sharply. "This is De Richleau. You know that stock I asked you to sell this morning? Yes? Well, sell up to twenty thousand."

CHAPTER XXII

"MALICE AND PAIN COMING FROM A FAIR WOMAN"

WHEN De Richleau had finished his conversation with James Ritherdon he rang up Rex at his little house in Trevor Square.

Rex was officially out, but actually at home. He had, however, given instructions to Mrs. Bottom that should the Duke or Simon Aron ring up they were to be put through.

The bell in the sitting-room tinkled and Rex stretched one long arm towards the receiver, with the other he shifted the slight but delicious weight of Felicia Standish to a more central position on his knees.

"Damn!" said Felicity.

"Hallo!" said Rex.

"I have news," said the Duke at the other end of the line.

"You don't say! That's great!"

"It's a long story, my friend, but interesting. I should like to see you. Moreover, I think we shall have need of your assistance."

"That's fine! I'll be right over—at least—" Rex suddenly remembered Felicity. "Wait a moment. Now, could you step round to me, in say half an hour, I'll be pretty occupied till then. You can? That's swell! In half an hour then. O.K." He rang off.

"Dar-ling," purred Felicity.

"Yes, honey?"

"Do you know what I really think about you?"

"I'll fall for it." Rex grinned doubtfully.

Felicity removed her slender form from his encircling arm.

142

She stood up and smoothed her neat golden head, emitting the faintest wave of her Chanel perfume as she did so.

"I think," she said slowly, regarding him steadfastly with her very blue eyes, "that persons who wear lemon-coloured boots and dickies are gentlemen, and that Eskimos who live upon the immoral earnings of blind women are desirable companions—compared to you. In fact, that you are the one original, authentic, undeniable and utter Cad!"

"Dar-ling!" protested Rex.

"Don't seek to deny it, my sweet. Bounder is your middle name. How else could you seduce a young and innocent girl like myself and then abandon her heartlessly for days? I shall sue this Duke man and your little Jew friend for alienation of affection, and get thousands by way of damages. At least I could do if we were in America. As it is I shall sell myself to a negro prince—then what will you do?"

Rex grinned and pulled her down again upon his knee. "Have a heart, honey!" he laughed. "It's serious this business. Honest it is."

"I know," said Felicity, twining a lock of Rex's rumpled wavy hair round one of her pink fingers and giving it a vicious tug. "Saturday you never bothered to turn up at Irma's until one o'clock in the morning; Sunday you lied in your imperfectly cleaned teeth about golf at Sunningdale—I know because Bobbie told me you never turned up, and let him down. Monday you put me off about dinner to dine with your queer friends, and now when I have got you to myself for five minutes I suppose I am to be packed off. What *is* the good of our having a love-affair if we never see each other—I ask you?"

"Now, honey, you must be reasonable."

"Pig. You can't even have the decency to remember how I loathe your nasty, cheap American endearments."

"I'm sorry, sweet. We did dine Tuesday, and lunch yesterday at that jolly little Punch's Club in Waverton Street. 'Twasn't my fault you wouldn't dine last night. I'm clean crazy about you, honest I am. You're just the most adorable thing that ever wore two shoes; but this is a big show I've got on with the Duke and Aron. I only wish I could let you in on it. You'll be just terribly interested when I can spill the beans, later on."

Felicity coiled herself round him in the manner of an affection-

143

ate python. "That's better," she cooed. "But what a big, important person it is to be sure, with its little secret, just like a nice grubby schoolboy who's got a robber's cave in the coal cellar with a couple of friends, and won't trust the girls for fear they tell. What are you going to do? Abduct Ishbel MacDonald, or blow up the King?"

"Say, cut it out!" exclaimed Rex, laughing and wriggling in his chair. "You're tickling! Stop it!"

"Worse will befall," whispered Felicity, "unless you tell. I see it all, as in a glass darkly, malice and pain coming from a fair woman who loves you."

"I can't, sweet, I've given my solemn word to the others I wouldn't let on."

"Here goes!" said Felicity, and her sharp little teeth seized upon the lobe of Rex's left ear.

"Hoi! You're hurting—you little slut." A scuffle followed. For a minute Rex held the girl stretched out across his knee, and managed to get in one resounding whack upon her behind; but next second with surprising strength and agility in one so slight she had managed to wriggle free and stood looking down upon him, flushed, breathless, hardly at all dishevelled, but adorably pretty in her excitement.

"Darling!" said Rex.

"My beloved!" said Felicity.

And rising, Rex folded the delectable femininity of Felicity into his huge male bosom, stooping his head quite considerably in order to bring his lips into firm and lasting contact with her lips, until the pain in his neck became such that he was forced reluctantly to take his mouth from hers, but even so he continued to hold her tightly to him for some little time. At last:

"Rex darling."

"Felicity sweet."

"I'll go now."

"Don't go—I don't want you to."

"Must, darling. Your silly old Duke will be here soon. Shall I see you at Archie's cocktail party?"

"Wish I could say, sweetheart." Rex frowned. "You heard. He wants me on a job. If it's this evening I'll just have to cut Archie's out."

"Poor sweet, what a shame. You don't mind my hating your old Duke, do you? I bet he dribbles in his beard."

Rex laughed. "You've got him all wrong, sweetheart. He's not that kind of Duke, an' he hasn't got a beard. You'd be crazy about him if you saw him. He's a great guy."

"All right," she smiled at him fondly. "Only don't let him take quite all your time. I feel so lonely, Rex, when I see so little of you."

He grinned. "Wish I could believe that. You've got lots of other men to take you to places."

She nodded rather sadly. "I know—too many. That's just the trouble, I suppose I'm an awful little fool to tell you so, but I just loathe going out with other men now. They're all so bothersome, and I didn't mind before. In fact, I thought it rather fun, but now I hate it."

Rex took both her hands in his and looked down into her upturned face. "You're not a fool, Felicity," he said earnestly, "you're great! And honest to God I am a whole heap fond of you. Listen, just to show I'm not kidding, I'll tell you a bit about what we're up against, and I wouldn't do that to another living soul."

"No, sweet," she shook her head violently. "I'd hate it if you went breaking promises. I'll be good and patient till it's over."

"Well, I'd just like you to know, Felicity, that the Duke and Aron and I aren't on a business deal. It's that Shoesmith case. You know they've gone and put that boy behind bars. Well, he didn't do it; and we've made up our minds to bring in the bird who did."

"Darling!" She laughed suddenly. "It's just like a flick, with you as Sherlock Holmes—No, Rex, I didn't mean that. It is a good show, I do hope you pull it off."

"You bet we will. Though really," he added modestly, "it's the Duke and Aron's party, they've got the brains, I'm a kind of looker-on."

"I don't believe that," she said seriously. "And if anything could make me more dippy about you than I am it only needed something like this; something outside dancing, and being just amusing and intolerably good-looking—oh, Rex, you are a pig."

At that moment there was a discreet knock upon the door. "Come in," cried Rex, moving quickly over to the window.

It was the little maid. "Please, sir, the Duke de Richleau is downstairs."

Rex looked at Felicity. "Like to meet him?" he asked, with a smile. "Don't worry if you'd rather not. You can slip right up the next flight, and then down after he's parked here."

She nodded quickly. "It would be rather fun."

Rex turned to the maid. "All right, show him up."

Felicity smiled. "You did mean that, dearest, didn't you? I'm just frantically curious."

"Of course, sweet, I've been dying for you to meet the big chief. He's a great man."

De Richleau paused in the open doorway. His quick grey eyes flashed from Van Ryn to the girl. He smiled as he took Rex's hand. "My friend, how nice of you to receive me, but how foolish. In your place I should have declared myself to be at liberty only when I was deserted."

Rex laughed. "Not a bit of it, I like my friends to get together. He introduced them. "Lady Felicity Standish—the Duke de Richleau."

De Richleau took the hand which the girl extended; his eyes twinkled. "What shall I say?" he murmured. "It's great to have you know me—or"—he paused, carrying her finger-tips very lightly to his lips as he bowed with a gesture which in anyone else might have seemed exaggerated buffoonery, but in him was the most charming of politenesses —"I have the honour, Madame, to be your obedient, humble servant."

Felicity's blue eyes lit up in the most entrancing smile. "I never could," she said, "abide Americans, but Your Grace's courtesy is overwhelming to so young a girl." With that she swept him a curtsy that would have done her credit in any Court.

As she rose again they laughed, that rich laughter which is only known among friends who understand and appreciate each other well.

"I think I knew your father," said the Duke, "or perhaps it was your uncle, Henry Standish. He was Ambassador at Madrid, but that was long ago, before the War."

"Oh, did you. Uncle Pom—how thrilling! He was a dear really, but we always used to call him Pom—short for Pomposity, you know." Felicity struck an attitude. "Lord Henry Augustus Standish, P.C., G.C.B., G.C.V.O., C.H., etc., etc., he was just like George Nathaniel Curzon—a most important person, but not half so clever, unfortunately for the family."

"Nevertheless, he had a fine taste in old brandy," smiled De Richleau. "A taste which unlike myself you were probably not old enough to share."

Felicity laughed. "I remember the story though. He used to take his own brandy in a medicine bottle when he went out to dine, and pretend he was a martyr to indigestion."

"A most ingenious idea, "the Duke nodded. "I must remember that. I have suffered considerably at times from drinking the inferior brandy of some of my less well-educated friends; but I'm glad that I'm unable to recall any occasion upon which Lord Henry was indisposed when he dined with me."

"I must fly." Felicity gave a pat to her hat and drew her fur about her. "You've got lots of awful business to discuss, I know."

"You have made me feel most guilty," De Richleau protested. "I arrive and immediately you run away."

"Not a bit of it." Felicity lifted her chin. "The woman who hangs around when men want to talk secrets is an utter fool. That's all." She held out a slim hand.

The Duke carried it to his lips once more, he smiled at Rex. "If only every woman were as wise as Lady Felicity and half as beautiful, what a glorious world it would be."

Rex grinned. "Now, just what wouldn't I give to be able to say things like that."

De Richleau held open the door for Felicity, as he replied softly: "My dear boy, every age has its privileges, that is one of mine, yours is—that it is quite unnecessary."

Rex ran quickly to the door. "Let me see you down, Felicity. I'll get you a taxi."

She shook her head, kissing her fingers to him behind the Duke's back. "No—I'm going to walk. Good-bye," and she was gone.

"A delightful child," the Duke, declared, sinking into the arm-chair lately occupied by Rex and Felicity. "Quite charming. How I wish that I were young."

"Well, I'm mighty glad you're not. Now let's have the low-down on the latest. Drink?"

"Not for me, I thank you," De Richleau waved him away from the bell. "Later perhaps—not now."

147

Rex squatted on the pouf before the fireplace.

"O.K., go right ahead."

"You'll remember that Aron and I considered it possible that Sir Gideon had employed an agent."

"Yep."

"Well, I do not now think that he did; on the other hand I do think it highly probable that he did it himself."

"You don't say!"

"I do. I talked this morning with a little man who attended the Park Lane Hotel dinner. He sat next but one to Shoesmith and peculiar circumstances gave him an opportunity for observing the various guests. From what he says, it seems that Sir Gideon left the table almost directly after the King's health had been drunk, and moreover was absent from the room for a period of at least half an hour. He only returned to say good-night to certain of the guests when they were leaving."

"My hat, that's interesting."

"Yes, particularly as I got information from another guest who left at ten minutes to ten, that Sir Gideon rose from the table before him. You understand what that could mean?"

Rex puffed at his cigarette thoughtfully. "I'll say I do," he said, "an' how! If he was away from that party all that time, he could have got to Errol House and back again on his head—and give Lady Shoesmith the works."

"Exactly." De Richleau leant forward. "I have further information still. The hotel servants have been questioned on my behalf. At a quarter to ten our man asked a waiter where he could telephone, the man told him, and ostensibly he left the room for that purpose, but he did not telephone. There is no record of his having put through a call. He did, however, at about that time collect from the cloakroom—the cloakroom at the back exit of the hotel, that is—a small brown paper parcel; after that, at ten minutes to ten, shall we say, he disappears. Our next information is that somebody answering to his description asked for a double brandy and soda in the downstairs bar, which you may remember is near the front entrance of the hotel. That was somewhere in the neighbourhood of ten past ten, he was then seen definitely in the dining-room at about twenty past."

"That gets the time down to twenty minutes," remarked Rex. "Even then it's plenty, if he looked slippy."

"Time was the essence of the alibi, but how clever!" De Richleau smiled. "I have little doubt now that it was he who was responsible. But even if it were proved that he was absent while the speeches were being made, he would reply at once: 'That is quite true, I did not feel well. I went out for a little air. I sat in the lounge or the drawing-room, and then I went and had a brandy and soda in the downstairs bar.' He could prove the last statement, but how difficult for anybody to disprove the first."

"You're right!" Rex nodded. "We couldn't make a case, so far."

"What do you suggest should be our next step?"

"We've got to find some guy that actually saw him on the way to, or coming, from Errol House."

The Duke smiled. "Exactly what I think myself. I propose, therefore, that we should divide up the locality for the purpose of a rigorous inquiry. I'll take the garages and flats in the cul-de-sac behind the Park Lane, there should have been a number of chauffeurs about at that hour, any of whom may remember seeing him. Aron can take the streets between the cul-de-sac and Errol Mews, they can't be more than five hundred yards in length, although the turnings make it seem more. However, there are one or two blocks of flats which Gideon would have to pass, and Aron can question the porters. You, I suggest, should devote yourself to Errol Mews, where there are garages and flats again. Since he did not arrive by the front door, the probability is that he came up the fire escape and that, as you know, descends into the Mews."

"O.K. by me," said Rex. "We'll get that bird before we're through."

CHAPTER XXIII

THE CURIOUS BEHAVIOUR OF MR. CARRINGTON SMYTHE

AT ten o'clock the same evening Rex stood at the entrance of Errol Mews. Although the night was cold, he wore no overcoat; but a thick muffler was wrapped tightly round his neck, the ends of which were buttoned beneath his double-breasted jacket.

He stood for a few moments at the opening of the Mews,

his hands thrust into his jacket pockets and a cigarette at an angle in the corner of his mouth, while he surveyed the locality.

The mews was plunged in semi-obscurity, lighted only by two lamps at a considerable interval apart, which served to throw a circle of pale light in their own vicinity, but hardly penetrated the surrounding gloom.

Upon the whole extent of the right-hand side towered the bulk of Errol House. Here and there pale squares of light showed curtained windows, but too high up to relieve the blackness, though, in places, they threw into relief the iron fire-escape which Rex had examined earlier in the week.

The left-hand side was occupied by a number of garages with chauffeurs' flats above. The far end consisted of a high brick wall, screening the small hidden garden of a mansion in Park Lane. If, therefore, Sir Gideon had entered Errol House by the fire-escape, he must have passed within a few feet of the place where Rex was standing, since there was only the one entrance to the mews.

He must have passed also at very nearly the same hour upon his way to commit the murder, if their theory were correct, and again some few minutes later on his return. If was for that reason that Rex had planned his visit for this hour of night. He reckoned, with some wisdom, that people whose business or habits caused them to be about the mews at this hour on one night were the more likely to be there at the same time on another.

Rex gathered from what he could see that there were six or seven garages in the mews; two stood with open doors. Of the nearest of these, the obvious occupant was leaning against the door, smoking a cigarette, while he gave his dog a run. In front of the other stood an old-fashioned Daimler, which an elderly chauffeur was hosing down, making as he did so that peculiar whistling sound to which in his younger days he had probably groomed a horse.

Apart from these two and the faint notes of a wireless which seemed to come from the lighted windows of what Rex judged to be No. 7, the mews seemed destitute of life.

Rex determined to tackle the obvious inhabitants first. He approached the man with the dog; at once the little terrier played up handsomely.

150

"Hallo, boy!" he stooped down and patted the terrier's head.

"Careful," advised the dog's owner. " 'E ain't too good with people 'e don't know."

"He'll be all right with me," said Rex. As he picked the terrier up with one hand: "Won't you, sonny? Nice little fellow."

"Oh, 'e's all right with people what likes dogs," the chauffeur agreed quickly, "but 'e's a bit difficult with people what don't, if you take my meaning."

"I certainly do," Rex smiled.

After that, conversation became reasonably easy, and in a little while Rex put it to the man. "Had he at any time seen a biggish elderly man in evening dress enter or leave the mews."

It is debatable as to whether Rex put the question clumsily or not, but the chauffeur became on his guard at once. "If you 'appen," he said coldly, "to be connected wiv the police, they've been 'ere already, and please to put down the dorg."

"You've got me wrong," Rex assured him. "Of course I've read about the murder in those flats, but this is a wager. Friend of mine lives in the block and he thinks the job was put across by someone who used the fire ladder as a get-away. Now I don't believe that at all, and he laid me he'd come down three nights in succession after dinner without being spotted by anyone in this mews. I've come around to see if I can't check up on him and draw the dough."

The chauffeur thawed again, but did not prove helpful. "I'm around here most nights," he confided, "and I'd be sure to spot anyone what comes down them escapes, but I haven't seen no one."

"Were you around Saturday?" Rex inquired.

"No, I had to take my lady up to Hampstead," the man replied. "Filthy night it was, too."

Rex nodded. "And you haven't seen an elderly man, my friend that is, snooping round here, last night or the night before?"

"No." The chauffeur was quite certain that he had seen no one, although on both evenings he had let his dog out for a run at round about ten o'clock.

"O.K.," said Rex crisply. "I think I'll move on and talk to the guy who's busy with that car. It wasn't a big bet, but I'd like to win it, all the same."

"Well, good luck to you," the chauffeur nodded, "but I doubt you'll get much change out of old George."

Rex sauntered up the mews in the direction of "Old George," and then stood smoking for some moments within a few feet of the ancient Daimler, hoping that the elderly man would look up and address him. Instead, the man took absolutely no notice; he went on hosing down his car to the accompaniment of his curious breathless whistle.

"Evening!" said Rex at last.

The elderly man threw down the end of the hose and seizing a sponge attacked the long flat bonnet of the Daimler whistling more breathlessly than ever.

"Evening," said Rex again more loudly.

The man looked up vaguely. "Ah!" he said, pausing in his work.

"Evening," said Rex once more, and still more loudly. "I'm looking for a friend "

"George," declared the old man promptly. "George Wend, chauffeur to Lady Lancastle, the Dowager lady as is now."

"Great!" Rex bawled in his ear, getting very close. "I reckon you'd rather be looking after horses though?"

" 'Orses," the elderly man gave an appreciative grin. "Ah, 'osses was creatures," he said brightly.

"I'm looking for a friend," Rex tried again.

"Friend, that's right. Friend of Man, that's what 'osses were," replied the ancient enthusiastically.

Rex took him gently by the arm and spoke slowly but distinctly into his ear: "I've made a bet."

"What on?" Old George asked with interest.

Rex tried a different angle. "Were you around on Saturday, here in the mews, at round about this hour?"

"Me—no." The old man shook his head. "We were in the country staying with the young lord. 'E ain't like the old lord, ain't got no heye for 'orse flesh, but a nice enough young chap."

"Well," thought Rex, "that'll be that. Thank you," he yelled. "Thank you, I'll get along now, so long."

The last garage but one had lights above and from it came the strains of the wireless which Rex had heard when standing at the entrance of the mews. He decided that this should be his next objective, and moved towards it, thinking how strange it was that the law of England should still allow such as old George to drive a car, when he felt a touch upon his sleeve, and whirling on his heel, found the old man had followed him.

"If you're a gentleman what likes 'osses," the ancient said, "you put a little bit on Tea Cup for the Lincoln."

Rex smiled. "That's mighty decent of you," but his thanks fell upon deaf ears, old George was already stumping back upon his bandy legs to the ancient Daimler. Rex rang the bell beside the tall, narrow door, and waited.

Heavy feet sounded upon the wooden stairs and an untidy female opened the door six inches or so to peer at him.

"Excuse me," he began.

"My 'usband's out," she said quickly, "and won't be back till I don't know wot hour."

"All the same," Rex smiled amiably, "if you don't mind I'd like to have a little talk with you."

She regarded him with evident distrust, closing the door another inch as she demanded suspiciously: "Wot for?"

"I've got a wager," Rex explained. "May seem fool nonsense to you, but you'll have heard of this murder in the flats here?"

She became interested at once, quite unconsciously allowing the door to swing freely open, as she regarded him with small, wide-open, greedy eyes. "You mean the young man wot killed 'is mother in the barth. I should say we 'ave, with us livin' opposite 'ere and all."

"Well," Rex went on, "friend of mine thinks the guy that did it made a get-away down the fire ladders."

"Corse not," the woman sneered. "'E walked out of the front door large as life, 'e bein' 'er son, and why shouldn't 'e?"

"But just supposing," Rex suggested. "D'you figure anybody in this mews would have seen him if he had?"

"There's no saying," the woman declared. "Maybe yes, maybe no." Then suddenly her eyes hardened. "An' 'oo are you?" she inquired, bringing the door nearly to again with a quick jerk. "We've 'ad the police round, or are you another of 'em?"

"Well, I'm making a kind of inquiry," Rex submitted.

"Ho! You are, are you," said the woman viciously. "Well, you go inquiring helsewhere, young man, or I'll 'ave the police on you." Upon which she closed the door entirely with a sharp bang.

Rex smiled ruefully to himself and considered the situation. No. 8 was in total darkness, No. 7 was the thin-faced suspicious woman whom he had already interviewed; No. 6, Old George; Nos. 5 and 4 had Jones Brothers, Builders, painted in large, white letters across the double doors, and were evidently a store used only in the day-time; No. 3 had a large board "To Let," and No. 2 was the man with the dog. There only remained No. 1, and he walked slowly back towards it.

Yes, No. 1 was occupied; a dim light penetrated the green curtains of the upper floor, and the narrow door had recently been painted a bright green, while the number-plate and letter-box were of polished brass. "Here goes," said Rex, and pressed the bell.

A moment later a clicking noise led Rex to guess that the latch was being released by a spring from above. He pushed the green door and it swung open. Squeezing past into the narrow space beyond, he looked up the steep, ladder-like stairs to see a fair, boyish face peering down at him.

"Oh, come up, do," called the owner of the flat in a quick, high, affected voice.

Rex accepted the invitation. He paused for a moment on the landing then followed the young man into the room which overlooked the mews.

It was a curious room, artistic, but in some queer way un-pleasant; the colour scheme was green, the decorations ultra-modern, there was a divan with piles of cushions, and a small table littered with books. Apart from two reproductions of drawings by Aubrey Beardsley, the walls were bare. Upon the mantelpiece were a number of photographs—but unlike the portrait collections of most young men, amongst them there was not a single woman. The light was dim, the atmosphere close and heavy—about it there lingered the faintest suggestion of stale scent.

Rex gave the young man a sharp glance and thought him one of the most unpleasant people whom he had ever seen. He was extraordinarily good-looking in the classic style, but he was not really young at all, and had he been a woman, one would have said he was thirty, made up to look eighteen. It was his boyish figure and his wavy golden hair that gave him the appearance of youth, on first sight. His bright, hard eyes

154

were full of knowledge and cunning, his thin-lipped mouth a line of determined viciousness.

Suddenly the thin mouth flashed into a bright smile. "How nice of you to come, do sit down. Will you smoke?" He proffered an elaborate platinum and gold cigarette-case.

Rex took one. "Thanks," he said and added, for want of something to say: "That's a marvellous case you've got there."

"Isn't it," the old-young man gushed in his quick, high-pitched voice. "I saw it in Asprey's window one day. I was with Victor Maradick, d'you know him, he's a perfect dear, and I said at once, 'Victor, isn't that case too divine,' and d'you know, next day he sent it to me. Of course, Victor's just lousy with money, but I do think it was sweet of him all the same. I do love getting presents, don't you?"

"I certainly do," Rex agreed.

The owner of the flat preened himself in front of the looking-glass, tilting his chin from side to side as if he were acutely worried by a high stiff collar, although actually his well-shaped neck was bare above his principal garment, a brightly coloured silk dressing-gown.

He suddenly started off again. "I should adore to be rich, wouldn't you? It must be such fun giving presents to one's friends. I had an awfully rich friend who took me to the South of France last year. We went to a tiny place near St. Maxime, I wonder if you know it, Cavalaire it's called. Look," he added, picking up a photograph of himself from among the group on the mantelpiece. "Don't you think my swimming-suit is too divine. I designed it specially to wear out there."

Rex regarded the portrait amusedly. The Greek God profile of the young man showed clear cut, turned at an angle over one shoulder, but the picture had been taken to commemorate the costume—it was some dark material, but differed from the usual pattern in that it was cut away in a sharp V from the shoulder to the waist-line, as was the fashion at that time for women's evening dress, thereby exposing as large a portion as possible of the wearer's back.

"It's a mighty swell costume," Rex agreed, handing the photograph back.

"Isn't it," the owner replaced it on the mantelpiece with a little wriggle of his shoulders. "Poor Owen took it. I hardly ever see him now, although I'm glad in a way. He became rather a nuisance after he'd lost all his money—don't you find that—of course, one's awfully sorry for people—but they might try to be amusing when they take one out. As I told Owen, it wasn't my fault if he'd made a silly mess of his business, but it's this filthy slump really, I suppose; nobody seems to have any money now."

Rex restrained an intense desire to pick up this extremely unpleasant young man and kick him down his own stairs. The conversation languished until the young man flashed his bright, insincere smile again.

"You're an American, aren't you? I've got lots of American friends. I say—I mean—would you think it too frightfully rude of me if I asked you who sent you along—don't tell me if you'd rather not, but I suppose we've got friends in common, haven't we?" He gave an unpleasant leer, and added: "Can't be too careful, you know."

"Well, as it happens, I was looking for a friend," said Rex.

"Oh, of course," the young man wriggled his shoulders again. "I'd simply love to go round with you while you're in London. I took to you frightfully, directly I saw you."

"I'm afraid you've got me wrong," Rex admitted. "I mean I was looking for a fellow who comes round here sometimes, old friend of mine."

"Oh, I see, I'm sorry," said the other with an offended air, turning for consolation to the looking-glass. "What's your friend like, and what's his name?"

"He's a big elderly chap, pale, heavy sort of face, looks like a churchwarden."

"Can't say I know him." The owner of the flat stroked a long eyebrow meditatively while he regarded his reflection. "Are you sure? I mean, that he's ever been to see me?"

"No, but I've got an idea he might have," Rex lied, deciding to try a shot in the dark. "Friend of mine thought he saw him walk out of this mews Saturday night, round about ten o'clock."

"Now that is *too* queer," the young man stopped plucking his eyebrows and turned to Rex. "I wonder if it could have been your friend I spoke to, a nasty, rude old man."

Rex leant forward eagerly. "Maybe," he said encouragingly. "He's a difficult chap, sort of nervous he'd be."

156

"Well I was just coming home. It must have been after ten, though, about five past perhaps, and I saw somebody who might have been your friend just outside my door. I think he must have been waiting for a car to pass that was backing into the mews, but I thought he might have come to see me, so I went up to him, ever so nicely, you know, and I said: 'Are you looking for No. 1?' and he was frightfully huffy, just turned his back on me, and scuttled out of the mews. I do think he might have been civil."

"That's him," said Rex excitedly. "Can you recollect how he was turned out?"

"Oh, evening dress, and a sort of a very thin mackintosh with the collar turned up, one of those silky things that do up into nothing at all. I remember thinking at the time what a queer get-up it was. I should positively have died of cold on a night like that, but I'm sure he was in evening clothes because I could see his white tie at the neck."

Rex stood up. "That's great," he said. "I'm tremendously obliged to you, Mr.—er—"

"Oh, not a bit, pleased, I'm sure. Carrington Smythe's my name, Cedric Carrington Smythe; but why you're so keen about that old brute, I just can't think; positively rude, he was."

"I'm obliged, all the same." Rex took up his hat.

"Oh, I say, you're not going, are you?" Carrington Smythe protested. "That would be too unfair. I wish I hadn't told you now."

" 'Fraid I must." Rex moved quickly to the door, ignoring the limp hand that Carrington Smythe held out to him. "But I'll be back," he added over his shoulder.

"Oh, rather, do come any time." Carrington Smythe's treacherous, unnatural smile flashed out. "I should love you to. I do hope you don't find your horrid old friend."

CHAPTER XXIV

HOW ADVANTAGE MAY BE TAKEN OF A MOST UNPLEASANT SITUATION

AN hour later they sat round a big fire in the Duke's flat, Simon, Rex, Superintendent Marrofat, Inspector Gartside, and De Richleau himself.

It had been agreed by the Duke, Simon and Rex that after they had made as many inquiries as possible, they should rendezvous at Errol House, and when De Richleau had returned with Simon, whom he had picked up on the way, they had found Rex already arrived, and in a fever of impatience.

After a short conference it had been decided that they should place the evidence they now had against Sir Gideon Shoesmith before the Superintendent without delay, and if he accepted the validity of their case, to press for Richard Elton's immediate release. They had endeavoured to get in touch with Mr. Granville Schatz, but here they had failed; with the Superintendent they had proved more fortunate, and at the Duke's urgent request he had come round at once.

The broad-shouldered police chief proved to be in a more genial humour than when they had last seen him, and not only had he consented to take off his great woolly overcoat and make himself comfortable, but he had accepted a whisky and soda and one of the Duke's long Hoyo de Monterrey Anillo d'Oro cigars.

It was the Duke who stated the case against Lady Shoesmith's husband, detailing clearly and lucidly the links in the chain of evidence which had gradually been built up against him.

The discovery that the pearls were false, that Sir Gideon had had them copied apparently without Lady Shoesmith's knowledge, and the financial difficulties with which he had been faced for some considerable time, provided a motive at least as strong against the husband as against the son. The Duke had then gone on to give details of his interview with Christopher Deacon, and the partial confirmation which James

158

Ritherdon would supply; followed in turn by the various statements which had been collected by Jacoby from members of the staff of the Park Lane Hotel; and finally the all-important fact that Mr. Carrington Smythe had seen and spoken to an elderly man—whose description agreed with that of Sir Gideon—in the mews at the back of Errol House upon the night of the murder, within the time that his absence from the Park Lane had been recorded and at about the time that the murder was proved to have been committed.

As he ceased, it seemed to Rex and Simon that there could be no shadow of doubt that between them they had probed to the bottom of this affair, just as surely as if they had actually seen Sir Gideon Shoesmith upon that fatal night. First, carefully releasing the switch within his flat that controlled the fire escape, then going out to his banquet, but only to slip away directly the King's health had been drunk, collect his little parcel from the cloakroom—undoubtedly the thin silk waterproof—slip it on quickly in some quiet corner, to hide his evening clothes, leaving the hotel and hurry through the foggy streets, slip into the mews and up the fire escape, through the window of his study—carefully left unlatched—listen for a moment in the silent flat, then cross the passage and commit the murder, answer the telephone promptly, and with great presence of mind before the servants were disturbed, leave the front door ajar—in order that suspicion might be thrown upon the stranger—then slip out of the window, down the escape into the foggy night once more; the one unfortunate nerve-racking encounter in the mews, and then the hurried walk back to the hotel to complete his alibi. From first to last the whole thing could have been done in under twenty minutes and not a soul the wiser.

The Superintendent ran his hand through his mop of ginger curls and looked round thoughtfully. "Yes," he said, at last, "you've made a case all right; whether you're right or wrong, it was first-class work, gentlemen, and I congratulate you."

De Richleau smiled. "That's very kind of you, Superintendent. I wonder if you'd mind telling us if any fresh evidence has come to light in support of your case against Richard Eaton?"

"No. We've questioned the maids again, and the porter, and Miss Eaton, but there's nothing fresh. We know all about his money troubles, of course, and that, together with his having had the pearls in his possession and having been the last person to see his mother alive—motive and opportunity, you know—made a pretty strong case, to my mind; but now we shall certainly have to readjust our ideas."

"That's great," said Rex. "And you'll let young Eaton out?"

"It all depends," Marrofat said cautiously. "Certainly, if I can substantiate all you say."

"I was hoping—er—that you might have let him out tonight," Simon suggested. "Like to go down to Brixton—bring him home, you know."

The Superintendent finished his whisky. "No, sir," he said promptly. "I'm afraid that's out of the question."

"He must be pretty worried." Simon took off his pince-nez and wiped them. "I mean, he's in a pretty bad muddle."

"Oh, another night in Brixton won't hurt him," Marrofat laughed, not unkindly. "Gartside and me'll put in a bit of night work with that young fellow at the mews and with the people at the Park Lane; then, if it's all right, you can go down with the officer who takes the order and collect your friend in the morning. In any case, it would have been against regulations to have let him out at this hour—it's too late tonight." He stood up and turned to the Inspector. "Come on, Gartside, we'll be moving. Mr. Van Ryn, I wonder if we might trouble you to step round the corner with us?"

"Sure," said Rex. "I'll come right along."

Marrofat nodded to the Duke and Simon. "I'm very grateful to you, gentlemen. We can't always be right, you know, and we don't run a man unless we're pretty certain in our own minds about him; we'd rather have no conviction at all than a wrong one, that's how so many people get away with it, though the papers don't give us any credit for that. If there's anything the Yard can do for you at any time, well, let me know, gentlemen. Good night to you!"

"Thank you, Superintendent." The Duke extended his hand. "I'm quite sure that what you say is true. Your work must often be beset with difficulties, but, despite that, the London Police Force remains the finest of its kind in the world. Good night."

Rex and the two officers walked downstairs together and round the corner into the mews.

"This'll be it." Rex paused before No. 1. Chinks of faint light still appeared between the heavy green curtains. He rang the bell.

This time there was no responsive clicking of the latch. He rang again, and after a short interval there was a noise above, the curtains were thrust aside, and the windows rattled as it was thrown up.

Mr. Carrington Smythe's head appeared. "Who is it?" he demanded crossly.

"It's me," said Rex, stepping back into the light which streamed from the open window. "Didn't I say I'd be right back?" The two detectives remained hidden one on either side of the door, in the shadow by the wall.

"Oh, it's you!" said Mr. Carrington Smythe sulkily. "But I didn't mean tonight. I've got a friend here now."

"Sorry," said Rex. "But I want to talk to you."

"Don't be unreasonable," Carrington Smythe pleaded querulously. "I've told you, I've got a friend with me. Come and see me tomorrow. Take me out to lunch."

"I want to talk to you now," replied Rex firmly. "Come right down and open this door."

The window was shut with a slam, the curtains drawn to. Footsteps descended the steep stairs furtively, and the door was opened enough to show Carrington Smythe's angry face.

"You beast," he hissed. "Can't you understand, I've got somebody here. I should have thought you'd have more sense than to go waking the whole mews. In a minute we shall have some nasty, snooping policeman round here, the very last thing I want. Do go away."

"That's all right," said Rex firmly. "I just want you to answer a few questions about what you told me tonight. I've brought a police officer along." Marrofat moved in the shadow.

Carrington Smythe's face went an unpleasant shade of green. "You're mad," he snapped, and quickly shut the door, but there was no sound of retreating footsteps, and almost they could hear his frightened breathing on the other side of the door.

The Superintendent rapped sharply with his knuckles. "Come on," he said. "I'm a police officer. Open this door."

161

Dead silence.

Marrofat rapped again. "Come on, sonny, don't waste my time. You'll be sorry if you do."

The breathless silence continued, then the Superintendent spoke once more.

"I've warned you, I'm on to your little game. But there's no harm coming to you if you act sensible. If you don't, you'll spend the night in Vine Street, and perhaps go farther than that. See?"

Slowly and noiselessly the door swung open. "All right, I suppose you'd better come in," said Mr. Carrington Smythe ungraciously, and led the way upstairs. They trooped up after him.

Rex and the Superintendent almost filled the small green room. The latter looked round with a baleful eye. "Pretty—very pretty," he said in a far from complimentary voice, and he took one of the Beardsley drawings from the wall. "That's a nice picture for mother's boy," he added venomously.

Carrington Smythe had partially recovered from his fright. He lit a cigarette and stood beside the mantelpiece, endeavouring to register martyred innocence, but he couldn't keep it up. "Of course," he said with a sneer, tilting his chin a little, "one can hardly expect people like you to appreciate art."

"Art," said the big detective, tossing the Beardsley from him on to the tumbled divan. "Filth!"

Rex, who had himself a certain appreciation of Beardsley's work, felt almost sorry for the wretched Mr. Carrington Smythe, so he intervened:

"I'd be glad," he said, "if you'd tell these gentlemen just what you told me earlier on—about seeing an elderly man in this mews, Saturday night, I mean."

Carrington Smythe shot him a venomous glance. "I've no idea what you mean," he said in an injured tone. "You haven't got any right to force your way in here like this, and I refuse to answer any questions. I simply won't."

"Ho, you do, do you!" boomed the Superintendent. "All right, my little innocent. Bring out your client—quick!"

Fear leapt into Mr. Carrington Smythe's shifty blue eyes. "I didn't mean quite that," he said hastily. His automatic smile flashed out. "How do I know you're not all having a joke with me?"

162

The Superintendent nodded heavily. "Take it from me, son, it's a joke you won't forget if you don't answer up."

"Well, if you must know, I did see a man," Carrington Smythe shot a quick look at himself in the glass. "Just after ten on Saturday, in the mews here."

"That's better." Marrofat nodded approval, while Gartside became busy with his shorthand notes. "What was he like?"

"Oh, I don't know—old and stuffy!"

The Superintendent drew out his pocket-book, selected a newspaper cutting and thrust it under Carrington Smythe's nose. "Was he anything like that?"

"Yes, that's him," the young man answered languidly, and then with a sudden movement he snatched at the paper. "I say, do let me look . . . why, it's Sir Gideon Shoesmith." A sudden comprehension dawned upon his handsome, shifty face. "I say," he whistled, "you'll want me to come into court as a witness, I suppose—I hate murders."

"Rather be a witness for murder than in the dock for something else, wouldn't you?" said the Superintendent tersely.

"You *are* a horrid man," declared Carrington Smythe petulantly as he turned away.

"Never mind about me," replied Marrofat. "How was this chap dressed when you saw him?"

"Oh, I don't know, evening clothes, with a light silky sort of waterproof over them. Awfully cold he must have been."

"What colour?"

"Didn't notice. Darkish stuff. What else do you want to know?"

"What you said to him?"

"Thanks, I'd rather not say."

"Dare say not, but I won't use it against you. Out with it."

"Promise?"

"Yes, I promise," Marrofat nodded grimly.

"Honest Injun, cross me heart?"

"Yes, I'll cross me heart—Queer what a lot of faith you've got in my promise, and how little I've got in yours, isn't it? Go on."

"There's no need to be rude," said Carrington Smythe sulkily.

"For God's sake get on with it."

"Well, I only said 'D'you happen to be looking for No. 1?'"

"And what did he say?"

"He didn't say anything, he just ignored me and walked away."

Marrofat nodded. "Well, that'll be a point in his favour when he comes to meet his God."

"Oh, I'm so tired," said Carrington Smythe peevishly. "I wish you'd go away."

"Don't worry, handsome, I wouldn't stay in the same room with you longer than I had to, not if I lost me pension."

Marrofat turned to Rex. "Any other points, sir?"

"No, I guess that covers it, Superintendent."

"Right. Then we'll get out of here. And listen, you!" He cast a meaning glance at Carrington Smythe. "You'll be here when I want you. Understand?" and turned away.

For a moment the young man's malice got the better of his discretion. His automatic smile flashed once more as he said: "Wouldn't it be fun if you broke your neck going downstairs?"

The Superintendent glared malevolently as he left the room. "Better be careful, sonny, else I'll put you through the hoop."

Carrington Smythe gave a high-pitched laugh. "Oh, no," he said with a leer. "You can't be unkind to me and then expect me to be a nice police witness too!" He glared at Rex, who was about to follow the others downstairs, and hissed: "You utter cad! I'll tell every soul I know about *you*."

Rex paused for a moment on the landing, and the temptation was too strong for him. Suddenly his long hand shot out and he seized Carrington Smythe by his curly golden hair. For a moment he rocked him steadily backwards and forwards, then gently cast him from him. "Do, sweetheart," he grinned. "I—should worry!"

Very soon after Rex and the detectives had taken their departure Carrington Smythe's other visitor slid silently down the narrow stairs and out of the green door.

Carrington Smythe sat for some time on the tumbled divan apparently in deep thought. "Oh, how I loathe England," he said suddenly, and standing up he took the portrait of himself in the swimming suit from the mantelpiece. "France *is* so civilized."

164

He replaced the portrait and took up the telephone directory, a few minutes later he was connected with Sir Gideon Shoesmith's flat.

"That *is* Sir Gideon, isn't it?" he asked in his high, affected voice. "Well, we have met, of course, but perhaps you might not remember it. That's not very flattering to me, is it? but it was a very short meeting. I remember you, perfectly well. It was last Saturday—yes, in the evening, about ten o'clock. I've got a tiny, tiny flat, you know, in Errol Mews. I should so love to see you again—What! Oh, don't be naughty now, we could be such friends. I do so hate any sort of trouble, don't you? I'd ask you to come and see me tonight, but I don't think that would be quite wise. You'd better meet me in the entrance of the Down Street Underground at nine o'clock tomorrow morning. It's filthily early, but we simply must have our little talk as soon as possible —nine o'clock." Suddenly the sweetness went out of Mr. Carrington Smythe's voice as he added: "And I *loathe* being kept waiting."

CHAPTER XXV

SIMON ARON GOES TO BRIXTON GAOL

HAVING spoken to Superintendent Marrofat on the telephone the following morning, Simon Aron decided to take a day off.

He rang up his office, from his bedroom in the Club—lying flat upon his back in bed, the receiver glued to his ear—and held long jerky conversations with at least four members of his staff. Then, having foreseen, as far as humanly possible, the contingencies of the day, he swallowed the orange juice which composed his breakfast, and got up.

By a friendly arrangement entered into with the Superintendent, a plain-clothes officer called for him at half past ten, and together they proceeded in a taxi-cab to Brixton Prison. It was peculiar to Simon Aron's psychology that although he was a young man of considerable substance, he did not own a car.

Having arrived at the grim, high-walled enclosure, with its bleak, barrack-like buildings, certain formalities were gone through, while Simon was left to cool his heels in a chilly reception-room. At last, however, Richard appeared, and apart from a rather strained look about the eyes, he seemed much as usual.

"Hallo, Simon!" They shook hands. "Awfully nice of you to come and get me out."

"Don't be silly," Simon laughed his nervous laugh, lowering his head to his hand. "Let's get out of this."

A prison officer saw them through the gates and they climbed into the taxi that Simon had caused to wait.

"Phew!" Richard let out a deep breath as they moved off. "I'm glad to be out of that."

Simon patted him affectionately on the arm. "I bet you are. I thought we'd go to the Club and—er—split a bottle."

Richard laughed. "It's great to hear you say that again! Got an Al Raschid?"

Simon produced his case. "Here, slip this in your pocket, we've got plenty more at the Club."

"Thanks." Richard lit a cigarette and inhaled contentedly. "I don't mind confessing, I was getting a bit nervy."

Simon's bird-like head nodded comprehendingly, as Richard went on: "I kept on telling myself that it was bound to be all right. Granville Schatz came to see me twice, I expect you know, and he told me you were doing your damnedest to get fresh evidence, and the Duke, and that nice American as well. I felt certain that one of you would tumble across something that would get me out, and at the worst I hoped that when the trial came on, the fact that the porter saw me leave the flats before ten, and you speaking to a man, when you telephoned later, would be sufficient to clear me."

"That was a strong card," Simon nodded. "A very strong card."

"Yes, but say anything had happened to you—or the porter. They won't take evidence at second hand, you know, or if they'd got a really first-class barrister on the job, who had persuaded or tricked the porter into saying that he was mistaken. You know what these clever lawyers are, they'd have said that it was me you spoke to all the time—what would have happened then? That was what I was beginning to wonder."

"We'd have been in a muddle," Simon agreed.

"That was the trouble. I kept on trying to persuade myself

166

that everything would be all right; but I couldn't be sure. Now and again I had that awful panicky feeling. I used to wake up about four in the morning and think to myself—just suppose that things don't go right—that there is no fresh evidence— and that I have to stand my trial—and then the trial goes wrong —and they bring me back here, and then there are three awful weeks—that terrible law that compels a man convicted of murder to wait until three Sundays have elapsed between his condemnation and execution, in order that he may make his peace with God. Then one cold and frosty morning to be weighed by the hangman that he may calculate the drop, and be led out with your hands bound behind your back! D'you know what I mean?"

"Rotten!" said Simon feelingly. "Rotten!"

"I couldn't help thinking of that marvellous story by A. E. Coppard. 'Judith,' I think it was called, but I forget which book it was in."

"The one about the schoolmaster who gave the boys pots of paint as prizes, d'you mean? That was in the *Field of Mustard*."

"That's right. You remember the man got hanged for a murder that he hadn't done. I think that and Aldous Huxley's 'The Gioconda Smile' are the two finest murder stories that I've ever read; both so true to life, so devastatingly possible and, if you remember, in both those stories the wrong man got hanged."

Simon laughed jerkily. "Well, anyhow, you're out of the muddle now."

"Yes, thank God, but who's in it? Was it a burglar or don't they know yet? I haven't heard a thing, not since I saw Schatz on Wednesday. I imagine there must be something new, or they wouldn't have let me out."

"It's Gideon's muddle now, and he can keep it," Simon said, with one of his quick, sideway glances.

"Gideon!" exclaimed Richard. "Good Lord, that's pretty bad, isn't it? Mind you, I never liked the man, but I didn't think he was capable of a thing like that. Are they certain?"

"Um," Simon nodded quickly. "Not a doubt."

"Old brute," said Richard slowly. "Well, I hope he swings for it. Mother was a damn good sort, poor dear, full of life and fun. It wasn't even as if she had been difficult or rotten to him— he hadn't the faintest shadow of excuse."

"Tell you all about it in a minute," Simon volunteered, as

167

they stepped out of the taxi. "We'll get our bottle first." They paid the man off and went into the Club.

Simon did not trouble to consult the wine list as he was very well informed regarding the contents of the cellar at the Club, and soon they were sitting in a comfortable corner with a bottle of Bollinger 1919 between them. Simon lowered his head to his glass and looked over his pince-nez. "Well—pleased to see you, Richard."

Richard smiled back. "Same to you, Simon. I say, doesn't champagne taste good?" He set down his glass carefully. "I feel as though I'd been locked up for a couple of years. Now tell me all about the old man."

"You know about the dinner he went to at Park Lane?"

"Yes."

"Well, he left the party early, just before ten. Lots of people moving about between the speeches, not difficult, you know—got home as quick as he could—wouldn't take more than four minutes at a fast walk, I tried it—entered the flat through the sitting-room window."

"D'you mean he went up the fire escape?"

"Um," Simon nodded. "Easy in that fog, the first floor is only about twenty feet up; did the job and came back the same way. Had a drink in the Park Lane bar, and got back to the dinner in time to hear the last two toasts. Clever, wasn't it?"

"Oh, he's clever enough," Richard admitted bitterly. "Cold-blooded brute. Your telephone call must have shaken him a bit, though?"

"Yes, rotten for him that—a pretty good performance answering it so quickly all the same. If that 'phone had gone on ringing the maids might have ruined the whole party."

"Queer," said Richard. "D'you know, I went over the whole thing time after time when I was at Brixton, and I never thought of him once."

"Well, I don't mind telling you," Simon admitted, "it never occurred to me until we found out that the pearls were false, then I began to see daylight, though the trouble was to get proof."

"Yes, Schatz told me about that; nice little chap Schatz, but even then I didn't connect Gideon with the murder. I tell you who I did think of—old Win."

168

"Who?"

"Aunt Winifred, you know, poor old thing. Of course, I didn't consider it seriously, but Mother was a bit of a bully, you know, unconsciously perhaps; but, nevertheless, she kept old Winnie on the run all day long. It was always: 'Oh, no, I can't leave it to the servants, Winifred will do that.' The poor old thing would never have stayed in the house another day if she'd had money of her own or anywhere else to go to. Although Father didn't like her I've always thought it was rather rotten of him to leave her absolutely dependent on Mother in his will."

"Ner." Simon shook his head emphatically. "We ruled her out from the beginning. It had to be a strong man to strike those blows." He carefully divided the remaining contents of the bottle between their glasses.

"I suppose it's early," Richard said suddenly, "but what about a little lunch?"

"Ah, that reminds me, I've an invitation for you. The Duke said, if you've no other arrangements, would you lunch with him, Errol House, one-fifteen? How's that suit you?"

"Splendid, love to. You'll be there, of course?"

"Um, and Van Ryn. Kind of celebration."

"They've been awfully good, those two I mean, considering they didn't know me from Adam," Richard remarked. "And as for you, my dear fellow, God knows what I should have done without you."

Simon waved his hand deprecatingly. "Oh, I love a muddle," he grinned. "What about walking round?"

They arrived a little early at Errol House, but the Duke was expecting them, and Rex was already there.

Richard had never met the Duke before except for the few hours on Sunday morning previous to his arrest, but he received a more than charming welcome, and became immediately interested in the wonderful collection of rare and beautiful things scattered about the big lounge-room.

De Richleau was always delighted to show his treasures to anyone of appreciation and understanding, and soon he was leading his guest from the sword which Francis the First had surrendered at Pavia, to the little *tabouret* upon which his ancestors had had the privilege of sitting in the presence of

169

the Kings and Queens of France. Mr. Granville Schatz arrived a little later, and, almost immediately after, luncheon was announced.

Luncheon was indeed a celebration. The Duke had spared nothing which he felt might give the released prisoner pleasure. A number of his oldest bottles had been removed from the place of their long rest, and carefully decanted earlier in the day. Wine followed with each well-chosen course, and it was not until after four o'clock that they rose from the table.

During the meal they had followed the precedent already set, and refrained from discussing Sir Gideon or the murder; but when the long Hoyo de Monterreys were lit Richard was told in detail, step by step, how the case against Sir Gideon had been built up, which had eventually enabled them to secure his release.

"You must, of course, have been exceedingly worried," said the Duke, "during your confinement, but I trust at least that you were not too uncomfortable?"

"Oh, no," Richard admitted. "They were really very nice. The Governor was an old Colonel, the real old 'Damn it! Shoot 'em! Fill 'em full of lead and teach 'em manners!' type, but really he was awfully decent. 'Man's innocent until he's proved guilty,' he blared at me when I arrived. 'Make you as comfortable as we can, but must observe regulations.' "

"Were the—er—regulations very stiff?" asked Simon.

"Not too bad, there's only one thing, and that's a disgrace to civilization."

"And what is that?" inquired the Duke.

"You're not allowed to smoke as much as you like. They admit, mark you, that you're innocent until you're proved guilty, so what right have they then to inflict what amounts to an absolute torture upon a man who's used to tobacco?"

"You're right," De Richleau agreed. "It is a scandal that your legislature should remain so callous and inhumane. In these days two-thirds at least of the entire population are habitual smokers; suddenly to cut one off from the practice of a lifetime must be torture."

"It makes one's nerves so rotten," said Richard bitterly. "After all, one's only occupation in prison is to think out one's defence, and when you've got heavy brain work that's the very time you want to smoke. You just can't think without it, and it's utterly unfair to rob a man of his normal capabilities for defence. I wish we could do something about it."

"Get busy with one or two of your M.P.s," suggested Rex.

"Trouble is, Parliament's grown so unwieldy," Richard replied. "Government bills take all the time! Unemployment, Disarmament, Reparations, India, Tariffs, there's hardly any time left for private members at all. The only chance is to try and get the public interested through the Press, but it's a thing that should be done. After all, anybody is liable to be detained by the police for a bad motor smash, or anything, at any time."

"We must see," said the Duke, "what we can do; it is a piece of official tyranny unlike the sporting fairmindedness of the British race." At that moment he was called away to the telephone.

When he rejoined them a few minutes later, he said softly: "That was our friend Marrofat. He thought we should be interested to know that he asked Gideon Shoesmith to call and see him at the Yard and quietly arrested him after lunch."

CHAPTER XXVI

THE DEFENCE TRIUMPHANT

AT twenty-five minutes to three upon the third day the case of Rex v. Shoesmith, the eminent counsel who led for the defence rose from his place in court and bowed solemnly to Judge and jury.

"My Lord, Gentlemen," he began. "It is with the fullest confidence that I rise to address you on behalf of the prisoner.

"In my long association with the Bar I can recall few cases in which so distinguished a man has been so wantonly submitted to all the hideous publicity, and appalling strain, that is involved by trial for murder, upon such slender and ill-founded evidence.

"You have heard the story of the prisoner's early life. By no means well endowed with this world's goods, we see him—a young man in a provincial town—slowly but surely earning the confidence of his employers, and winning his way to the front.

171

Not because of any financial advantage, not because of any special aptitude for sport, not owing to influential relations, or any unusual degree of social acceptability—but solely upon account of his industry, his capability, his honesty.

"Later, we see him setting out on ventures of his own. Not—*not*, mark you—as one avid for wealth and success, ruthlessly casting aside old associations, but modestly, prudently, with the blessing and the backing of those who had previously been his masters.

"There follow years of industrious, conscientious labour, largely devoted to business, but even more largely devoted to the welfare of his fellow-men. We see the prisoner climbing life's ladder, ever mindful of the teaching of his parents, religious people in the best and truest sense; so that today it would be difficult to estimate the debt of gratitude which the poor of Sheffield owe to Sir Gideon Shoesmith.

"Sir Gideon is not—has never been—a wealthy man. Undoubtedly with his abilities applied to no other end, he might have been; but of him it may be truly said, his charities have kept him poor.

"Indeed, it was for this lifelong devotion to the interests of others that, in 1928, his Sovereign decided to honour him with a knighthood—a fitting recognition of a long and honourable career.

"This, then, is the man who, according to the suggestion of the prosecution, has abandoned the principles of a lifetime, and for what, to him, must be a paltry sum, committed a crime, the brutality of which fills us all with horror.

"And, to pile absurdity upon absurdity, they persist in their accusation, in the full knowledge that the victim was, of all people in the world, the prisoner's but recently married and dearly cherished wife.

"Let us examine the flimsy motive upon which the prosecution base their case. They argue that because the prisoner had financial embarrassments of a temporary kind he sacrificed a position of permanent ease and brutally murdered a woman to whom he was undoubtedly devoted in order to secure temporary relief.

"What are the actual facts? What exactly did Sir Gideon hoesmith stand to gain?

172

"Lady Shoesmith had, as is required by the law, made a new will at the time of her marriage. Under that will the prisoner was the principal beneficiary. But is there anything surprising in that? They were man and wife. Lady Shoesmith's only son was already handsomely provided for under her late husband's will. What could be more natural than that she should decide to leave the bulk of her estate to Sir Gideon, a matter of some eighteen thousand pounds.

"But what did he stand to lose?

"Only a comparatively small portion of Lady Shoesmith's handsome income was derived from her personal estate. Her principal revenue came from a different source entirely. It came from the Trust formed by her late husband in which she had interest for life. A Trust, I ask you to remember, in which Sir Gideon had no sort of interest and over which he had no shadow of control, which passed absolutely to Richard Eaton in the event of Lady Shoesmith's death.

"We have been told that Lady Shoesmith's income amounted to the considerable figure of some eight thousand pounds a year, and it was, we are told, very largely from this source that the establishment in Curzon Street was kept up.

"How, then, can the prosecution suggest that to acquire an estate, almost entirely consisting of a piece of property at Slough, a property which may be worth fifteen or sixteen thousand pounds, but which I am advised may not fetch more than ten in the open market today, a man would be foolish enough to sacrifice the benefits of a steady income totalling eleven thousand a year, of which the wife with whom he was living in all amity and happiness was in receipt?

"We have heard a great deal about the episode of the pearls. What does this actually amount to? A loyal wife happy to help her husband in a business difficulty.

"There is no shadow of proof for the rash statement that Sir Gideon had the pearls copied without the knowledge of his wife. You have heard the truth from Sir Gideon himself. Last July his bank pressed for a reduction of his overdraft; he had at that time no liquid assets which he could realize and, pressed by his wife, he disclosed to her the reason for his anxiety.

"Naturally, Lady Shoesmith was anxious to assist him, but the question was—how? Her income was almost entirely derived from this Trust which she was powerless to touch, and therefore she suggested to him the sale of the Slough property, this being her own to dispose of if she wished. Sir Gideon was opposed to this; as a business man he realized how great the appreciation in value of this property was likely to be in years to come. He felt that he could not allow his wife to make this sacrifice. It was then that the question of the pearls arose, and the pearls, mark you, were the only other free asset of any considerable value which Lady Shoesmith possessed.

"If Lady Shoesmith ceased to wear these beautiful necklaces, which had been the admiration and envy of her friends for many years, it would excite comment and inquiry. This was obviously to be avoided in the circumstances, and the remedy was a simple one—the pearls could be copied and nobody would be the wiser. Nobody, that is, except Sir Gideon and Lady Shoesmith herself, for we can hardly accept as serious the suggestion of the prosecution that a woman of Lady Shoesmith's position, who had been accustomed to wear jewels all her life—and moreover, as we are told, had worn these actual necklaces every day since she had received them from her first husband many years before, could for one moment be deceived by a set of imitations, let alone remain unaware of a substitution during as long a period as four months.

"It was then decided to have the necklaces copied. Sir Gideon very wisely avoided unnecessary expenses by having the work carried out by a wholesale firm in the city rather than Lady Shoesmith's jeweller in the West End.

"The next question was the disposal of the jewels, and here again it was desirable that the utmost privacy should be observed. Necklaces of such considerable value are known and recognized among the trade, to break them up would be to destroy a great part of their value, to sell them openly to a London firm would have been to risk the knowledge of their sale becoming public, and any rumour of such a kind might have proved seriously damaging to Sir Gideon's credit at that time.

"Sir Gideon and Lady Shoesmith had already arranged to take a short holiday at Deauville. After some thought it occurred to them that they might find a possible buyer in that fashionable resort, where so many wealthy people from all parts of the world congregate during its brief season. The idea proved a fortunate one since within a few days of their arrival they made the acquaintance of a rich Brazilian who subsequently bought the pearls.

"From start to finish this affair was one in which the maintenance of secrecy was essential, unless Sir Gideon's credit was to be seriously impaired. It was an entirely private matter, and there was no reason of any kind why Lady Shoesmith should have informed her relations or her friends.

"Transactions of a similar nature, where a woman of property seeks to assist a husband in business difficulties, must, in one form or another, take place every day. In a great city like London, I do not doubt that there are, at this very moment, innumerable conversations taking place with a precisely similar object in view.

"I submit, there, that there is not the slightest reason to doubt Sir Gideon's relation of this affair, and the ready willingness with which Lady Shoesmith sacrificed her pearls last summer can be taken as one more indication of the happy accord in which this couple lived.

"We come now to the history of the Sheffield and Kingslade Estate Development Company, of which the prosecution have made so much.

"Evidence has been brought before you that this Company came into being under Sir Gideon's auspices shortly after the War.

"What was the object with which this Company was formed? Largely, we have learned, to relieve the over-crowded and insanitary conditions in which—in common with the less fortunate elements in all the other great cities of Britain—the poor of Sheffield live.

"All of us realize how important it is that the slums and tenement houses of the past should become nothing but a hideous and disgraceful memory, and instead, people of the most moderate means enabled to secure accommodation which gives them light and air and sunshine at a rental which they can afford.

"The Government has been doing what it can to rectify the social scandal of the slums, but the Government has many calls upon it, and in the face of the burden upon industry of the present high taxation it is utterly unable to bear any but a small portion of the cost for this most necessary work.

175

"How, then, could this work progress at all if it were not for men of high practical ideals, men of Sir Gideon's stamp, who fill the breach by the creation of concerns such as the Sheffield and Kingslade Development Company?

"What actual benefits has Sir Gideon received for all the time that he has devoted during the last ten years to this Company's affairs? A few hundred pounds in director's fees and a modest return upon his capital; during the past year he has received no dividend at all.

"And it is for the sole purpose of investing further sums in this excellent but unremunerative undertaking that the prosecution allege the prisoner committed this unnatural crime!

"Had Sir Gideon been involved in financial speculation—gambling in shares or foreign currencies—there might have been some grounds for an assertion by the prosecution that he sought to obtain this money for further speculation by which he hoped to retrieve his failing fortunes, but their contention that he did this thing for the purpose of further investing in a profitless concern is manifestly absurd.

"So much for the shadowy, unsubstantial motive alleged to be the reason for the crime. Let us now examine carefully the actual events upon the night in question.

"In his opening for the Crown, my learned friend told us that he proposed to show beyond any shadow of doubt that the prisoner had absented himself for a period of half an hour or more from a public dinner at the Park Lane Hotel with the deliberate intent of returning to his flat and committing the crime of which he stands accused.

"In addition, my learned friend proposed to bring evidence that the prisoner was actually seen during the time of his alleged absence from the hotel, in the mews at the back of Errol House, from which we are told access could be had by way of the fire-escapes to his flat.

"Later we learn that this evidence is not forthcoming, but the innuendo has been made, and I should be guilty of neglecting my duty to the defence if I allowed the faintest doubt to linger in the mind of any member of the jury as to the complete worthlessness of this evidence, which the prosecution has been unable to produce.

"Upon inquiry it appears that the young man who was

reported to have seen Sir Gideon was one of those parasites who batten upon the vice of all great cities—suspected of being concerned in the illicit drugs and other illegal practices, and of such dubious character that, dreading the light which questions in this court might throw upon his own nefarious way of life, he has elected, or been persuaded by his wealthier principals, to leave the country.

"It has been suggested that Sir Gideon himself provided the means for the man's departure because he drew a certain sum in notes from his bank upon the morning of his arrest. That Sir Gideon should have had his pocket picked with such a sum upon his person is for him a most regrettable coincidence. That he should not have mentioned this to the police is perfectly understandable, since within an hour of the event he suffered the terrible shock of being arrested upon a charge of murdering his wife; a shock that would most certainly put all other thoughts out of any man's mind. But the suggestion that this money was used to bribe this man to leave the country is malicious and absurd. No evidence whatever has been brought to show that Sir Gideon had the faintest idea of this person's existence, and since at that time Richard Eaton was being held by the police in connexion with the crime, Sir Gideon could have had no possible idea that he was even under suspicion.

"The prosecution begged leave to read a statement purporting to have been taken from this man. If such a thing were possible you will see how easily a man's life might be sworn away by irresponsible people, without any opportunity for the court to verify the facts alleged, or assess the reliability of the witness.

"Fortunately for the interests of justice such a procedure cannot take place in a court of law, and His Lordship very rightly ruled that this statement should not be read and could not be admitted as evidence.

"But my learned and able friend was not content to let the matter rest at that. You have seen during the trial how again and again he has reverted to the question of this missing witness, and by searching and often irrelevant questions to the police Superintendent and the man Van Ryn, sought in the most skilful manner to bring before the Court the story alleged to have been secured from this untrustworthy and disreputable young man.

177

"So much so has this been the case that His Lordship has found it necessary, upon more than one occasion, to exercise his authority in order to restrain the ardour of my learned friend.

"Now let us face the innuendoes regarding the statement of this young man. It is inferred that he saw somebody that he thought was Sir Gideon Shoesmith leaving the Mews. Let us assumed that for once in his evil life he was telling the truth. How could he possibly be sure?

"There is no suggestion even that he had ever seen Sir Gideon before; it seems that he made this criminally rash statement upon being shown a reproduction of a photograph of Sir Gideon taken from the daily press. All of us know how misleading such a reproduction may be.

"You will also recall that the night was foggy and the mews ill-lit. At that hour of night the streets adjacent to Piccadilly are more frequented by elderly gentlemen in evening dress than the streets of any other quarter of London—one might perhaps say than the streets of any quarter of any city in the world. Indeed, it would be difficult between eight o'clock and midnight to walk two hundred yards down any of these turnings which lie between Mayfair and the Clubs without meeting an elderly gentleman in evening dress.

"How then, can this man presume to say that the figure of which he caught one glimpse in the foggy darkness was that of Sir Gideon Shoesmith?

"I feel that the defence has been hampered by these innuendoes, and it would have been better—far better—if the prosecution had been able to produce this witness; we should then—once and for all—have had the opportunity of exposing before the court how utterly baseless and unfounded is this suggestion of identification, and how impossible it would be to place credence in the word of such an unreliable and abandoned creature.

"What, then, is the actual evidence brought before the court?

"You are asked to believe that because Sir Gideon was absent from one room in an hotel for a matter of from twenty to thirty minutes, he did, in that incredibly short space of time, traverse a number of streets, climb a fire-escape—an elderly man, mark you—commit this crime, unheard, unseen, although there were a number of people present in the flat, answer a telephone call in a manner that can only be attributed to an

178

actor or a trained criminal, descend the fire-escape, return through the streets, and once more take his place at the table among his friends, unruffled, unperturbed.

"Sir Gideon has himself informed you regarding his movements during that critical half-hour. Only in the previous week he had consulted a doctor, who advised that social engagements of any kind should be entered into with the greatest moderation.

"How can we be surprised that after the strain of the long dinner Sir Gideon felt unwell—the heat—the atmosphere of some one hundred and twenty persons gathered together in that confined space would naturally tend to aggravate any previous indisposition. In such a case who would not leave the table at the earliest opportunity for the freer air of the hotel lounge, and that is precisely what Sir Gideon did, sitting for some little time quietly in a corner until he felt somewhat recovered.

"And then what do we find? Sir Gideon does not wish to trouble his friends with his temporary indisposition, so instead of returning immediately to the banqueting-room he prescribes for himself the old-fashioned remedy of a brandy and soda, and spends at least ten minutes, one-third, I would ask you to remember, of this half-hour of which the prosecution have made so much, consuming it and completing his recovery in the downstairs bar.

"How, I ask, in the short space of twenty minutes, to which the limit has been reduced, could an elderly man, such as the prisoner, accomplish all these activities that have been alleged against him? A boy of twenty could not accomplish half as much!

"To recapitulate, then.

"We have seen Sir Gideon, an honourable and industrious man, carving for himself a distinguished career, devoting much of his time to charities and works of the highest public utility.

"Not until he is well past middle age does he have the time and opportunity to seek the amenities of marriage, but when he does he is fortunate in meeting a woman suitable in age, position and temperament. We have ample evidence that the marriage was a happy one, and I aver that the very fact that Lady Shoesmith sold her pearls to help her husband in his difficulties is an additional proof of their mutual confidence and trust.

179

"It has been plainly shown that whoever might benefit by the death of Lady Shoesmith, it could certainly not be Sir Gideon. For him it is a tragic blow, by which at one stroke he is robbed, not only of the considerable financial support of a rich wife, but of a pleasant home with all the comforts of life and that happy companionship during his declining years, to which, after all his labours, he was entitled to look forward.

"We have gone into the history of the Sheffield and Kingslade Development Company and find that this concern was promoted by the prisoner, largely with the aim of bettering conditions for the less fortunate members of the community; and it has been made clear that had Sir Gideon been able and willing to assist that company in its present difficulties, no considerable benefit could have been derived by him, for at least a number of years, by so doing.

"We have dealt with the insinuations made by the prosecution regarding the statement of the witness whom they were unable to produce, a miserable creature, utterly unstable, and capable of making any rash assertion through his fear of the police; and it is obvious that it was the intention of the police to endeavour to fix the crime upon Sir Gideon. Moreover, we have made it clear that even if this person were of the highest integrity he had not sufficient opportunity which would enable him to identify the prisoner, one brief glimpse, in a foggy, ill-lit mews being totally inadequate.

"Lastly, we have examined the suggestion that the prisoner left the Park Lane Hotel, and we have proved conclusively that at ten minutes to ten he was talking to a waiter in the lounge, and at ten minutes past ten he was quietly consuming a brandy and soda in the downstairs bar.

"The prosecution have signally failed to produce one scrap of evidence regarding his either going out or coming in to that hotel.

"I maintain that the defence has proved that Sir Gideon was in that hotel within the narrowest possible limits of time, and that the prosecution have failed to show any reason for supposing that he ever left it.

"Once more I say that in all my long association with the Bar never have I seen an honourable man submitted to such a hideous ordeal upon such slender and ill-founded evidence."

CHAPTER XXVII

LADY FELICITY VALETS REX VAN RYN

AFTER the court rose the Duke offered Simon and Rex a lift westward in his car.

"You can drop me at the American Club," said Rex, "an' I'll be grateful. I've got to do a spot of work, not having been near the office all day an' I'll be able to have a word there with one or two of the boys."

The Duke looked at Simon.

"Um," the latter nodded. "You can drop me there, too, if you will, it's quite near the National."

When they were settled in the car Simon proffered his cigarette-case.

"Thanks," said Rex. "I think I'd have had to quit that court to get a smoke if they'd sat another half-hour."

After that they sank back in gloomy silence, each one revisualizing certain episodes that had taken place in court that day, while the big car alternately rushed and crawled its way through the traffic of the Strand, Lower Regent Street and Piccadilly.

"Come along in and have one," Rex proffered, as they drew up before the Club.

"Thank you, I will," the Duke agreed, getting out.

"'Fraid I can't," Simon shook his head. "Got to meet Richard, he'll be anxious to know how things went. See you tomorrow," and he hurried off down the street.

"Two Manhattans, and heap the peel," was Rex's brief order to the white-coated steward who served the bar. "Over to that corner there."

"Hallo, Mike!—Evening, Nickie!—See you later, Jerry"— he waved salutations to half a dozen friends who beckoned him to join their groups as he piloted the Duke through the babble of sound to the quietest spot available.

Another white-coated steward appeared and paused before their table. "Your office called you, Mr. Van Ryn."

Rex shrugged. "Oh, let 'em keep calling."

The man presented a large envelope. "Feller left this for you, Mr. Van Ryn."

Rex took the packet and tossed it on the table. "Thanks, Andy, those birds'll be the death of me."

"Don't mention it, Mr. Van Ryn," the man replied in his sing-song voice.

"D'you mind," Rex looked at the Duke.

"Of course not, please open your letter," De Richleau smiled.

Van Ryn tore the packet open and glanced down the long typewritten sheets. "Batavian Shelling down again," he grunted, "and Eden Copera going into liquidation. I'd hate to play the market these days."

De Richleau nodded. "And, my friend, I fear things will be worse before they're better."

"Two Manhattans and a heap, Mr. Van Ryn," the steward chanted, setting the drinks on the small table.

"Do it again," said Rex briefly.

"O.K., Mr. Van Ryn."

Rex pushed his papers from in front of him, and swallowed his drink. "That guy's going to get away with it," he said suddenly.

"I fear so," De Richleau agreed. "Personally I thought the Superintendent would drop the case when I learned that Carrington Smythe had fled the country. I imagined that the death of Lady Shoesmith would be added to that long list of murders where the police are perfectly well aware of the identity of the murderer, but lack the evidence to bring a case."

Rex groaned. "Who'd have thought the police of this country were all that bum; little Cedric would never have put foot on a dock-side in the States."

"Perhaps not," the Duke smiled. "But Shoesmith would have got bail, and appealed for retrials every six months for the next ten years."

"Say! Where'd you get that stuff?" Rex grinned. "All the same, I'll allow there's a heap in what you say. Pity Marrofat didn't pull Cedric into Vine Street that night, though."

"Yes, I've little doubt that he got in touch with Shoesmith on the morning of his arrest, or even the night before, perhaps. It was an opportunity for blackmail that such a person as Carrington Smythe could hardly be expected to neglect."

"How do you think things'll go tomorrow?"

"There'll be the closing speech for the Crown, then the Judge will sum up. I almost doubt if the jury will retire and a verdict of 'Not Guilty' is certain to be returned. It will be all over by lunch-time. That, at least, is some consolation, luncheon in comfort, for the first time in four days."

"I just can't get over the way that attorney twisted everything upside down. To listen to him all afternoon you'd think the old man was God's own uncle!"

"It was a clever speech," the Duke agreed. "I admired the manner in which he dealt with the Sheffield and Kingslade Development Company. If Aron is correct it is one of the biggest swindles in the country."

"And all that stuff about the old man being come over queer and parking in the lounge."

"He was clever, too, when dealing with the pearls. From all that I have heard of Lady Shoesmith, they were the very last thing with which she would have parted."

"I'll tell you, though!" Rex swallowed his second cocktail. "He hit on one great point, the old man did stand to drop a packet on the deal!"

"You mean the income of the Trust going to Eaton, that's true; but I think it was a question of great urgency. He had to have a certain sum at once or he would have gone under."

"Maybe you're right, but doesn't seem to me it would have been much fun if he'd re-financed his company and had no income to live on."

The Duke raised his slanting eyebrows. "I had a long talk last night with Simon Aron," he said slowly, "and Aron's ideas on this subject are interesting. He points out that Shoesmith was his own accountant, that is to say, his firm acted for his company; he may have been in difficulties for a long time, and in his capacity of accountant it would be easy for him to fake the books. He may have counted upon his marriage to set everything right, having no knowledge of the Trust, and only discovered that Lady Shoesmith was in no position to help him, later."

"I get you," Rex nodded.

"I think Aron may be right in his suggestion that Shoesmith has falsified the Company's accounts. Now, if that has been going on over a period of years, all would be well as long as the

Company prospered and the other shareholders received a reasonable dividend, but when times are bad, it is then that people are apt to look into things. You'll remember the Company passed their dividend this year; there was a scene, I understand, nothing serious, but a certain discontent. Perhaps Sir Gideon was scared and felt the time had come when things must be put right. I'll tell you another thing."

"Go right ahead," Rex called to the passing steward: "Andy, two more Manhattans. Yes, go ahead, I'm listening."

"Aron points out that if he had falsified the accounts in any way, he could not deal, sell the majority holding, or amalgamate with a similar concern; not, that is, until he had straightened things out. Do you remember the copy of the Articles of Association that Aron procured?"

"Yes, he gave me a loan of it."

"Then you'll remember the nice block of shares which Shoesmith got for the original concession. If everything had been in perfect order he might have turned those over at ten shillings, in addition to unloading his ordinary and preference shares. Aron worked it out, and at that price he would have received some forty thousand pounds."

"Even that wouldn't have seen him happy compared to sitting pretty with the dame."

"I wonder." The Duke drew thoughtfully at his cigarette. "Has it ever occurred to you that a confirmed bachelor might not find marriage in itself so altogether wonderful, especially when it is with a middle-aged woman who has been spoilt all her life?"

"Maybe it wouldn't be all that funny," Rex agreed.

"It would have been still less funny, my friend, if he'd been made bankrupt, or sent to prison, or perhaps both—not a little bit funny. And upon the other hand," De Richleau finished his second cocktail, "no inquiry, no bankruptcy, no prison, but forty thousand pounds, all ready to start in the game again, and—no wife." He stood up slowly.

"Have another before you go," Rex suggested. "I'll have to beat it myself in a minute, I've got an early dinner at the Embassy tonight. Bum party, it's sure to be, every one of them dead from the neck up, and before I go I'll have to try and get the hang of what those guys have been doing in the office all day." He picked up his papers from the table.

184

"Thank you, no," De Richleau smiled. "Another cocktail now and I should have no appetite for the excellent sherry which I hope to drink at Clarendon House in a few hours' time."

Rex escorted him downstairs. "So long," he grinned as the Duke carefully buttoned his fur coat about him. "See you in the morning."

For an hour and a half Rex put in some hard and conscientious work, annotating and digesting the reports which had been sent up from his office, in the quiet library of the Club. Then he placed his papers in his locker and made his way to Trevor Square.

As he left the Club he studied his watch with a rueful face, realizing that if he were to change and arrive at the American Embassy in decent time for dinner, it would be impossible for him to ring up Felicity and get half an hour with her. His work had taken longer than he thought, and after all, he reflected, it was better not to go to the Embassy at all than to arrive there late for dinner. If he did that he'd get the boring evening that he expected, anyway, and instead of kudos for having done the right and proper thing, nasty reports would find their way across the Atlantic, to the great old man on the other side.

But at Trevor Square a pleasant surprise awaited him. Felicity lay curled up on the Chesterfield in his sitting-room, all arms, and legs, and loveliness.

"Dar-ling!" said Rex.

"My Sweet," said Felicity.

"Isn't it just the top of the world to see you, after a long, hard day. I'll say it's marvellous, but who let you in?"

"Mrs. Bottom, of course, silly. Mrs. Bottom's a friend of mine."

Rex dropped down on to the cushions beside her. "You witch!" he grinned. "You'll make friends with Peter when the last trump sounds."

Felicity smiled. "Very tired, my treasure? Tell me, have they hanged the poor old man?"

"No—not a hope, he's put it across the whole party. He'll get away with it—you see."

"Darling, what does it matter if he does?"

"Honey, you don't understand!"

"Of course I understand, Rex. He's done something frightful, cut his wife's throat, and all that, I know; but he's old. His youth has gone for ever, and that's the only thing really worth

185

having. What's it matter if he lingers for a few more years; he'll die of cancer or angina, or cirrhosis, or some filthy disease like that. Why should you spend your time hustling that poor old man to his death."

"Perhaps you're right, Felicity. I don't know. It all started with us trying to get Richard Eaton out."

"I know, darling, that's different. He's young, and I thought him awfully nice, that time you brought him for cocktails with us, but he's been cleared now. You said yourself last night that the porter's evidence had been accepted in court about the time that Mr. Eaton left, and about Mr. Aron's telephone call, and so whatever happened, Mr. Eaton wouldn't have to worry any more. Besides, the story that you got out of that filthy little swine in the Mews made it as plain as plain who did it, and so now it will be just like all these cases. The police know that it was the old man, but they simply haven't got enough evidence to get a conviction."

Rex suddenly caught sight of the clock. "Darling!" he exclaimed. "I'm the world's worst lover. I haven't even given you a little drink, and I've just got to beat it and change right now. If I don't I'm ruined, and no mistake. If you're late for dinner at the Embassy it's known from Kamchatka to Table Bay before you've finished the soup. It's just awful how the United States has gone and overlapped the world to my especial detriment."

Felicity smiled sweetly. "Never mind, darling, I'll come up with you, we can talk while you change—Oh, don't look so shocked! I won't look through the keyhole while you're having your bath."

"What about the old dame?" said Rex hesitating. "I wouldn't like her to start getting ideas."

"And she never will," said Felicity sweetly. "As long as you never ask anybody except nice respectable girls like me to the house."

"Oh, you're marvellous!" A broad grin spread over Rex's ugly attractive face. "Gee! I just hate the thought of going out tonight."

"My dear, you needn't," Felicity smiled. "I'm being taken by a friend of my childhood to the Savoy, so you'd be awfully lonely doing nothing."

"Damn!" said Rex tersely, and he picked Felicity up in his arms. With a quick motion of his knees he had the sitting-room door open, and had run upstairs and flung her down on the bed.

"Now!" he laughed, just a trifle breathlessly. "You stay put, I'll get busy with the bath."

For a few moments Felicity lay at full length upon the crumpled bed, then Rex returned, wrapped in a dressing-gown.

"Aw, hell!" he exclaimed. "Of course I've been and forgotten every darned thing about telling Bottom to put my clothes out again. Say, Felicity, that's the valet." He pointed to a big mahogany wardrobe. "Just take a little practice in doing what a woman ought to do for a man, while I have my bath." He disappeared with a grin, slamming the door of the bathroom after him.

Felicity sat up, straightened her hair, and putting her long legs to the ground, went over to the wardrobe.

She opened it and for some minutes took out and put back the things inside, with care and amusement. She examined the pants, vest, polo sweaters, shirts, pyjamas and socks, fingering each garment carefully to assess the texture and quality with a woman's natural interest in material. At length she started to put out such things as she considered he might want, and although she had never done such a thing in her life before, it is interesting to note that Felicity put out every necessary garment and not a thing too much.

The resounding splashing from the bathroom ceased and Rex returned. He cast his eye over the array of clothing, and a broad smile lit his face.

"Oh, Felicity, that's swell of you. I didn't mean it. I was only joking, but how perfectly marvellous of you to have put out just the things I want."

Felicity was almost conscious of a blush. "Have I done it right, Rex? I'm so glad. I'll run downstairs again till you've changed."

"It's perfect!" he regarded the carefully arranged clothing, "'cept for just one thing, that's my best evening suit. You weren't to know, sweet, but I keep him for swell parties. Let's swop it for the one I use for dull dinners, like I'm going to tonight. It's in the valet all handy." He picked up the trousers as he spoke.

Felicity took up the coat. "Rex," she said suddenly. "What on earth do you keep in your pockets? There's a thing like a piece of cardboard stuffed in here—that's not the way to treat your best suit."

"I don't know, darling," he replied gaily. "Maybe it's an invitation from the Prince of Wales to meet Mr. Mount's shrimps from Morecambe Bay at the Five Hundred Club."

Felicity pulled it out. After a moment: "Rex," she said softly, "what queer parties you do go to," and she read out the title, printed in gold upon the square cardboard booklet which she held:

"The Thirteenth Annual Dinner of the London and Sheffield Commercial Association, Park Lane Hotel, London, November 22nd, 1931."

"Say that again," said Rex suddenly.

"The Thirteenth Annual Dinner—" she had only got so far when Rex snatched it from her.

"Where did I get that," he exclaimed.

"My love, how in the world should I know?" she answered sweetly. "It sounds a dull party, anyhow."

"It's Gideon's copy—look," he held it out to her excitedly, "got his name in copy-hand on the top corner." He opened it rapidly.

"Take a look at this, honey." He spread out the table plan which was pasted in the back. "Here it is again, top table, Sir Gideon Shoesmith, underlined in red. They always have these things at banquets, hand 'em out to each guest as he comes in, so they can find their place easy.

Felicity looked troubled. "But, beloved, how did you come to have it in your pocket, and why are you so terribly het up?"

"Say! Give me that telephone!" shouted Rex suddenly, and he began to dial furiously upon the instrument beside the bed.

"Hallo! Hallo! Is that Grosvenor 8383? . . . Give me the Duke—and make it snappy. . . . Hallo, is that you? Listen here, I've got the goods on Shoesmith. It's just marvellous. A programme of the dinner with a table plan and all—Gideon's own copy marked with his name. Where'd I find it? Why, stuffed away in the pocket of my best suit—suit I haven't worn since the Ingram party. . . . How did I come to have it? Say, can't you guess? Picked it up off the desk in the Shoesmith apartment. . . .

yes, I used it to fan the hired girl when I was trying to pull her round out of that faint. . . . You get what that means, don't you? These programmes wouldn't be issued before the show; the old man must have brought his copy back with him and when Aron called the flat he got rattled, laid it down beside the 'phone, right where I found it. It just couldn't have got there any other way, I knew it again the moment I saw it, and I'm prepared to take oath as to where I found it and the time I picked it up."

The Duke's clear voice came back over the line. "My dear fellow, how intensely interesting and, by Jove, you're right! This will alter the entire aspect of the case. It's not too late, and this fresh evidence can be brought tomorrow. We must certainly hold a conference tonight. I'll get hold of Marrofat, I am very glad for his sake; this case has been particularly difficult for him. I'll also get Aron and Schatz and Eaton; we must have the people for the prosecution, too. They must get particulars from the man who handed out these programmes at the Park Lane Hotel. If all these programmes were in his possession until the guests actually arrived for dinner, the case is complete."

"I'll be along, the very moment I can break away after dinner," said Rex, as he hung up the receiver.

"Felicity, sweetheart," he lifted her off her feet with a laugh. "I'm going to cut that bum party and take you out to eat."

*   *   *

Upon the following day His Lordship allowed that it was not too late, and that he would hear fresh evidence brought by the prosecution. A little under a month later Sir Gideon Shoesmith paid the final penalty, upon a February morning, which belied its nature and held every promise of an early spring.

SIMON ARON TAKES A HOLIDAY

I

ONE Wednesday afternoon some five months later, Simon Aron and the Duke de Richleau were enjoying the pine-laden air of the Surrey hills, as they were borne smoothly and rapidly along in the latter's great, silver Hispano.

Earlier in the day the Duke had invaded the tall, grey building in the city where—summer and winter—Simon Aron sat, hedged in between his desk telephones, narrow-shouldered and stooping a little, nodding and peering over his pince-nez from one set of stock reports to another. Hesitant of speech, diffident of manner, but so quick and active in mind, busy, for ever busy, weaving and unweaving the complicated threads of finance.

It had been no easy matter to drag Simon from his desk out into the summer sunshine, but the Duke had succeeded because he was a wily man. Finding the more ordinary methods of appeal to be useless, he had lied shamelessly, pleading his loneliness and advancing age, and Simon, who never spared himself, could never resist an appeal from his friends. He had, therefore, put through two long-distance calls and then abandoned work for the day.

The great car took the long rise from Milford to Hindhead with an even purr of its many hidden horses. Upon one side was spread the lovely panorama of the Punch Bowl and, on the other, the sunlit valleys that lie between Whitley and Dunsford. With a long musical note upon the siren they sped through the village and on down the hill towards Liphook, but when they were still half a mile away from the cluster of houses, the car slowly drew to the side of the road and stopped.

"Let us," said the Duke, removing the rug from his knees, "stretch our legs a little."

Simon agreed, and they got out. De Richleau placed his

hand upon the younger man's arm and led him slowly down a little lane, a cave of cool shadow in the sunlight, flecked and speckled with the tiny patches of light that penetrated the roof of boughs and leaves above.

"I'm taking you," De Richleau remarked quietly, "to tea with an old friend, at least, I hope there will be tea, since she is not informed of our coming."

"She?" said Simon, casting one of his quick sideway glances at the Duke.

"Yes, a spinster lady of our acquaintance. Behold, my friend, this charming old-world cottage, as a house-agent might say—with Tudor garden and a sunken lawn. Indeed, a pleasant place to spend one's old age in. How I wish that I were not cursed with this restless spirit of mine, ever seeking companionship and excitement. Look, too, at the tiny orchard and the kitchen garden. I wonder, do you think there will be strawberries for tea?"

They had paused before a wicket gate, beyond which a neat tiled walk led up to something between a cottage and a country house. Upon either side a blaze of colour met their eyes, steep banks of July blossoms, delphiniums, phlox, and marigolds, tall hollyhocks, and little blue love-in-the-mist, lupins and daisies and golden Aaron's rod.

"An English Eden," murmured De Richleau, lifting the latch. "Almost I am sorry that I have come—but we are here— let us go in."

To all appearances the place was deserted, sleeping for ever in the sun; it seemed impossible that winter or death could come to such a spot. The silence was only broken by the murmuring of hovering bees; one bright blue dragon-fly paused for a moment, almost completely still, above the walk and, then, with a flight ability far surpassing that of bird or man, wheeled without warning and disappeared aloft in a curve of flashing light.

De Richleau pulled the hanging bell, and a faint tinkle sounded from the interior distance. There was a pause while Simon thoughtfully prodded a piece of moss that grew between the tiles, and then the door was opened to disclose Miss Eaton.

The Duke stood hat in hand upon the doorstep. "We are indeed fortunate," he smiled, "to find you at home. My car has broken down here just at the end of the lane. My man tells me that it will take at least an hour to put the trouble right, and I was wondering if we might seek the hospitality of this charming house in the meantime. I am a little old to walk very far; by good chance a farm-lad informed us the name of the owner, which has emboldened us to try."

"Oh, please come in." Miss Eaton held open the door which led into a cool and comfortable lounge hall.

Simon regarded her closely. She was a trifle greyer, perhaps, and she seemed smaller than ever, but certainly more lively, when she had first opened the front door—but after, he thought, she went a little dead, speaking quite naturally, but avoiding his eyes and those of the Duke.

"What a lovely garden," De Richleau went on, as Miss Eaton led them to a low-ceilinged, chintz-hung room, at the back of the house.

"It is nice, isn't it?" She smiled nervously. "I was lucky to find a little place like this. I like it better every day."

Simon held a chair for her near the open window. His dark eyes flickered rapidly from Miss Eaton to the Duke. "What was the purpose that lay behind this visit?" he wondered. "Why the Duke's excuses to get him here? The lie about the car having broken down, and the farm-lad whom they had never met?" But the Duke gave no sign.

"Of course you'll have some tea?" Miss Eaton went on hurriedly. She pressed a bell behind her chair as she spoke.

De Richleau bowed again. "You are most kind, nothing could have been more welcome, if we do not trouble you too much."

"Oh, not at all, not at all." A diminutive maid appeared from a door in the oak panelling. "Visitors, Hetty," said Miss Eaton quickly. "Tea, China tea, as quickly as you can." And the girl departed with a quick grin.

"What a—er—nice little maid you have," remarked Simon, for lack of something to say.

"Yes, oh yes, Hetty's a good girl, a little awkward, but I took her straight from the village school," Miss Eaton nodded.

"You take perhaps an interest in the life of the village?" inquired De Richleau.

"Oh yes. There's the women's institute, you know; I find the people very nice, so helpful, I'm not a bit lonely, and I have

192

Hetty to sit with me in the evenings. Of course, some people might not think that quite right, but I'm sure I don't see why."

Simon laughed into his hand. "Very silly of them, and anyhow, why should one worry what other people think?"

"That's just what I say," agreed Miss Eaton.

"May we, I wonder, walk round your lovely garden?" De Richleau asked. "It looks so very lovely."

"Oh yes, we'll go round while we're waiting for tea." Miss Eaton led the way out with the Duke beside her.

Simon brought up the rear. He was amazed at the knowledge that the Duke displayed of plants and flowers, their seasons, and the soil most suitable to each; while Miss Eaton was obviously pleased and happy to show them her small domain. The atmosphere was easier than it had been in the house, yet Simon—trained and sensitive to receive and qualify impressions and reactions—was aware of an undercurrent, a spirit of fear and tension that had invaded the slumbering peace of the garden. Twice his quick eye caught Miss Eaton looking furtively at the Duke, and he felt more certain than ever that the clever, charming epicurean had a definite purpose in having brought him there.

On their return to the house they found tea awaiting them. Hot buttered toast and apple jelly, little rolls of thinly cut bread and butter, and a great heaped dish of strawberries flanked by a pot of fresh cream.

Simon never ate tea, but today he made an exception. The country air had sharpened his appetite, besides it was impossible to resist Miss Eaton's pressing; moreover, he felt it preferable to eat than to sit still and say nothing, for he certainly had nothing to say. Indeed he was unhappy, almost miserable. He was anxious to get away—out of this, to leave the little spinster to her flowers, her institute, and Hetty. Not to stir up things that were better left unstirred.

The Duke, too, had ceased to make conversation, his grave, bright eyes regarded Miss Eaton steadily across the tea-table, while she kept looking at him, and then nervously away.

"You greatly prefer," the Duke addressed her suddenly, "living here to living in Curzon Street, do you not?"

"Yes," she said, almost in a whisper.

"I imagine that you often dreamt of having such a home when you were there?" he went on evenly.

She nodded, avoiding his eyes.

"Lady Shoesmith was not your sister, was she, Miss Eaton, only your sister-in-law? She was not over-considerate, I think, for those dependent on her."

Simon Aron rose quickly to his feet. He spoke abruptly, rudely almost for him. "Come on," he said, "let's get back to London."

Perhaps Miss Eaton thought he was addressing her. In any case, she stood up suddenly with a little wail. Wringing her small hands together, her eyes wide with fear flew from one to the other. "Oh," she cried, "I knew they'd find out, I knew it, and now you've come to take me away."

2

At the same hour that Simon and the Duke were sitting down to tea with Winifred Eaton, by a curious coincidence Rex and Felicity were not very far away.

They, too, had been tempted by the sunshine to drive into the country, and a neat little sports car with Felicity at the wheel was making its way up the long pull round the corner of the Devil's Punch Bowl.

It had been a silent and unhappy drive. Rex's stay in England was nearly over, orders had come from the big chief, his father, on the other side, and he was sailing for the States in the coming week.

Rex knew what was in Felicity's mind well enough, but he was stubborn about it, endeavouring to evade the issue, and he would not give her a lead.

Felicity, dreading the possible blow to her pride, did not wish to open the subject herself, and had been hoping for days that he would do so of his own accord. It had, in fact, been with that particular object in view that she had, with some difficulty, lured him away from his office to come upon this drive. But by the time they had passed through Goldaming, she had decided that he was determined not to help her, and that if she wished to discuss the matter she much broach it herself.

All the way up the long hill she was keying herself up, and at last, just as they passed the Sailor's Stone, she said it.

194

"Rex why won't you marry me?"

Rex shifted uncomfortably in his seat. Here it was at last—just what he'd been expecting, ever since he'd broken the news about going home. "I never said I wouldn't," he parried clumsily.

"Isn't that rather cowardly?" said Felicity. "If you'd wanted to, you'd have asked me weeks ago."

"You're right," he admitted. "I'm just terribly fond of you honey, but I don't want to marry."

"Why not, Rex? You love me, don't you? I believe you do, but don't lie to me, tell me the truth. Do you love me, or are you tired?"

"I love you, sweet. Honest I do, and I'm just hating the thought of how I'll miss you when I get back home."

"Then why not, Rex? I know it sounds terribly old-fashioned and all that, but one must settle some time. Surely you have had enough gadding about, or is it the awful truth that I have made myself too cheap?"

"No, darling, no," he protested quickly. "Don't say that. It's horrid and it's not true. But be honest, Felicity; there wasn't any question of marriage when it all started months ago, was there? We met, and well—we liked each other terribly—I reckon we just did what most people in our set do, that's all."

"Yes, I suppose you're right," Felicity said softly. She was driving very slowly down the Liphook road. "I'm not complaining, darling, but hasn't our friendship grown into something more than just one more affair?"

Rex squirmed. "Oh, sure, darling! You know it has. It's been different, different altogether, but all the same we'd be fools to marry. All marriage is a mess these days, you've only got to look around."

"Not all, Rex. There are people who pull it off. Why not let's try? After all, we've got everything in our favour; all our friends would be delighted. Mother would simply faint with joy at my netting an American millionaire's son, and I hardly imagine your people would be exactly sniffy at having a Duke's grand-daughter in the family. We could afford to do up Glanely and live there for the hunting, and have a little house in London; you could run the English business for your father; or, if need be, I wouldn't mind living in the States."

"That's just the rub, sweet. It's too darned easy. We'd

have nothing to fight, too much money, and too much time; that's how all our kind go on the rocks. If you do find a happy break in marriage, you may bet it's because the people are hard up, and with lots of worries; then they've just got to stick together. We'd be like all the rest, divorced in a couple of years."

"I don't believe it, Rex. That's only because people are weak and don't know what they want. We could go straight if we meant to from the start; it's having one's eyes open that matters, and when it comes to marriage, that's the only kind I'd ever try. I could go straight with you, my dear, that's why I'm being such a bore."

"Oh, sweetheart," Rex hung his head unhappily, "why will you hurt yourself and me? I know you mean it now, and I feel that way myself. But I'm older than you, and I've seen such a packet of it. If we got married we'd be just asking for trouble."

Felicity felt that he was weakening, and decided to play her last card.

"Rex," she said softly.

"Yes, sweet?"

"Guess what I've got in my bag?"

"How'd I know, honey?"

"I've got a seven-day licence that I took out last week, and a hundred pounds; we could use that licence tomorrow and go a long way on the hundred pounds. Let's go off into the blue, darling. Just leave everything and love each other. I promise you, Rex, I promise you whatever happens afterwards, I won't complain."

Rex was sorely tempted—after all, why not? Get married tomorrow and cut out all the fuss, just a couple of telegrams, "Married this morning, off for long honeymoon, love to all, Rex and Felicity." Ship the little car over to France. He could easily get passports and more money in a day or two. Then he'd be with Felicity always, for weeks on end, seeing all sorts of queer places together up and down Europe. No nonsense about her having to go home each night. What fun! What gorgeous fun. . . . But then Rex had been spoilt by women ever since he was a likely lad. He'd been fond of so many and adored by them. Not quite as fond as he was of Felicity, perhaps, but nearly, and always, always, there had come the little casualnesses, the tiny irritations,

196

the tension, and then at last the staleness and the rotten going on together; waiting, seeking, generally on both sides, for a decent excuse to break. Felicity was very young, she would get over him sure enough, as he would her; she'd be bitter for a bit perhaps, and as far as that went, he wouldn't feel like making love to anyone for a long time to come. He'd miss her terribly; but all his reason and experience told him that the wisest thing to do was to break.

"Can't be done, sweet," he said solemnly at last. And then with a sudden foolish impulse to save her pride whatever it might cost him in her estimation, he added: "Not that I don't want to, but I've got a wife in the States, though even the Old Man doesn't know."

Felicity sat back from her wheel as though she had been stung. "What!" she gasped, and turning her small fair head, her eyes blazed at him; then she looked back quickly to her wheel and, swerving the car, just managed to avoid the ditch.

"Steady," said Rex.

She laughed, jamming her small foot upon the accelerator; the car leapt forward. "Oh, I didn't ask for marriage," she cried scornfully, "not till today, but at least I expected truth. You utter beast, how could you? I shall never, never be clean again!"

"Felicity!" he pleaded. "Felicity!"

The car sped on. "Why didn't you tell me?" she stormed. "If you had had an unhappy marriage, do you think I should have cared—if you had told me—but to live a lie. . . . Oh, how ashamed I am to think that I should have cared for anything like you."

They flew round the corner at terrific speed. Rex tried to seize the wheel. "Felicity!" he cried. "You'll crash us, sure!"

"I see!"—she flung at him—"It only needed that—you're just a funk as well!"

Rex was not a coward, he was as brave as most men and had, on occasion, performed certain definite feats of personal courage, but the sneer stung him badly, as it was meant to do. He shrugged his big shoulders and for one second took his hand off the wheel. At that moment they were going downhill with a left-hand bend ahead, and his reaction to the taunt proved fatal. Felicity, with set teeth and dead white face, seized the opportunity to switch the wheel the other way, with head thrown back and a gasping laugh, she charged the bank at fifty miles an hour.

3

It was the Duke who saw them first. He had turned to the window in an endeavour to avoid Miss Eaton's panic-stricken eyes. He had felt certain for many months that she had a hand in the murder, and his interest in psychology had tempted him into this visit. He wanted to see just how well a woman who had committed a murder without being found out stood the test of success, and thinking that it would interest Aron, he had brought him too. But the Duke was no moralist, and now he was ashamed and unhappy at having shattered this poor lady's quiet and peaceful life.

"Dear me!" he exclaimed. "What's this?"

The others turned to see a great dark hulk of a man, his face smeared with blood, stooping and staggering across the lawn. In his arms he carried something slim and white. At the second glance it could be seen that a pair of long silk-stockinged legs swung aimlessly on one side of him, and on the other wobbled slackly a fair, girlish head.

With a common movement the group within the cottage made for the garden door. The man lurched nearer, and as Simon ran forward he saw a great crimson splash upon the body of the girl. At every step the man took splashes of crimson fell from his hands upon the sunlit lawn.

With a final lurch he came to a halt before the porch, shaking his head dumbly as Simon proffered his arms to relieve him of his burden.

"We crashed," he said simply, in a weak, husky voice.

"Rex!" exclaimed the Duke and Simon almost simultaneously, but De Richleau lost no time. He seized Miss Eaton by the arm, every sign of his recent distress had passed completely from him.

"A bed, woman!" he said. "Quick—which way?"

Simon had disappeared almost before the Duke had spoken. With an agility surprising in so unathletic a figure, he was pelting down the lane. The Duke's car—a doctor—were the immediate ideas which animated Mr. Aron's legs. After that,

198

Harley Street—best man—who? How far to London? How long there and back? Then he came up against the tragic fact that able brains can never function best when their attendant body is moving at any speed. So ill-conditioned are the bodies of mankind that all his blood had left his head and rushed to the support of his thumping chest and aching legs. Nevertheless, even as a drowning man has the sense to cease struggling with the problem of getting anywhere, and reserves his strength to keep afloat, so, he abandoned thought, drew a long breath, and yelled: "The Duke's car! Doctor wanted! Start her up!"

The drowsing chauffeur jerked himself erect, and as Simon Aron touched down on the running board, the car leapt forward to Liphook and skilled help.

In the meantime Miss Eaton had led the way. Under the Duke's urging her limbs regaining their animation. She turned down her own bed, and ran with quick, frightened footsteps for hot water, brandy, bandages.

Rex laid the inert body on the bed. With quick fingers the Duke rummaged Miss Eaton's work-basket, he seized the scissors and flung the other contents on the floor.

"She's mine," said Rex huskily. "Nobody's to touch her 'cept me."

De Richleau gave him one look only, a long, commanding look. "You will sit down, my son," he said, "and leave this to me."

Rex sank into a chair and the Duke turned his back upon him. With rapid snips and tears he stripped Felicity of her thin summer garments. With the practised hands of one long since trained to tend wounds, he felt her limbs gently and then rolled the sheets above her thighs. Her face and head were dead white, yet scatheless, so also were her lower limbs, but between her little breasts there was an ugly jagged hole that continually welled blood. Without compunction De Richleau rummaged in the chest of drawers, made a pad of Miss Eaton's best handkerchiefs, and tore a petticoat into strips to tie it on.

"Steering-wheel?" he demanded of Rex tersely, when he had tucked the sheets under Felicity's chin.

"Yes," Rex nodded drunkenly. "Damn' car turned over on us. Thank God it didn't burn."

Footsteps upon the stairs, a murmur of voices, Simon and

the local doctor, a fresh-faced, youngish man. Miss Eaton with a bowl of steaming water, and wide-eyed Hetty with bandages gripped in her clumsy hands.

De Richleau turned to Aron as to an older man. "Take him away," he said nodding in the direction of Rex. "He's no use here."

"I'm not going," said Rex thickly, but Simon got him out.

"Come on, old chap," he said softly, taking the big man by the arm. "I'm Simon—I understand."

Rex heaved himself up, and allowed himself to be led away.

4

Later, out upon the lawn in the stillness of the early summer evening, the Duke talked to the doctor.

"The spine. Yes, I feared as much, and the loss of blood must have been frightful. Poor child—so young—beautiful. Have you told the boy?"

"No." The doctor shook his head.

"Then I think we'll leave that for a little. How did you find him—much hurt?"

"Nothing serious, a nasty cut above the eye, and a twisted ankle, his hands are badly damaged. He must have literally torn that car to pieces to get her out. I've patched him up and he's with her now."

"I see," the Duke nodded. "Then there's not much more we can do. You must remain, I think, to spare her all the pain you can."

They walked on in heavy silence, unheeding the perfume in the twilight, down the border of sweet peas.

It was just about this time that Felicity regained consciousness.

"Darling," she murmured when she saw Rex sitting beside her bed, then she gave a little moan of pain.

"Felicity, sweetheart." He took both her hands in his. "It wasn't true, Felicity, it wasn't true—'bout me being married, I mean."

She smiled faintly. "Wasn't it? Oh, I'm so glad about that. Are you hurt, Rex?—Much?"

"No, honey, I'm all right. It's you we're worried for."

"I've got an awful pain in my chest, every time I breathe—and Rex. . . ."

"Yes, sweet?"

"I can't feel my legs, Rex . . . I—I believe—I've done myself in."

"No, you'll be all right, sweet—and listen, Felicity. Yesterday when—what a fool I am—I mean, this afternoon, when we were talking 'bout getting married . . . You were right all the time, I was just a big piker, scared of getting tied up. When I was trying to get you from under that car I saw it all, clear as can be. God, how scared I was! I thought you were dead, and I'd lost you for keeps!"

She patted his hand fondly. "I'm afraid we must forget all that now, Rex."

"And why?" he demanded. "I stuffed that bag of yours in my pocket. We've got the licence, we can get married any time—now if you like."

"You foolish darling, it's after three o'clock, and we couldn't use the licence till tomorrow, anyway."

"All right, let's make tomorrow the big day."

She considered for a space, frowning a little, then she said slowly: "If you really want to, Rex, marry me tonight, the licence will be all right after midnight."

"Marvellous!" he grinned. "Will you be all right here for a bit? I'm just crazy to get busy on it. I'll send somebody right up."

"Yes." She coughed and a spasm of pain crossed her face. "I feel awfully tired," she said.

As soon as Rex launched this astounding news upon the people downstairs, Simon brightened up at once. He had been hanging about with his head well down and his hands in his pockets, utterly miserable at having nothing to do.

"Look here," he said, "if you'll leave it to me, I'll—er—fix it all up for you. Love to, no trouble. Ner—Just give me the licence." He turned to the Duke.

"Don't mind if I take the car, do you? Like to slip up to town, after I've been to the village—I'll be back before ten."

"Of course, my dear fellow, by all means," De Richleau agreed. And five minutes later Simon had gone off in the Hispano.

The doctor went with him as far as the village, to pick up

some drugs that might be needed, while Rex went back to Felicity's bedside.

5

For the first time Miss Eaton and the Duke were left alone. He found her looking at him curiously.

"What do you mean to do with me?" she asked him suddenly.

The Duke was thinking of other things. "Do?" he repeated slowly. "Ah, yes, of course. But, my dear Miss Eaton, there is nothing to be done, only to express my very great regret at having disturbed your tranquillity here."

"You mean—you're not going to give me up to the police?"

He placed his hand upon her arm and led her to a chair. "indeed, no. Why in the world should I do that?"

"And the young Jewish gentleman—won't he say anything?"

"Most certainly not. And, let me take this opportunity to reassure you with regard to others who might have their suspicions that you knew more of that matter than you declared at the time. British justice is such that, Sir Gideon having paid the penalty, the affair is over and done with. Even if you confessed to the police, they could not try the case again."

Winifred Eaton let a little sigh escape her and she relaxed in her chair. After a moment she looked curiously at him and asked: "Then what made you come down here? Or had your car really broken down?"

"No, I fear I deceived you there," De Richleau confessed. "I came deliberately, but if I were to tell you the reason, I should have to speak plainly, and I might hurt you by so doing."

"I think," she said slowly, "that I'd like to know."

"As you will," he smiled slightly. "Then you must understand that I have been convinced for many months that you were at least partly responsible for Lady Shoesmith's death. I was filled with a great curiosity to see you and to establish for myself whether, having committed a successful murder, without having attracted a shadow of suspicion to yourself, hou were a prey to suffering and remorse, or if you were living yappy and untroubled upon the proceeds of the crime?"

"Elinor was a hard woman," said Miss Eaton softly, "and it was she who prevented my brother from providing for me independently in his will. I'd always lived with them and she found me too useful to let me have my freedom."

"Yes," he nodded. "The lot of a poor relation in a rich household is not always a happy one. I was astonished that the police did not appreciate that motive at the time. They were, of course, too certain that it was Richard Eaton, to investigate other possibilities very closely."

"I—I wouldn't have let anything happen to Richard," she said. "I would have given myself up."

"You could have given Gideon up," the Duke suggested, "and saved both Richard and yourself. Or didn't you know about the part Gideon played, and only find her after he had gone?"

"No, it wasn't quite like that."

"Does it distress you to talk about it?" De Richleau inquired kindly. "If so, let us say no more."

"No—oh no," she smiled faintly. "It's rather a relief, really —now I know that I can't be arrested. That's been the worst part, in a way, not being able to talk to anyone about it. If I tell you, I think I shall be able to put it in the back of my mind."

De Richleau nodded. "I should be most interested to hear."

She gave a little cough. "Well, it was this way. It was all through that telephone call of Mr. What's-his-name—the polite young man. I'd been sitting in the sewing-room where I always sat, ever since Richard and his mother had gone into her bedroom. I didn't hear Richard let himself out, but I did hear the telephone go, and I was just coming along the passage to answer it, when I saw Gideon. He slipped out of the bathroom across the passage to the lounge where the telephone was and I knew he'd answered it because it stopped ringing.

"I was so surprised to see him, thinking that he was out at one of his banquets, that I just stood where I was. Then, just as I had made up my mind to go down the passage and see why he'd come back so early, he popped out again, slipped down to the end of the hall and opened the front door a little; after that he ran back to the bathroom. You've no idea how quiet and quick he was for such a big man. He had a habit of moving very quietly—you could never tell when you were going to come upon him suddenly in the flat; I found it most upsetting. Well, as I was saying, he'd only just got to the bathroom door again when a door opened somewhere; it must have been one of the maids going to her room, or from the kitchen to their sitting-room, I don't know—it was just round the corner of the passage from where I was standing, but he heard it, and quick as quick could be he'd closed the bathroom door again, and slipped back into the lounge. That was all I saw of him."

The Duke leaned forward. "Yes," he said. "Yes. But I wonder greatly that he never saw you. Please go on."

"He was so intent the whole time, I think that was partly the reason. Then you know how long that passage is, don't you; there was only the one light on by the hall door, and my end was in complete darkness; besides, I had on my black frock and was standing almost round the corner. He only gave one quick look in my direction, just once when he heard the door open. I'm quite sure he had no idea I was watching." She paused thoughtfully.

"What happened then?" the Duke prompted her.

"Well, you see, I thought something strange was going on as you may say, so I walked down to the lounge to ask Gideon what he was doing, but he wasn't there. I was ever so puzzled because that room only had one door, and I knew he hadn't come out into the passage again. I didn't know what to think."

"He was, of course, going down the fire-escape."

She nodded. "That's what I came to think myself, when I was wondering about it afterwards, and that's how they said it was at the trial, didn't they? But at the time I just couldn't imagine what had happened to him, so I went into the bathroom."

"By the door in the corridor, or the door from Lady Shoesmith's bedroom?" asked the Duke.

"By the door in the corridor, and that was another strange thing. Only those two ever used that bathroom, so the door in the passage was always kept bolted. I thought about that afterwards, too, and I think he must have slipped the bolt back himself that evening when he had his bath, so that he could come upon her from behind, if you take my meaning."

"Of course," De Richleau agreed. "Seated in the bath she would have her back to that door. I imagine that she never even saw him. He must have timed it well, but that would not be difficult since he knew her habits, and before he went in, I don't doubt that he listened to hear the water splashing, to make certain that he would be able to take her unawares. . . . But tell me what happened when you went in?"

204

"I found her lying in the bath, her eyes were shut, and she was groaning, she—she wasn't dead then."

"She would probably have died of her injuries," De Richleau suggested comfortingly. "Those blows upon the head were heavy ones, so heavy, in fact, that for that reason I knew you could not have delivered them."

Miss Eaton shook her head. "I don't know," she said in a whisper. "I should like to think so." She paused for a moment and then went on more evenly. "Elinor was a hard woman. I could have had this cottage years ago if it hadn't been for her. She made my brother leave her everything, not a penny for me or the boy, and she kept me running—morning, noon and night with all her little fads, just as the price of a roof over my head—that's what made me do it. I was so tired of it all, her tempers, and her always changing her mind, so when I saw her like that, I wasn't sorry, not a bit. I only just thought it was a chance to escape from it all, so I turned on the tap."

They sat silent for a while in the gathering darkness; at last, Winifred Eaton spoke again; "I don't think there's much else to tell. I went into the bedroom for a few moments while the water was running in, and when I came back to turn off the tap, the water was over her mouth and she was quite still; that's the only thing that worries me a little now, I don't like the sound of running water—but otherwise I'm very happy here."

"It happened much as I had imagined," said the Duke gently, "and I don't think you have any real cause to reproach yourself. I think we may consider it certain that Lady Shoesmith would have died in any case."

"Thank you," said Winifred. "I'm glad you think that."

6

Ten o'clock came and shortly afterward Simon Aron returned from London. If there were to be a wedding, he had determined that he would do his utmost to make it as like a proper one as possible.

Having made special arrangements with the Rector, he held one of his short jerky conversations with the Duke's chauffeur. There was vague talk as to what the Hispano could do—more particularly in the hands of a good chauffeur, who understood Hispanos as opposed to one who did not. Further there was talk of journeys which Simon had accomplished in Hispanos with French and Spanish chauffeurs—whereby the element of patriotism was aroused. A complete guarantee of immunity in case of accidents was given, Aron pledging his word for the Duke. A time was mentioned—and a bet offered and accepted, in which the odds were at the unusually long figure of ten shillings to fifty pounds; with understanding that any unforeseen delays were not to be counted in the time concerned—and finally a trust was placed as between friends, whereby the chauffeur became of the convinced opinion that the Jewish gentleman was "a rare fine sport."

As a result, therefore, of some seven minutes' expenditure of time, they fled to London as though all the devils in Hell were after them—a roaring comet of speed and light. Simon was enabled to spend over two hours in the West End, and having carefully planned his campaign on the way up he was enabled during that time to deal with a multitude of affairs; and with a dozen well-placed telephone calls, he had sent as many people upon his business, reopening their shops and scouring their hotels.

He arrived with a carload of boxes and packages; a wedding breakfast for half a dozen people, a couple of cases of champagne, flowers by the basketful, masses and masses of them, a wedding-cake and silver horseshoe confetti; he had even tucked away in a special box for Felicity a little white satin bed-jacket to be a wedding dress and a fine piece of old Brussels lace to be a bridal veil. Nor had he forgotten a wreath of orange blossom for her hair; but his triumph of triumphs was that at his side he brought Maestro Gian Cappello, the world-famous violinist, and upon his knees Maestro Cappello carried his precious violin.

"Why did you do all this, my friend?" De Richleau asked seriously as he watched the unloading of the boxes and the baskets.

Simon gave his nervous little laugh, then he looked up quickly. "You know as well as I do," and that was all he said.

After that all was a bustle of preparation. The choir-master arrived with his boys as Simon had arranged; they were to be stationed beneath Felicity's window, and then the Rector came, a little fussed and worried about the unusualness of everything,

206

but reassured after a few moments' conversation with the Duke.

Everything was arranged so that Felicity should be disturbed as little as possible. At a few moments before twelve the doctor, together with a nurse that he had brought back with him, and Miss Eaton, raised Felicity a very little on her pillows, draped the little coat about her shoulders and the veil with its crown of blossoms upon her head. Then a table already disposed as an altar was carried in, and all the flowers that Simon had brought back from London, already arranged in vases. In a surprisingly short time the preparations had been completed.

At a signal from the window the fresh young voices of the choir rang out, the Duke gave the bride away and Simon acted as best man. Miss Eaton was the only bridesmaid, and the doctor and nurse all the congregation. It was a strange wedding, but so it was that Lady Felicia Standish married her big American.

The service was the shortest possible, and there was no address, instead the divine music of Cappello's violin filled the summer night.

When the service was over, for a few moments only the newly-married couple held a reception. The cake was carried in and cut beside Felicity's bed, and she was allowed half a glass of champagne. Cappello played again, and after that everything was quickly cleared away, so that before half past twelve Rex and Felicity were alone once more.

"Oh, Rex, darling," she smiled as the door closed softly behind the doctor, who was the last to go, "aren't people marvellous?"

He grinned. "Marvellous, honey, why yes, I suppose they are."

"Of course they are, Rex. Think of that boy, Simon, going all the way to London and finding Cappello, and the wedding-cake and the flowers and everything. I think he must have known."

"Known what, sweet?"

"Don't *you* know, Rex?"

"I don't know what you're talking about."

"Surely you didn't think I'd let you marry a girl who was going to be a cripple all her life, did you?"

A shade of fear crossed his face. "Just what d'you mean, Felicity?"

"I'm going to die, dear."

"You're not, Felicity, you're not."

207

"Yes, sweet." She smiled again. "People who're going to die can tell, you know, and I don't think I'll be very long, that's why I wanted to be married tonight."

7

Downstairs they drank champagne and ate caviar sandwiches, but quietly, because of the invalid above. The parson was a jovial man and liked his glass. Cappello at times could be a wit; but the doctor, the Duke and Simon were only putting up a show—they knew.

As soon as was consistent with decency they got rid of the Rector, who promised to find Cappello a bed, and took the great musician with him; Miss Eaton was persuaded to retire to her own spare bedroom.

"How long do you think she will last?" De Richleau asked the doctor.

"Not long at this rate," the other shook his head.

"She'll go some time tomorrow, maybe tonight. The moment I saw her I knew it was useless to get anybody down from town. I wonder if we ought to tell him?"

"Ner," said Simon Aron. "Kinder not."

"Poor child, do you think she's in much pain?" asked the Duke.

"Not much," the fresh-faced doctor replied. "I'm managing to keep it under pretty well. Of course that will shorten things if I go on, but then I'm no believer in torturing hopeless cases for the sake of keeping them alive, I learnt that in the War."

The others nodded silently as the doctor glanced at his watch. "Think I'll go up now and give her another shot."

8

For some time Felicity had been lying pale and silent, but after the doctor had gone again she spoke once more.

"Rex."

"Yes, sweet?"

"I've been thinking, you were right about things yesterday —I mean today—it was possible that we might have made a do of it—but with chaps like us the odds were all the other

208

way. I'm awfully lucky really. I've had all the fun there was to
have and I've even got married after all—but I shall never see
you running after another woman—and we shall never be divorced.
I've eaten my cake and kept it, too. Isn't life fun?"

9

The doctor was taking a nap in the hall; the nurse sat knitting
on the landing outside the bedroom door, ready for any emergency. The Duke and Simon sat alone, they were half-way through
a bottle of old brandy, which was one of the things that Simon
had brought back from town.

De Richleau had been giving the details of his conversation
with Miss Eaton.

"And who do you really think was—er—responsible?" Simon
asked.

The Duke lifted his fine head to exhale a cloud of tobacco
smoke from the fragrant Hoyo de Monterrey that Simon had
given him.

"My friend," he replied slowly, "there can be no doubt
whatever that it was Sir Gideon's intention to murder his wife,
but your telephone call arrested him in the act. Afterwards,
he returned, undoubtedly to finish what he had begun, but he
was disturbed again by the opening of a door, and he had to
leave the thing half done. Miss Eaton arrived on the scene when
there was still life in Lady Shoesmith's body; quickly and effec-
tively she extinguished that life." He shrugged eloquently.
"To take life so is murder in the first degree."

Simon nodded his head up and down. "Yes," he agreed.
"But—er—tell me—how did you tumble to it?"

"It wasn't difficult," the Duke smiled. "You see, I did something which nobody else thought to do. Almost immediately I
arrived on the scene I was puzzled by the amount of steam,
and when I put my hand in it, the unusual heat of the bath water,
therefore I took the temperature. It was 112 degrees Fahrenheit."

"Really? Wouldn't have meant anything to me," said Simon.

"Well, it did to me. I happen to know that the ordinary
temperature for a bath is blood heat, that is to say round about a
hundred. After that, if you have never tried, I think you would

be amazed and interested to discover how with every extra degree water becomes almost unbearably hotter. Few people, I believe, would care to get straight into a bath at a temperature greater than, say, one hundred and five, or remain in it for long having gradually brought it up to one hundred and ten. I realized at once, therefore, that as a certain allowance must be made for cooling since the bath had been filled or replenished by the dead woman, some person had added hot water after the murder had been committed. If there were finger-prints upon the hot tap, therefore, they might tell a tale."

Simon grinned. "Clever!" he said with a chuckle, "Oh! clever! I suppose you got the prints from Scotland Yard—Miss Eaton's?"

"Exactly," smiled the Duke.

"But—er—wait a minute now; why didn't you tell us, or the Superintendent?"

"Because that alone was not sufficient explanation. Miss Eaton lacked the physique to have given those blows to the head, and I will confess I was a little sorry for Miss Eaton, therefore I kept that little piece of information in reserve hoping that we should discover fresh evidence. The moment we had Sir Gideon I saw everything, excepting only if they had acted separately or together."

"Clever," said Simon Aron, chuckling into his hand. "Oh, clever!"

10

"Darling," whispered Felicity, some little time later.

"Yes, sweet?" said Rex.

"I'm so sorry for you. You won't worry too much, will you? All—all this is rotten luck on you."

He shook his head slowly. "Don't worry about me, sweet."

"But I do, darling—I—I'm not worried about myself. After all, death is the great adventure, isn't it? Tomorrow there'll be nothing—or else I'll know all about everything. . . . Oh, Rex, isn't death fun!"

She gave a little sigh and lay very quietly for a while. And then the gallant spirit of Lady Felicity Van Ryn went out into the bird song of a summer dawn.

This book
designed by William B. Taylor
is a production of
Heron Books, London

Printed in England by
Hazell Watson and Viney Limited
Aylesbury, Bucks